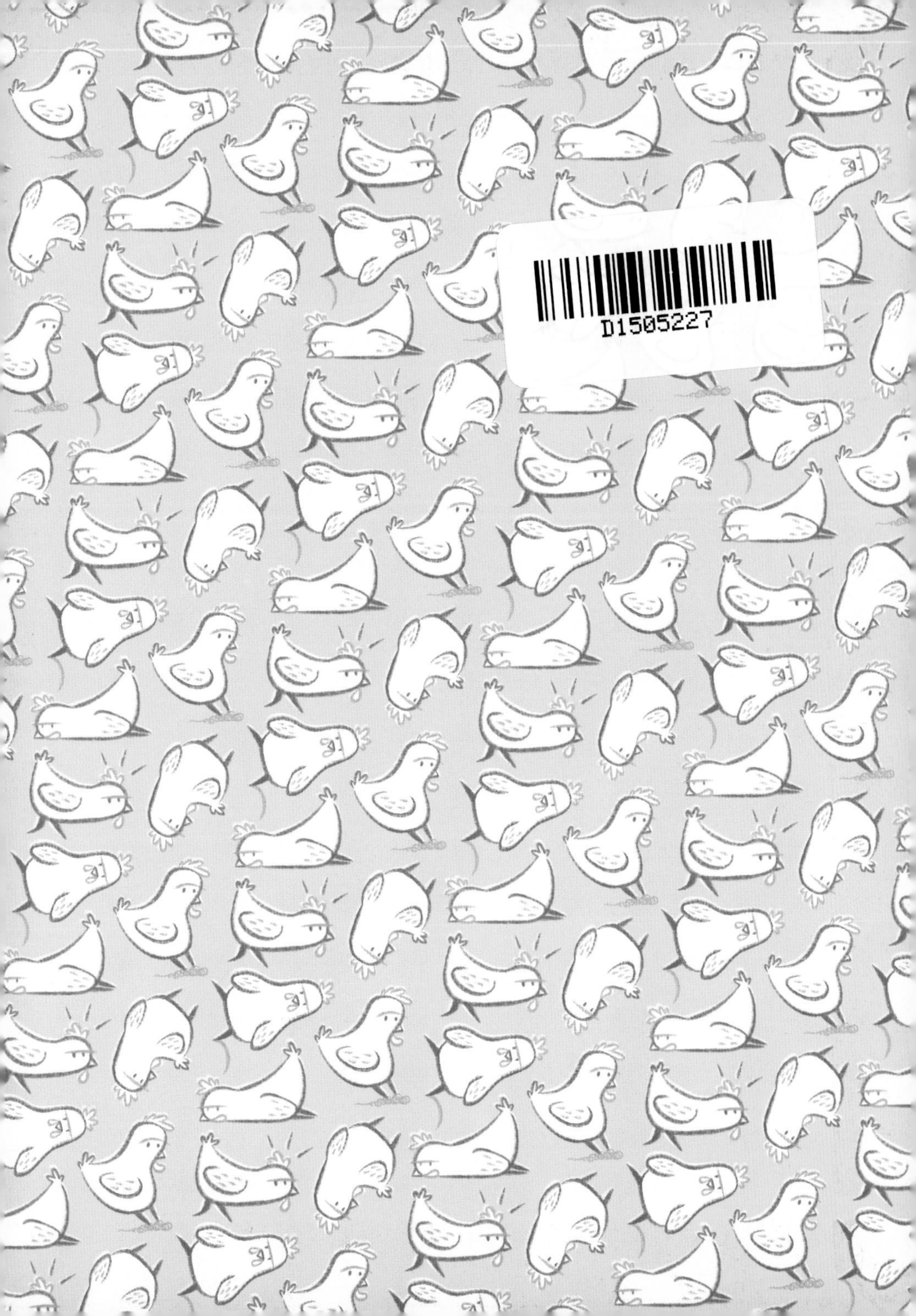

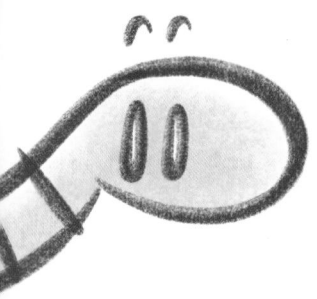

Cranky and Speedy have **more** adventures in these books!

Cranky Chicken

Cranky Chicken: Party Animals

NKY CHICKEN

CRANKOSAURUS

ROAR!

KATHERINE BATTERSBY

MARGARET K. McELDERRY BOOKS

NEW YORK   LONDON   TORONTO   SYDNEY   NEW DELHI

For the Cranksters—all the reader
(young and not-so-young) who have
shared their cranky love with m

MARGARET K. McELDERRY BOOKS . An imprint of Simon & Schuster Children's Publishing Division .1230 Avenue of th
Americas, New York, New York 10020 . This book is a work of fiction. Any references to historical events, real people,
real places are used fictitiously. Other names, characters, places, and events are products of the author's imagin
tion, and any resemblance to actual events or places or persons, living or dead, is entirely coincidental. . © 2023
Katherine Battersby . Book design by Rebecca Syracuse © 2023 by Simon & Schuster, Inc. . All rights reserved, includi
the right of reproduction in whole or in part in any form. . MARGARET K. McELDERRY BOOKS is a trademark of Simor
Schuster, Inc. . For information about special discounts for bulk purchases, please contact Simon & Schuster Spec
Sales at 1-866-506-1949 or business@simonandschuster.com. . The Simon & Schuster Speakers Bureau can bring autho
to your live event. For more information or to book an event, contact the Simon & Schuster Speakers Bureau at 1-86
248-3049 or visit our website at www.simonspeakers.com. . The illustrations for this book were rendered digitally usi
custom chalk, pastel, and watercolor brushes. . Manufactured in China . 0123 SCP . First Edition . 10 9 8 7 6 5 4 3 2
. CIP data for this book is available from the Library of Congress. . ISBN 9781665914550 . ISBN 9781665914574 (eboc

We acknowledge the support of the Canada Council for the Ar

Conseil des arts   Canada Coun
du Canada   for the Arts

CONTENTS

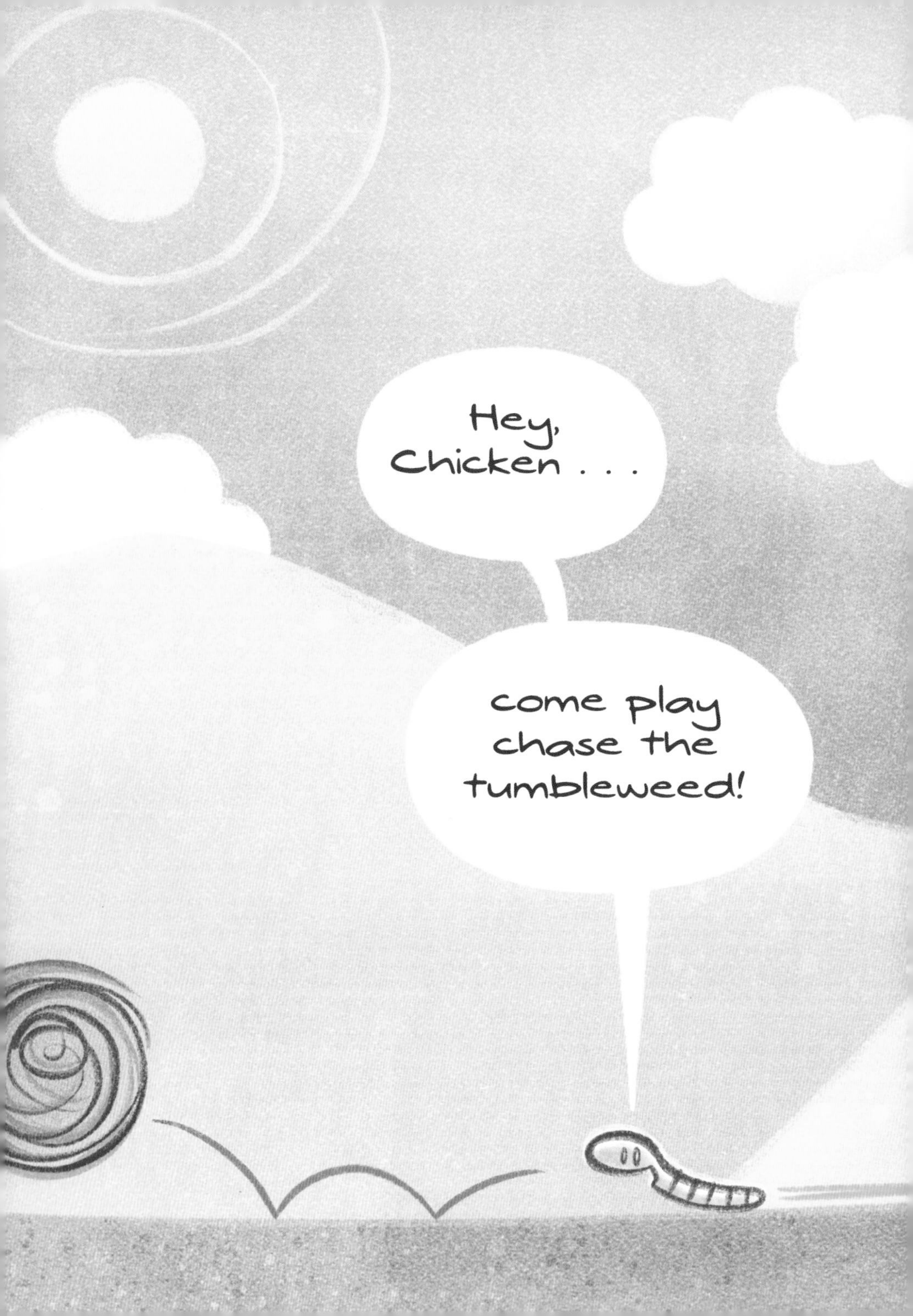
Hey, Chicken . . .
come play chase the tumbleweed!

1 The Happiest Nap Ever

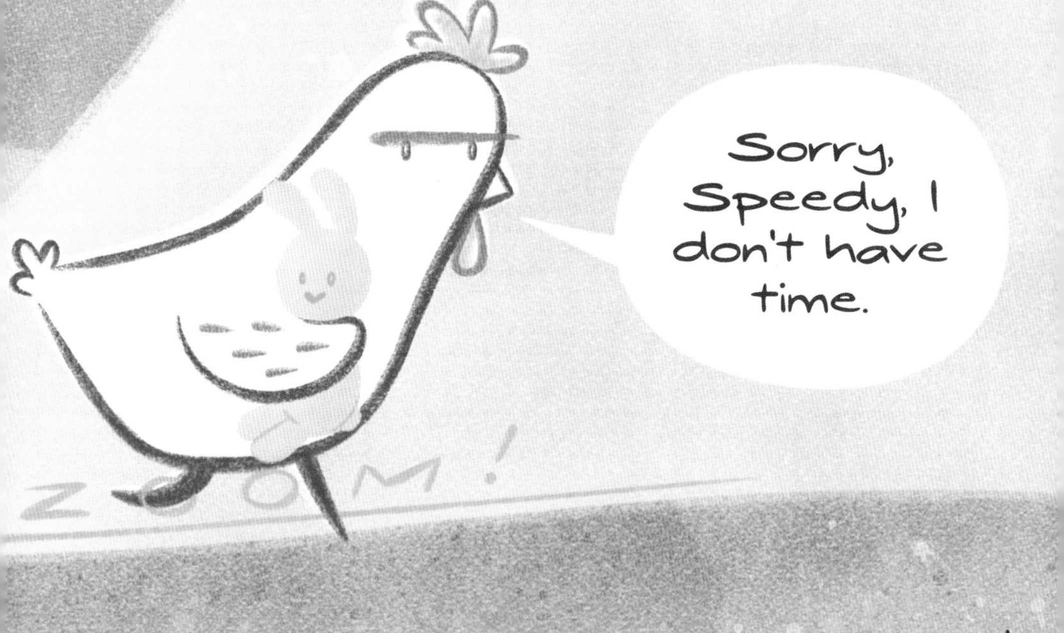
Sorry, Speedy, I don't have time.
ZOOM!

You don't have time?
To play??
Nope.
But all we do is play!
ZIP!
It's not all we do.

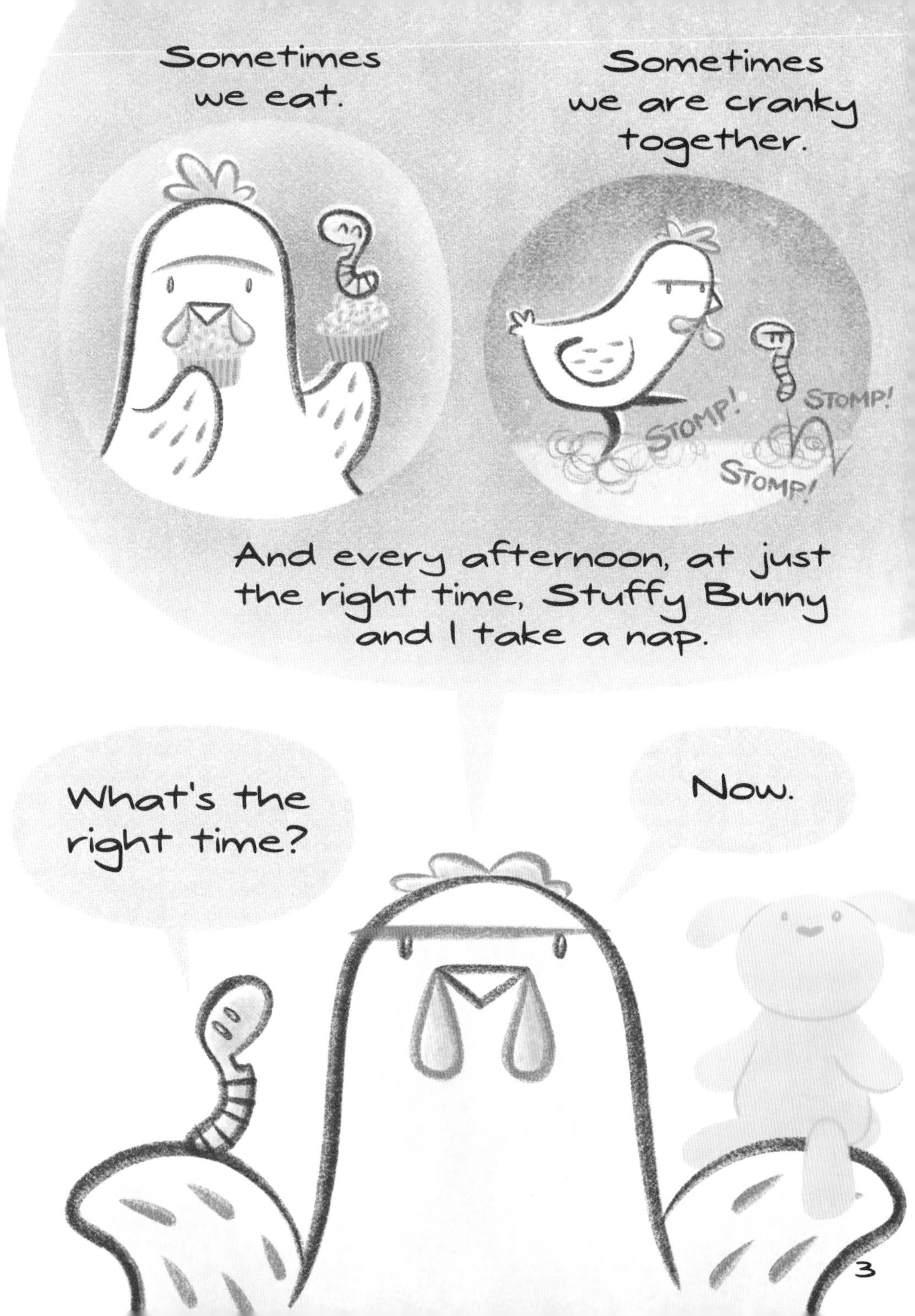
Sometimes we eat.
Sometimes we are cranky together.
STOMP!
STOMP!
STOMP!
And every afternoon, at just the right time, Stuffy Bunny and I take a nap.
What's the right time?
Now.

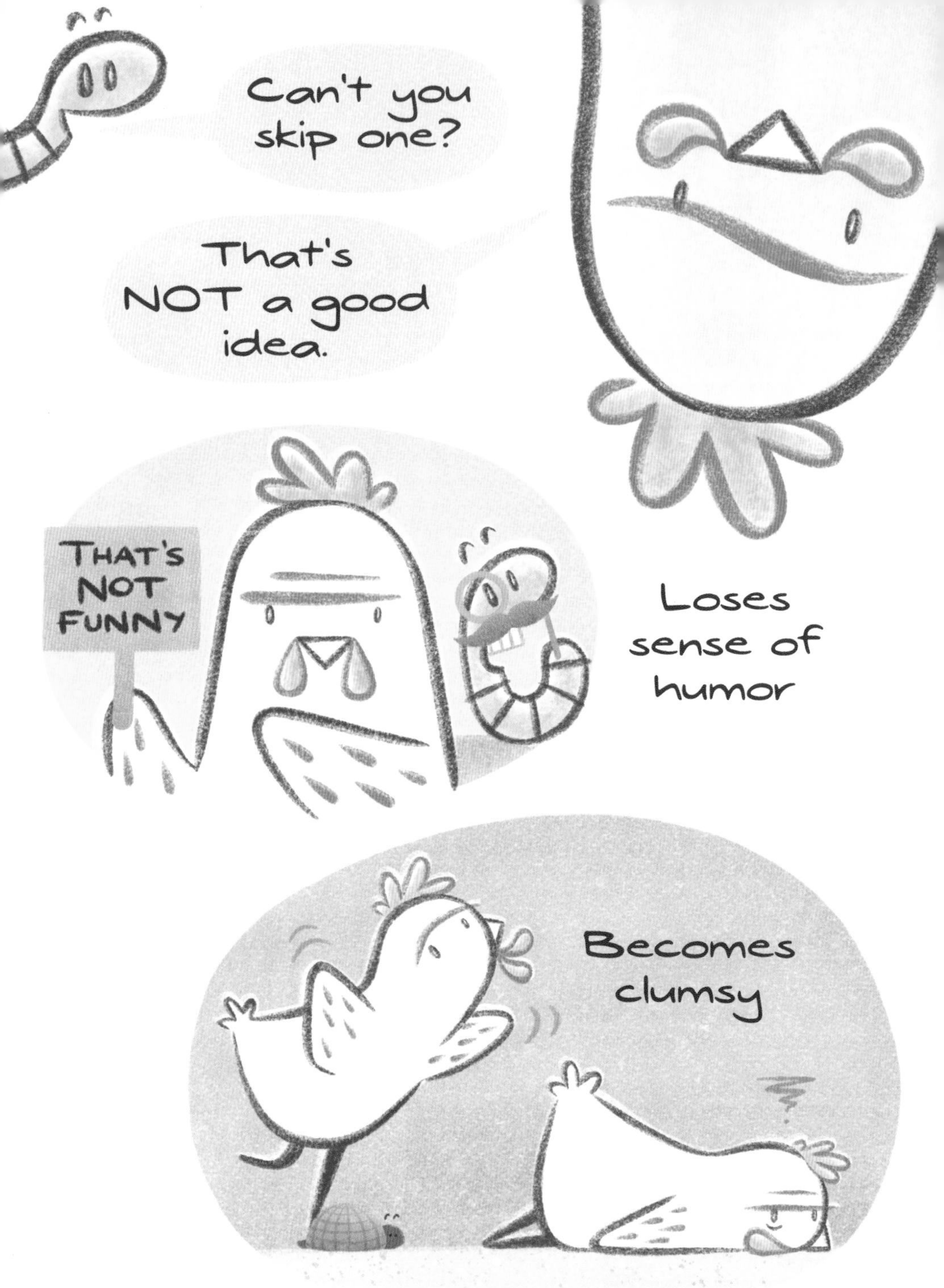
Can't you skip one?
That's NOT a good idea.
THAT'S NOT FUNNY
Loses sense of humor
Becomes clumsy

What Happens When Cranky Chicken Skips a Nap

Gets silly

HIC!
HIC!
HIC!
HIC!
HIC!
HIC!
HIC!
HIC!
HIC!
HIC!
HIC!
HIC!
HIC!
HIC!
HIC!
HIC!
HIC!
HIC!

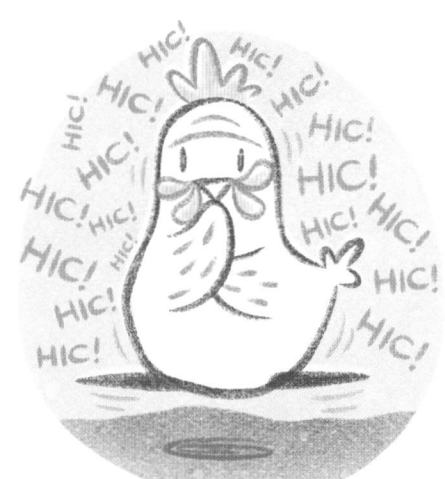

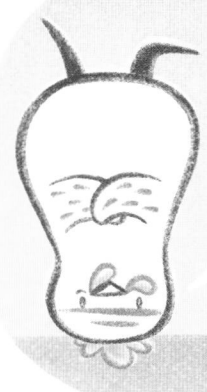

Why are you upside down?

Gets the hiccups

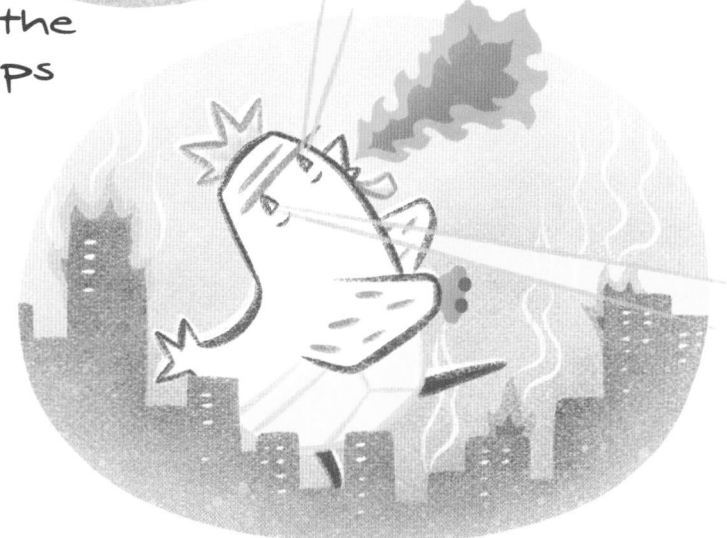

Turns into super monstrous cranky pants

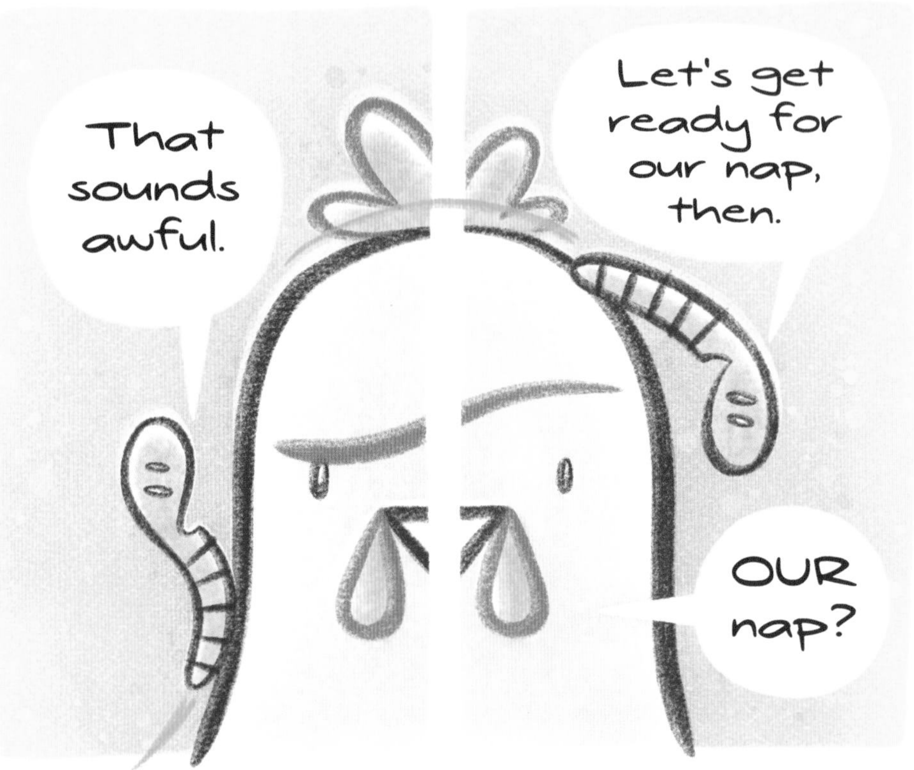
That sounds awful.
Let's get ready for our nap, then.
OUR nap?

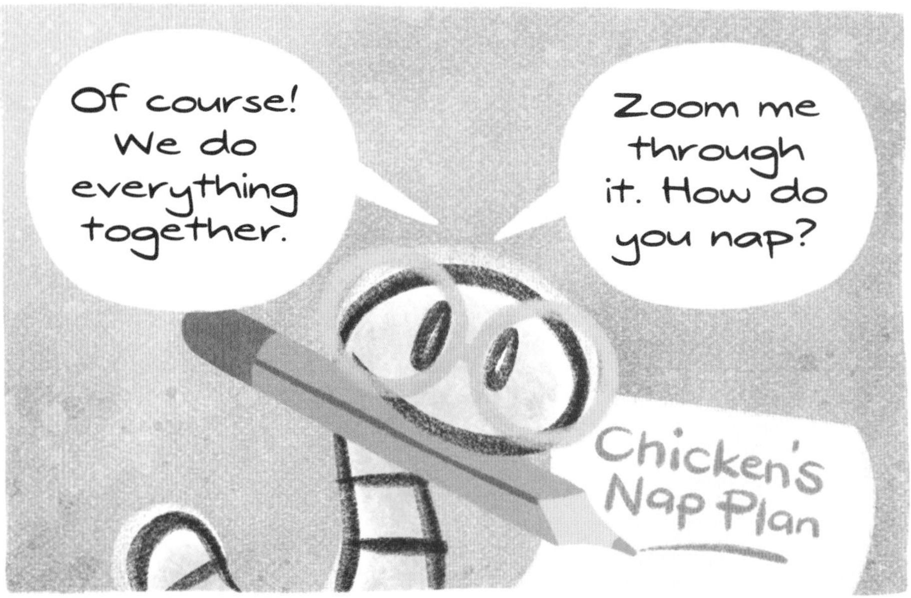
Of course! We do everything together.
Zoom me through it. How do you nap?
Chicken's Nap Plan

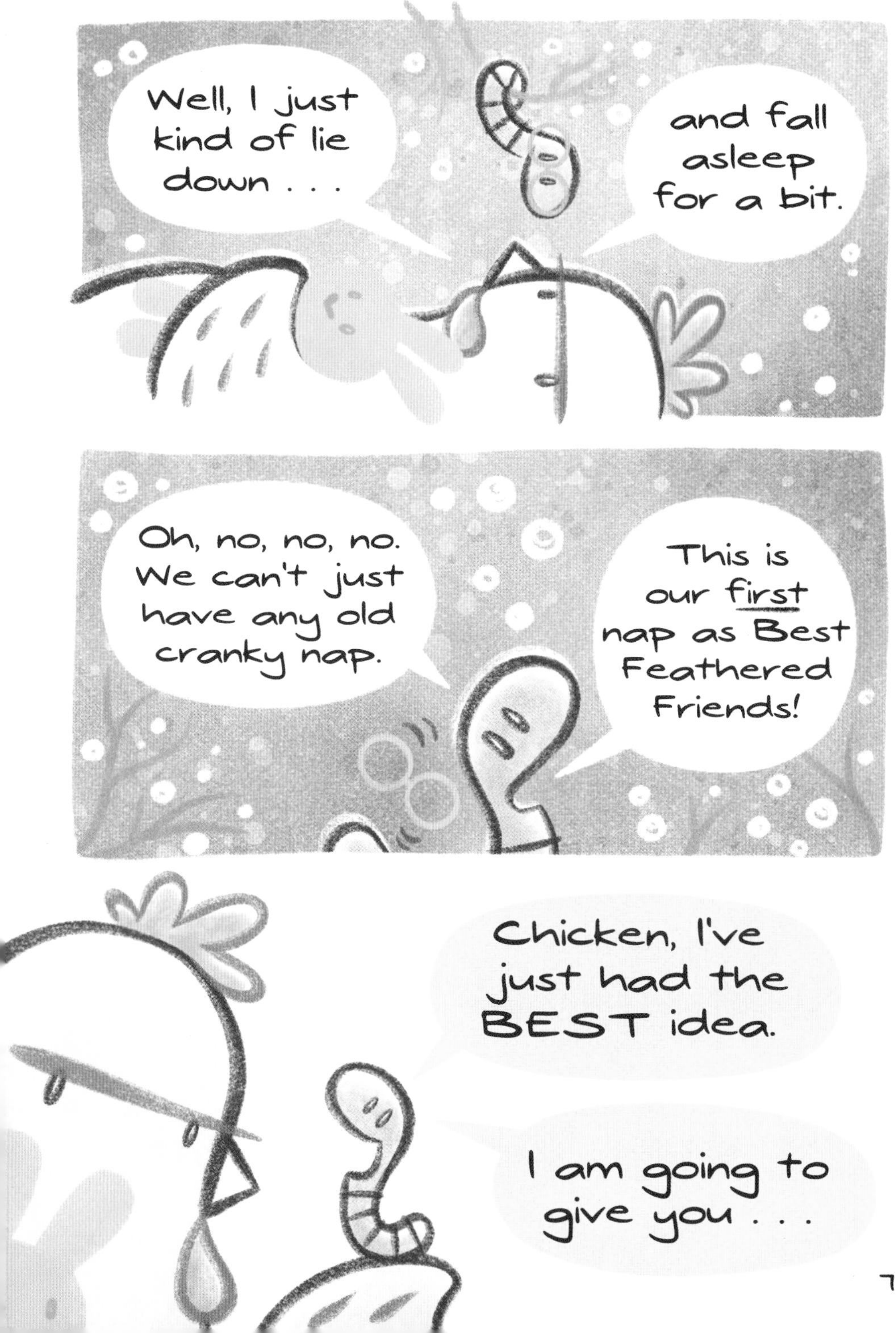
Well, I just kind of lie down . . .
and fall asleep for a bit.
Oh, no, no, no. We can't just have any old cranky nap.
This is our first nap as Best Feathered Friends!
Chicken, I've just had the BEST idea.
I am going to give you . . .

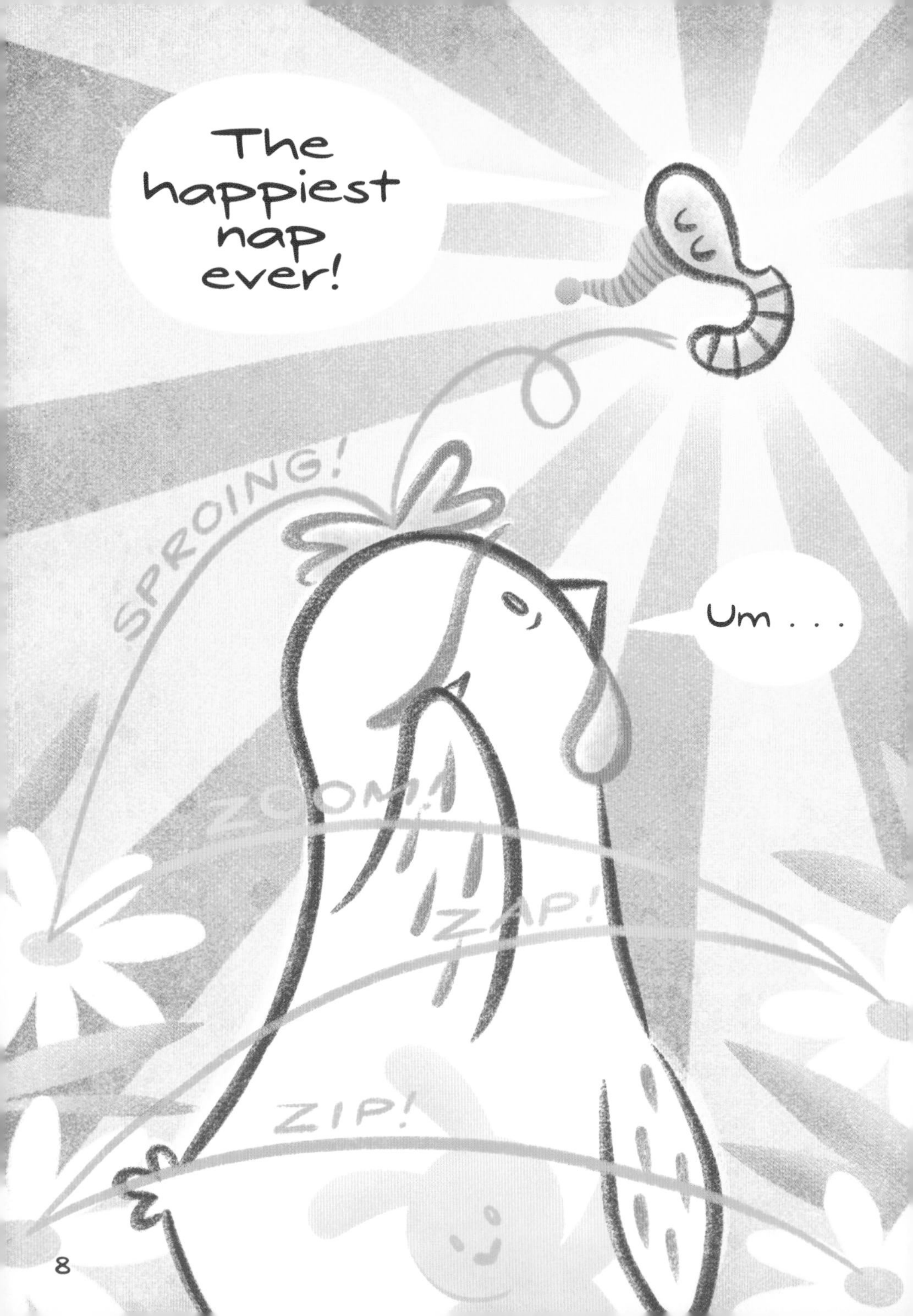
The happiest nap ever!
Um . . .
SPROING!
ZOOM!
ZAP!
ZIP!

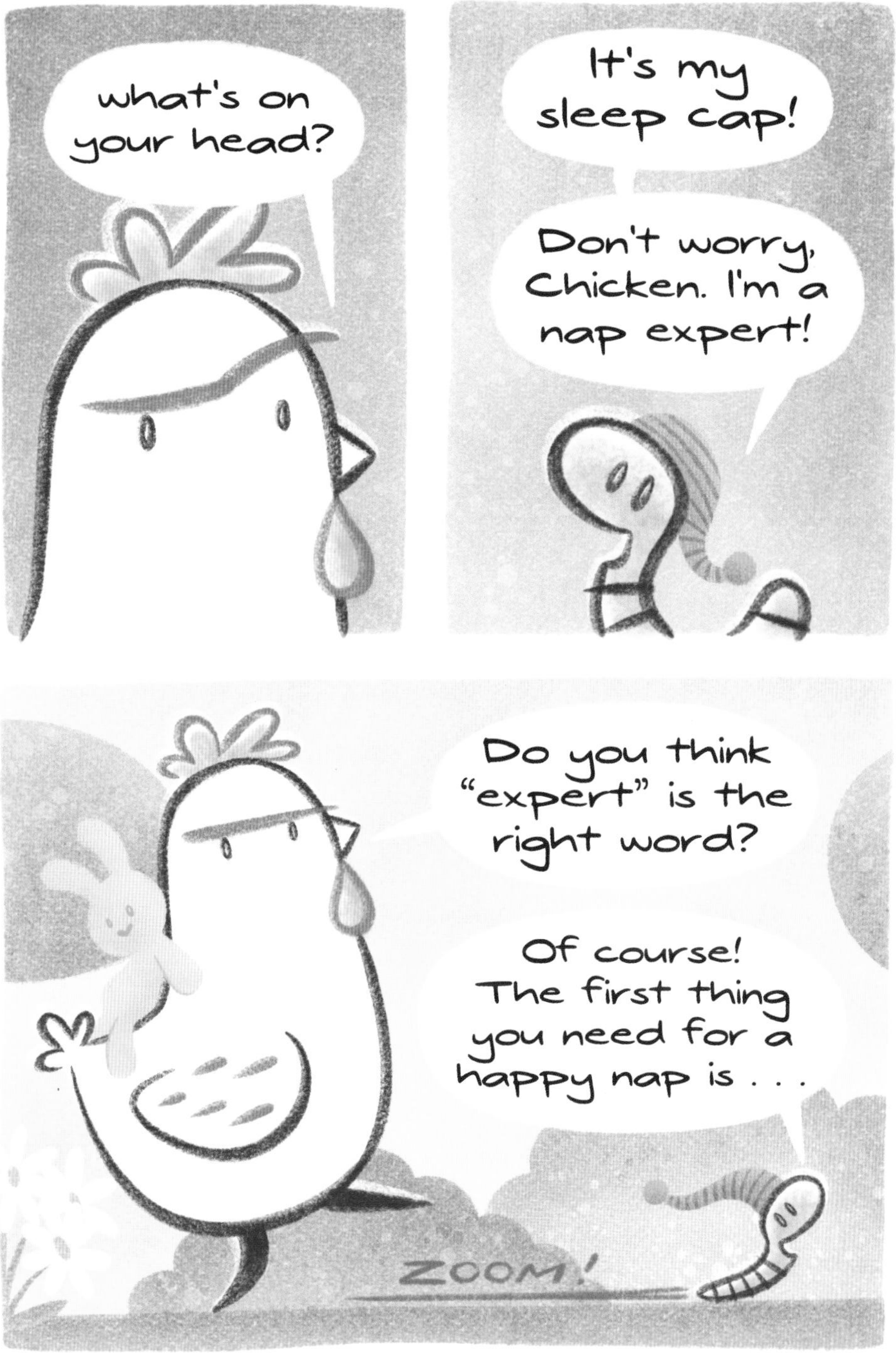
what's on your head?
It's my sleep cap!
Don't worry, Chicken. I'm a nap expert!
Do you think "expert" is the right word?
Of course! The first thing you need for a happy nap is . . .
ZOOM!

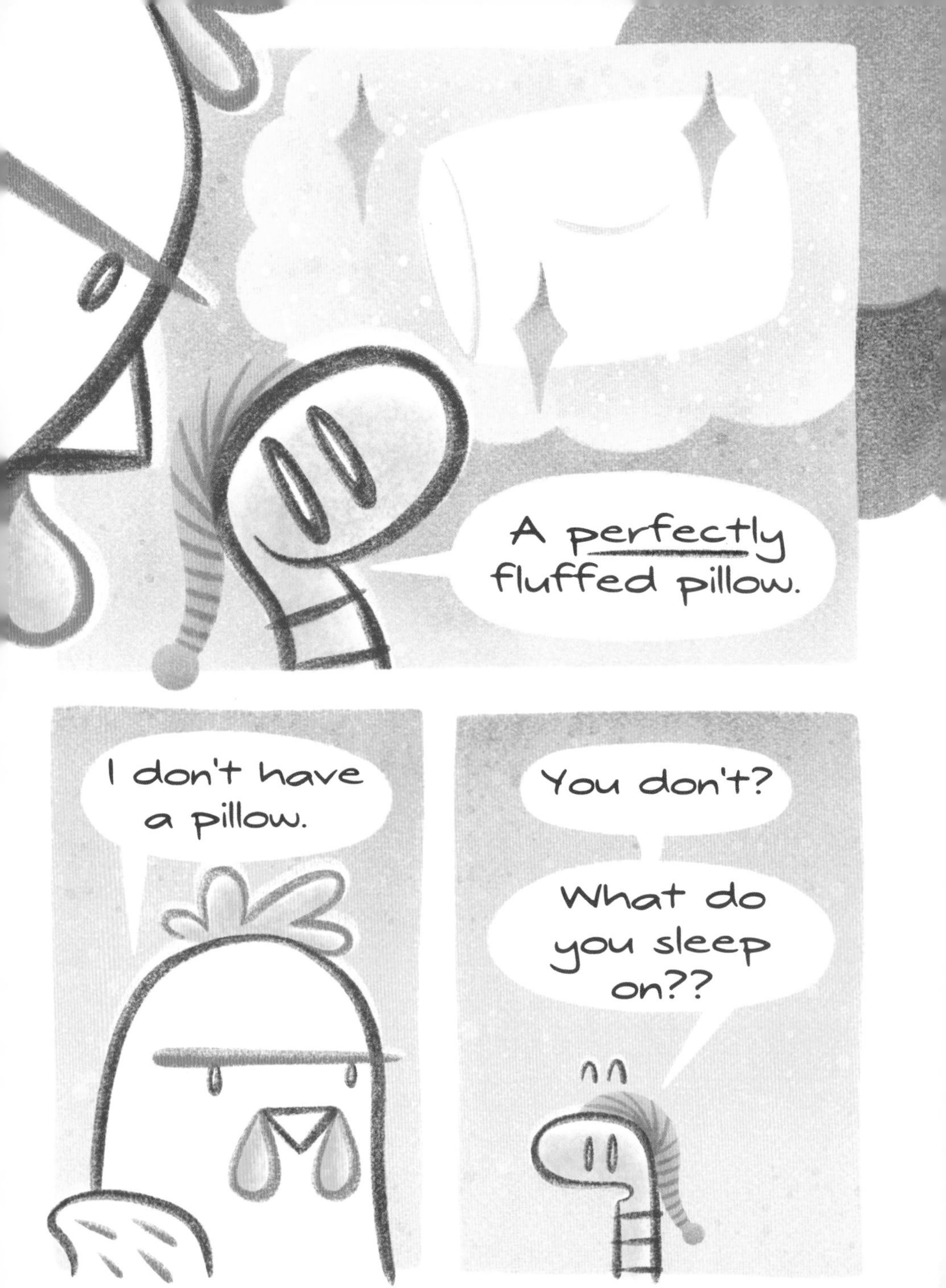
A perfectly fluffed pillow.
I don't have a pillow.
You don't?
What do you sleep on??

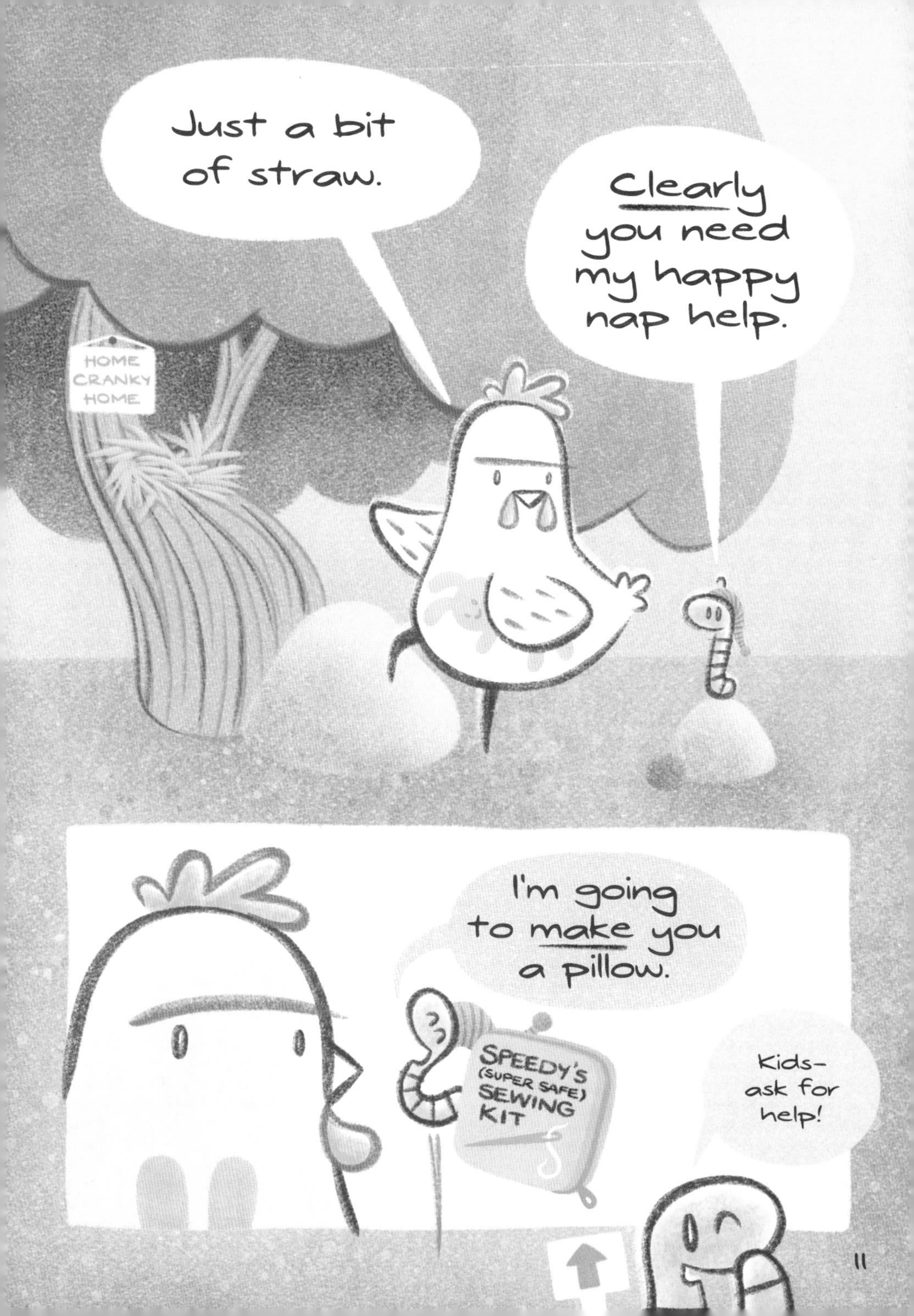
Just a bit of straw.
Clearly you need my happy nap help.
HOME CRANKY HOME
I'm going to make you a pillow.
SPEEDY'S (SUPER SAFE) SEWING KIT
Kids- ask for help!

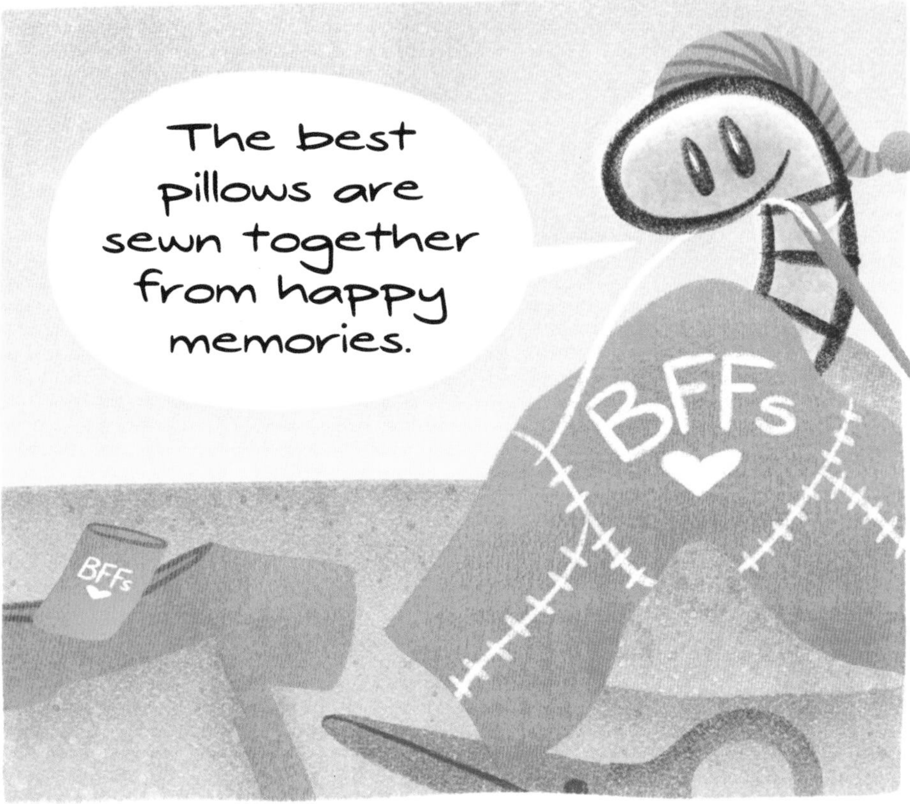
The best pillows are sewn together from happy memories.
BFFs
BFFs

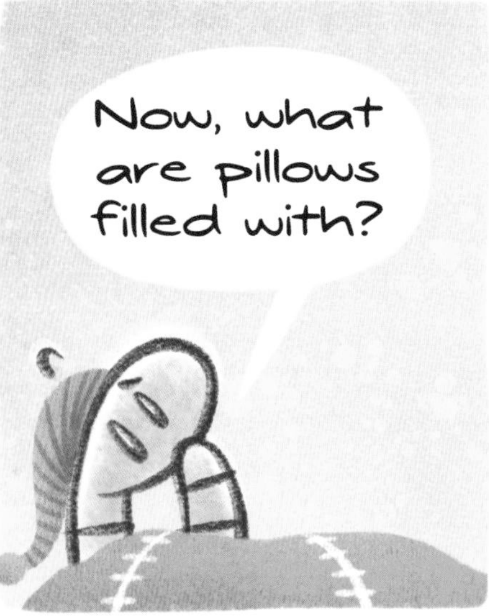
Now, what are pillows filled with?

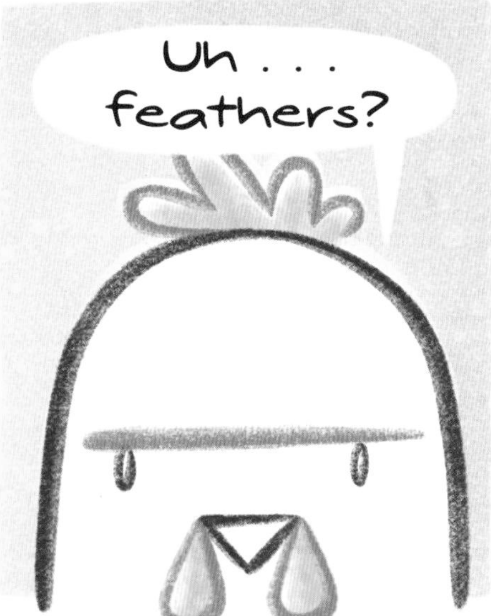
Uh . . . feathers?

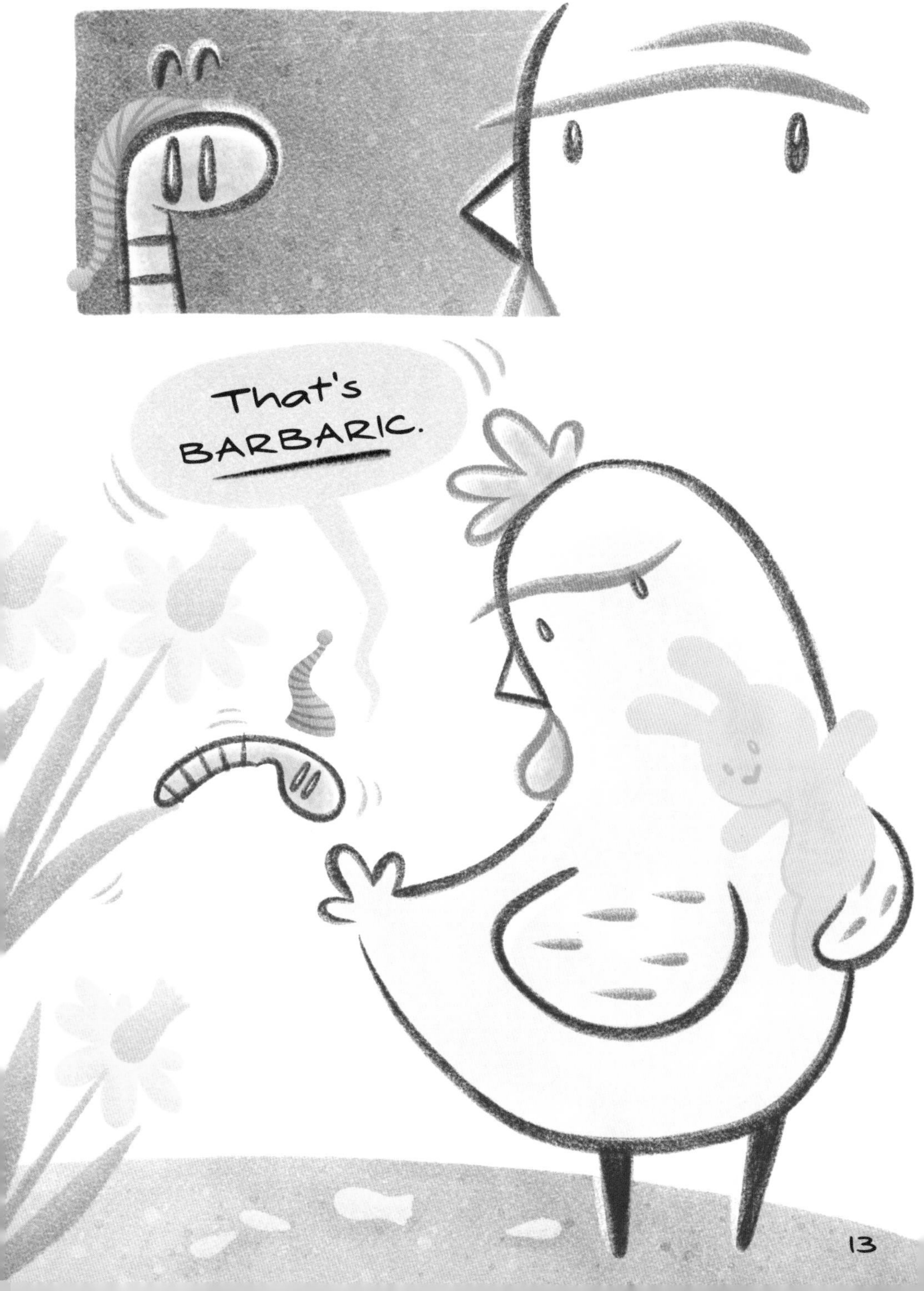
That's BARBARIC.

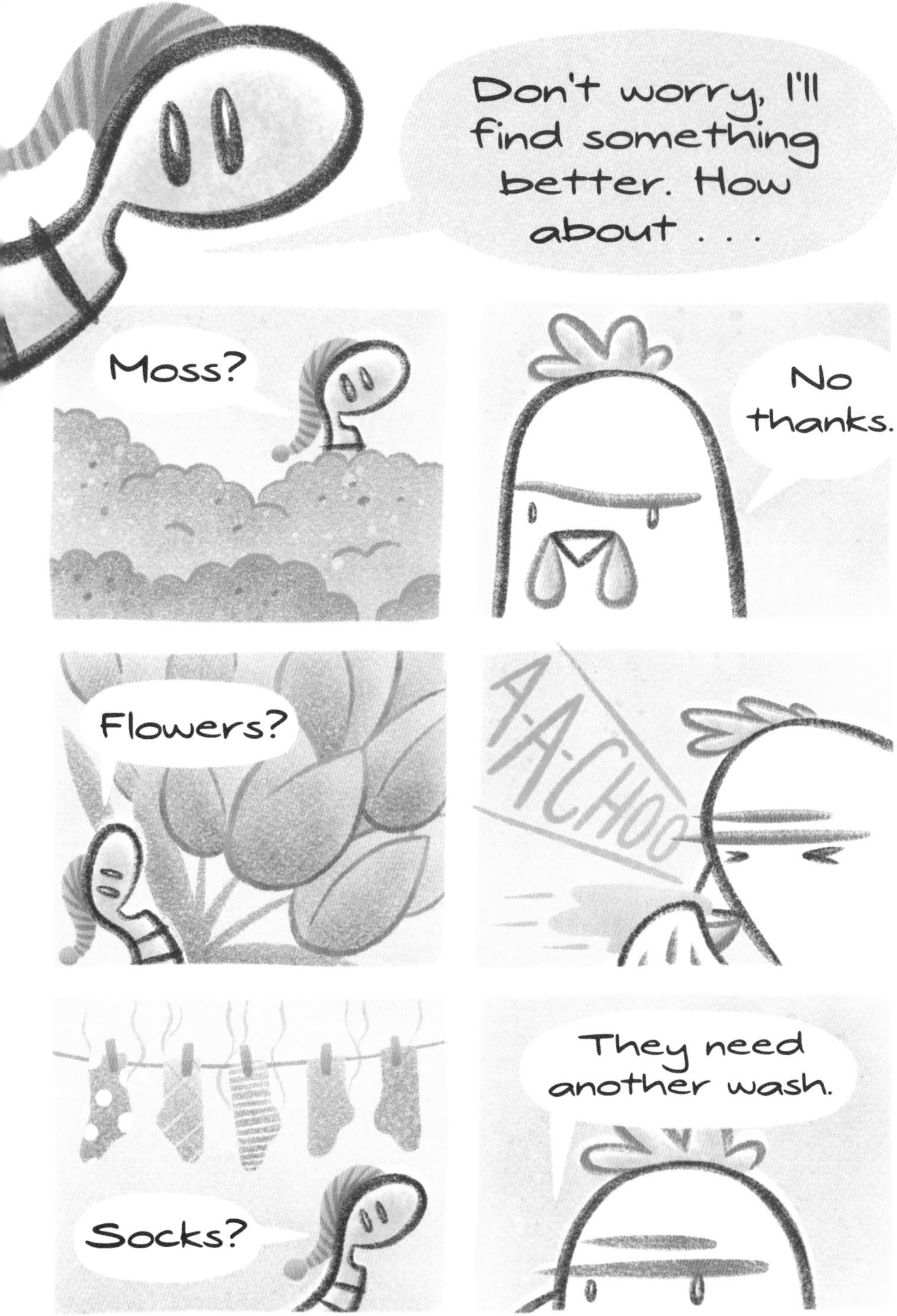
Don't worry, I'll find something better. How about . . .
Moss?
No thanks.
Flowers?
A-A-CHOO
Socks?
They need another wash.

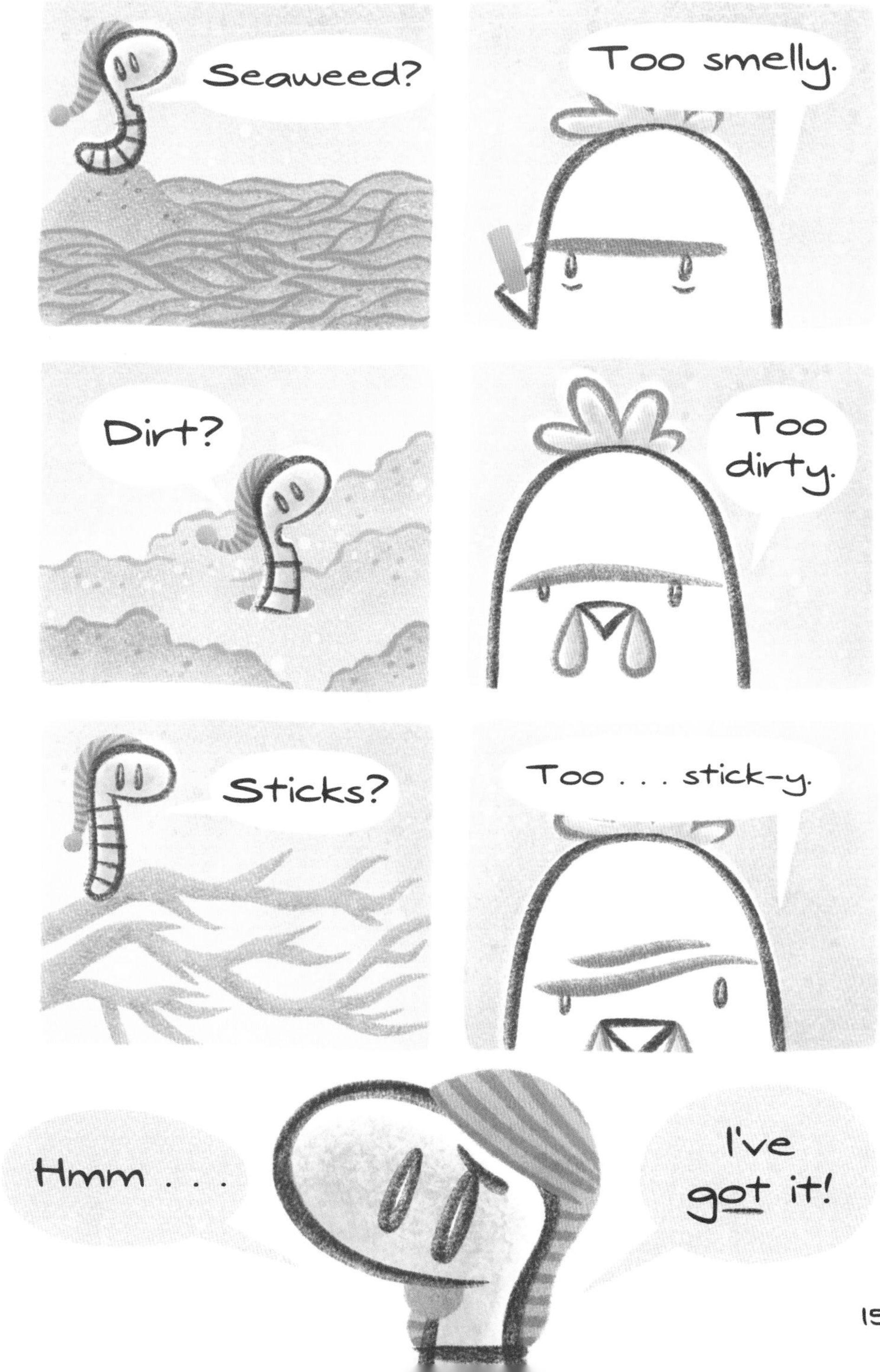
Seaweed?
Too smelly.
Dirt?
Too dirty.
Sticks?
Too . . . stick-y.
Hmm . . .
I've got it!

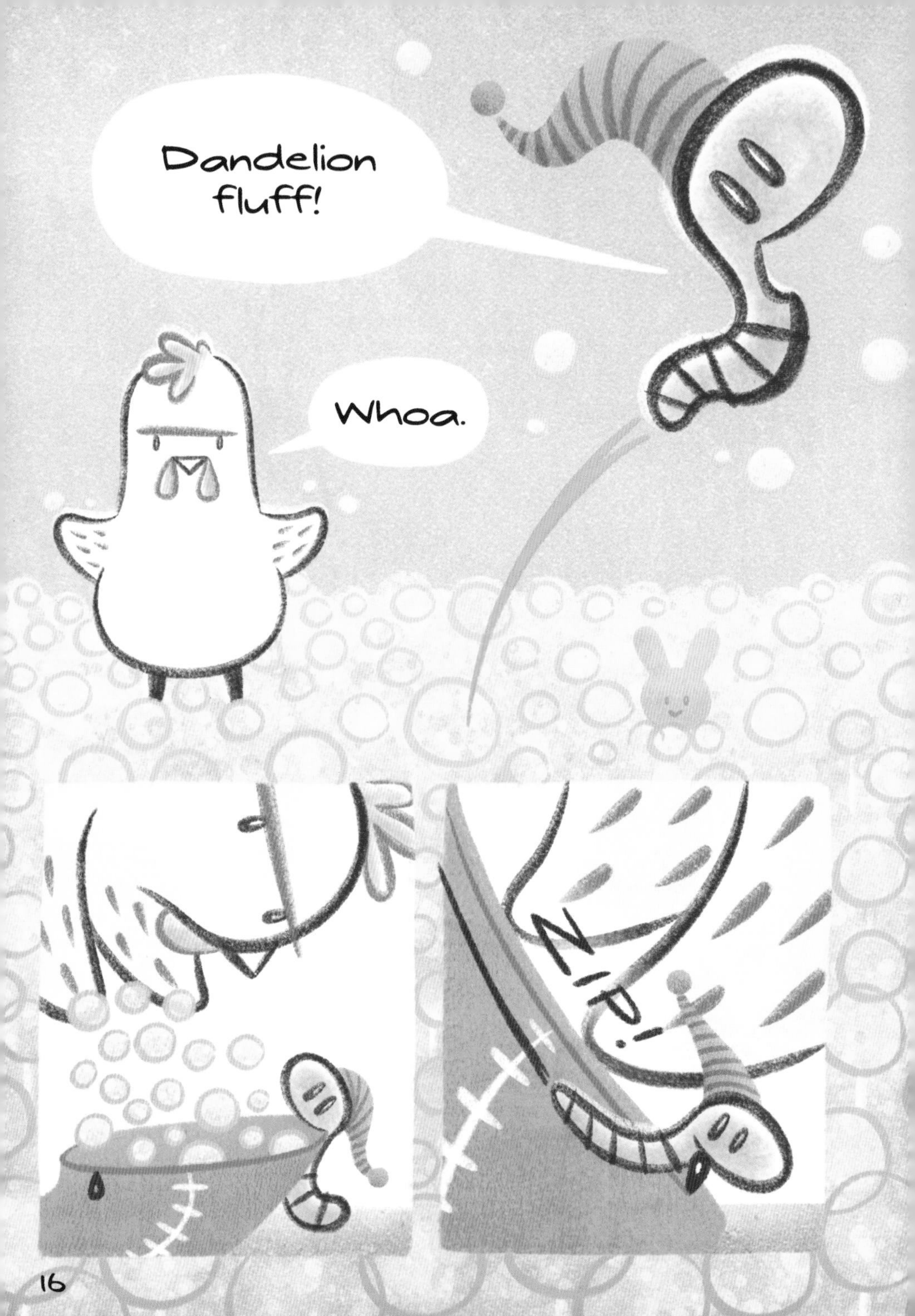
Dandelion fluff!
Whoa.
ZIP!

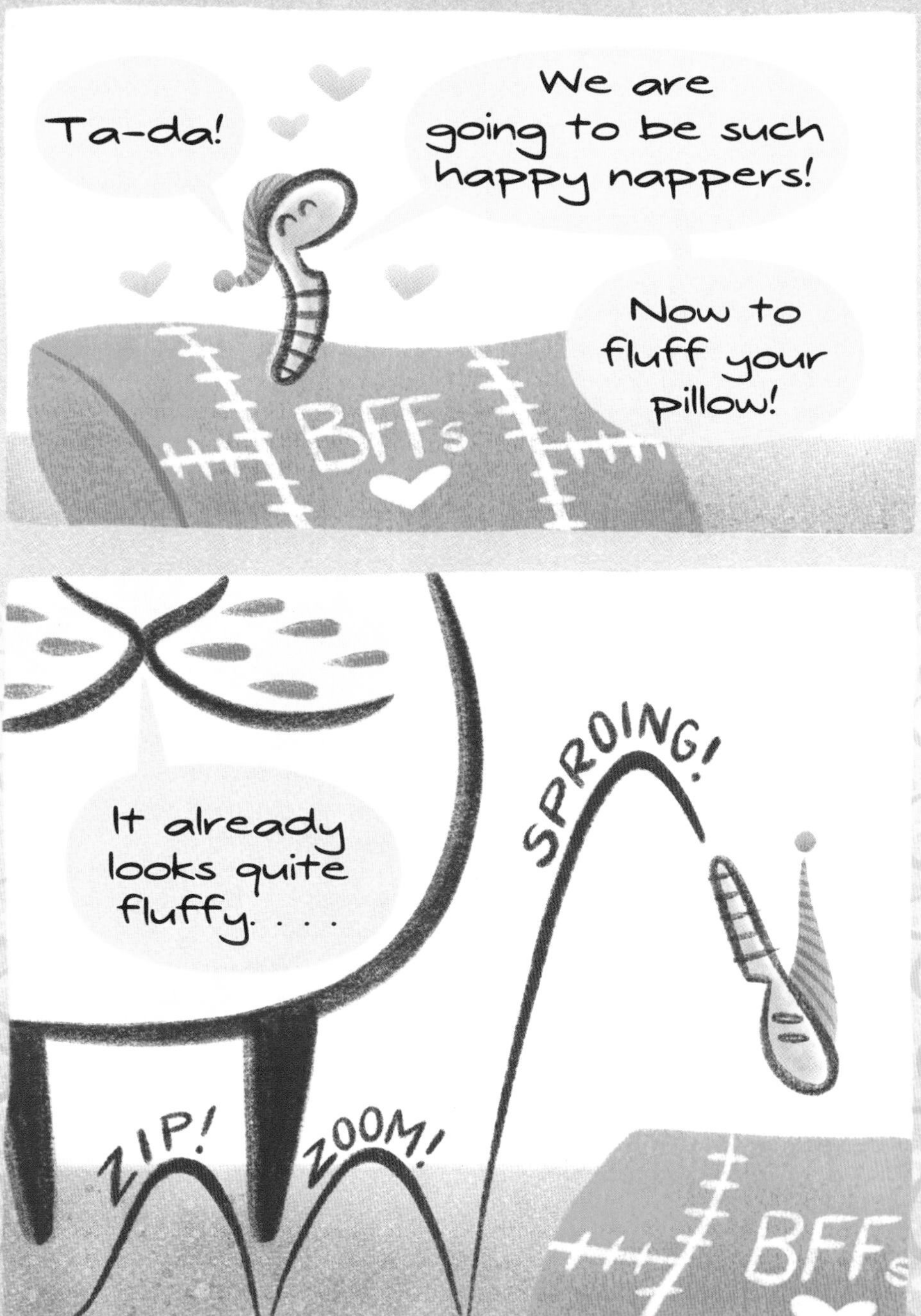
Ta-da!
We are going to be such happy nappers!
Now to fluff your pillow!
BFFs
It already looks quite fluffy. . . .
SPROING!
ZIP!
ZOOM!
BFFs

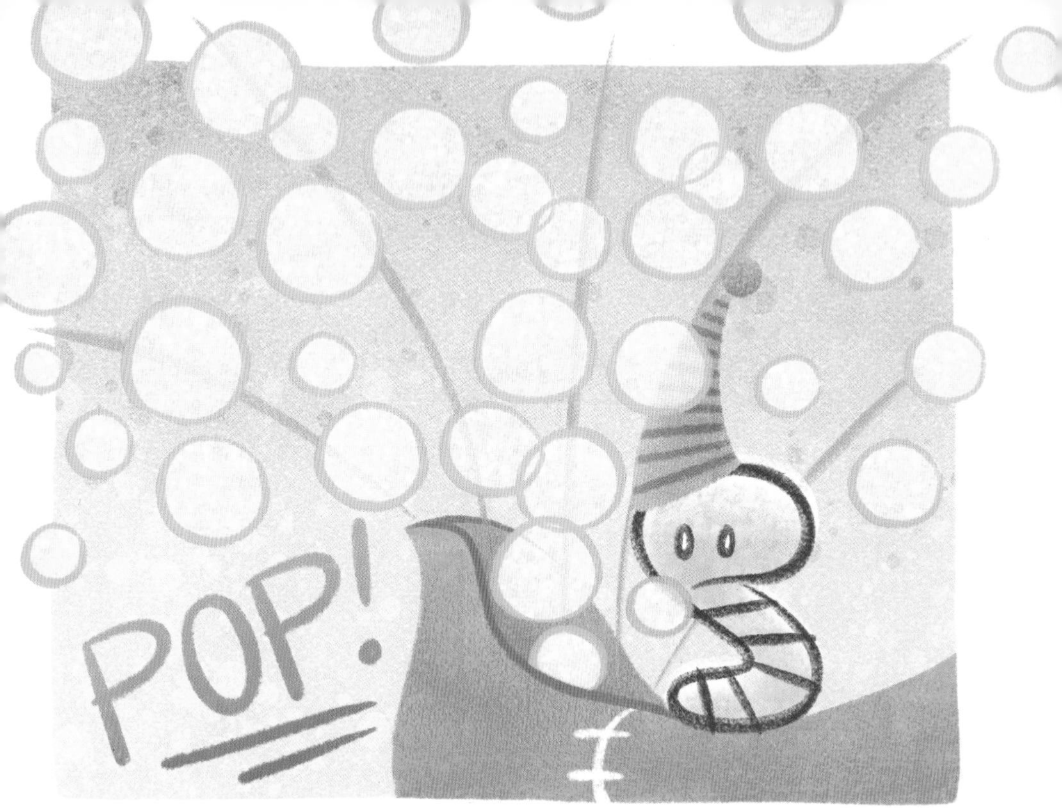
POP!

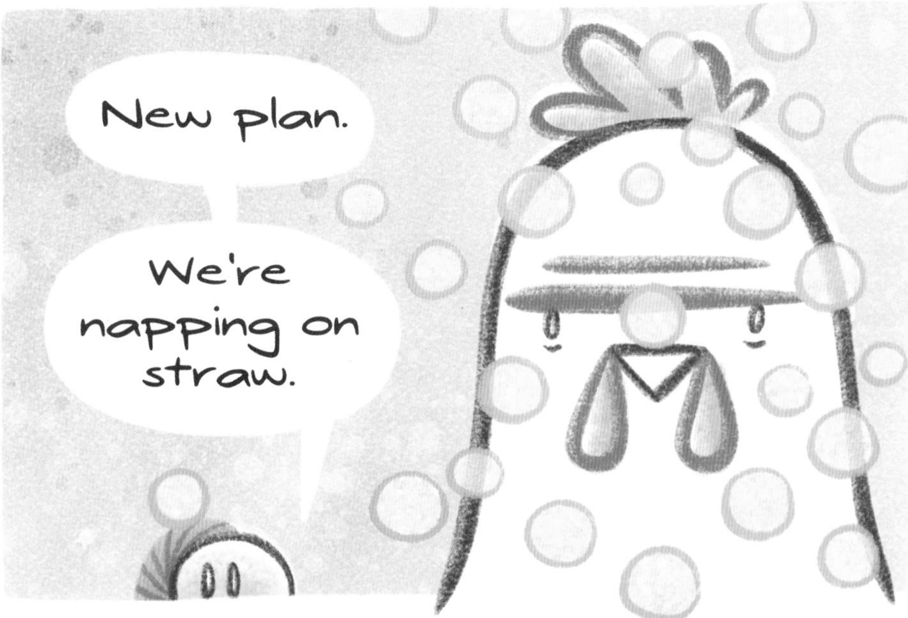
New plan.
We're napping on straw.

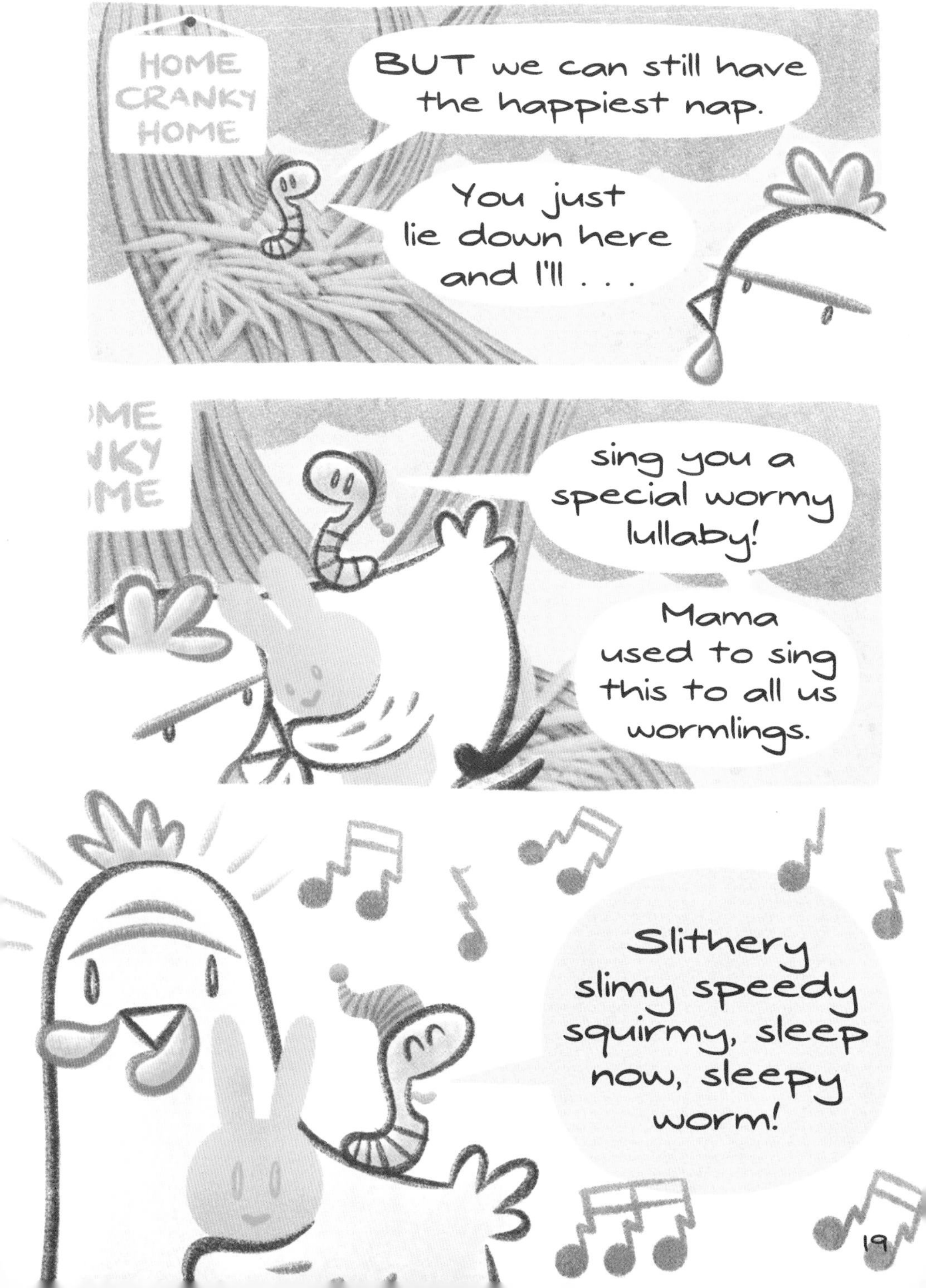
HOME CRANKY HOME
BUT we can still have the happiest nap.
You just lie down here and I'll . . .
sing you a special wormy lullaby!
Mama used to sing this to all us wormlings.
Slithery slimy speedy squirmy, sleep now, sleepy worm!

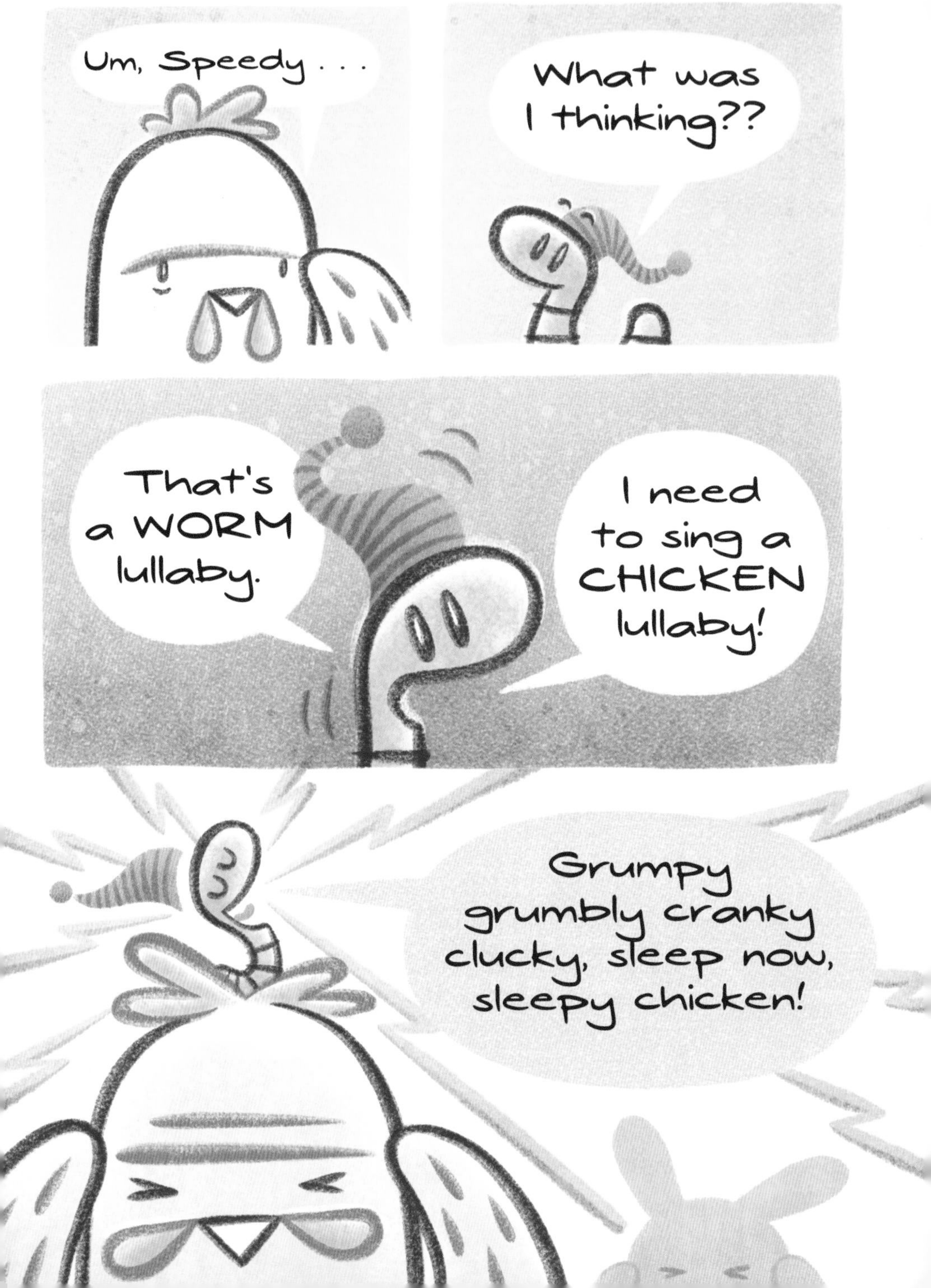
Um, Speedy . . .
What was I thinking??
That's a WORM lullaby.
I need to sing a CHICKEN lullaby!
Grumpy grumbly cranky clucky, sleep now, sleepy chicken!

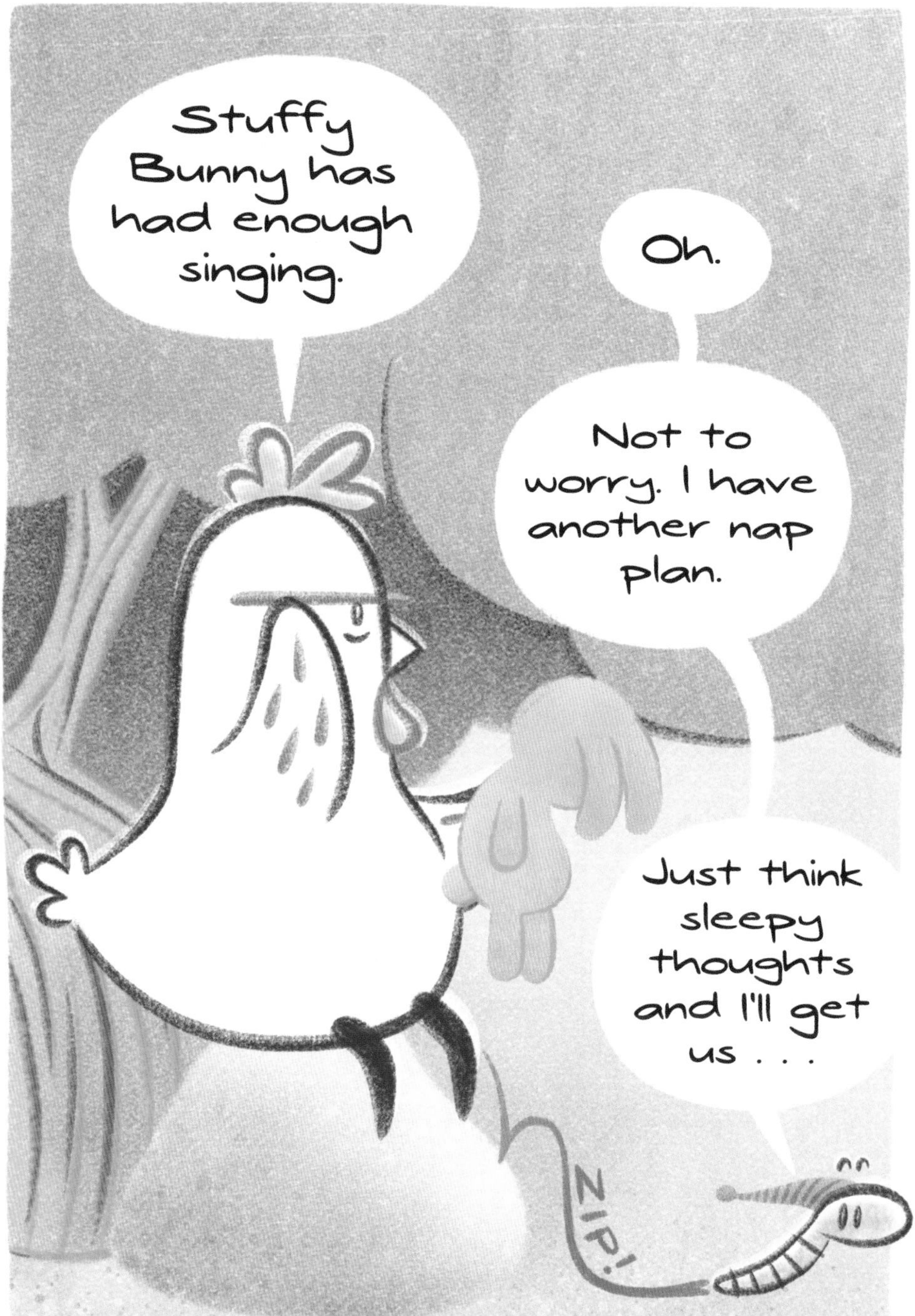
Stuffy Bunny has had enough singing.
Oh.
Not to worry. I have another nap plan.
Just think sleepy thoughts and I'll get us . . .
ZIP!

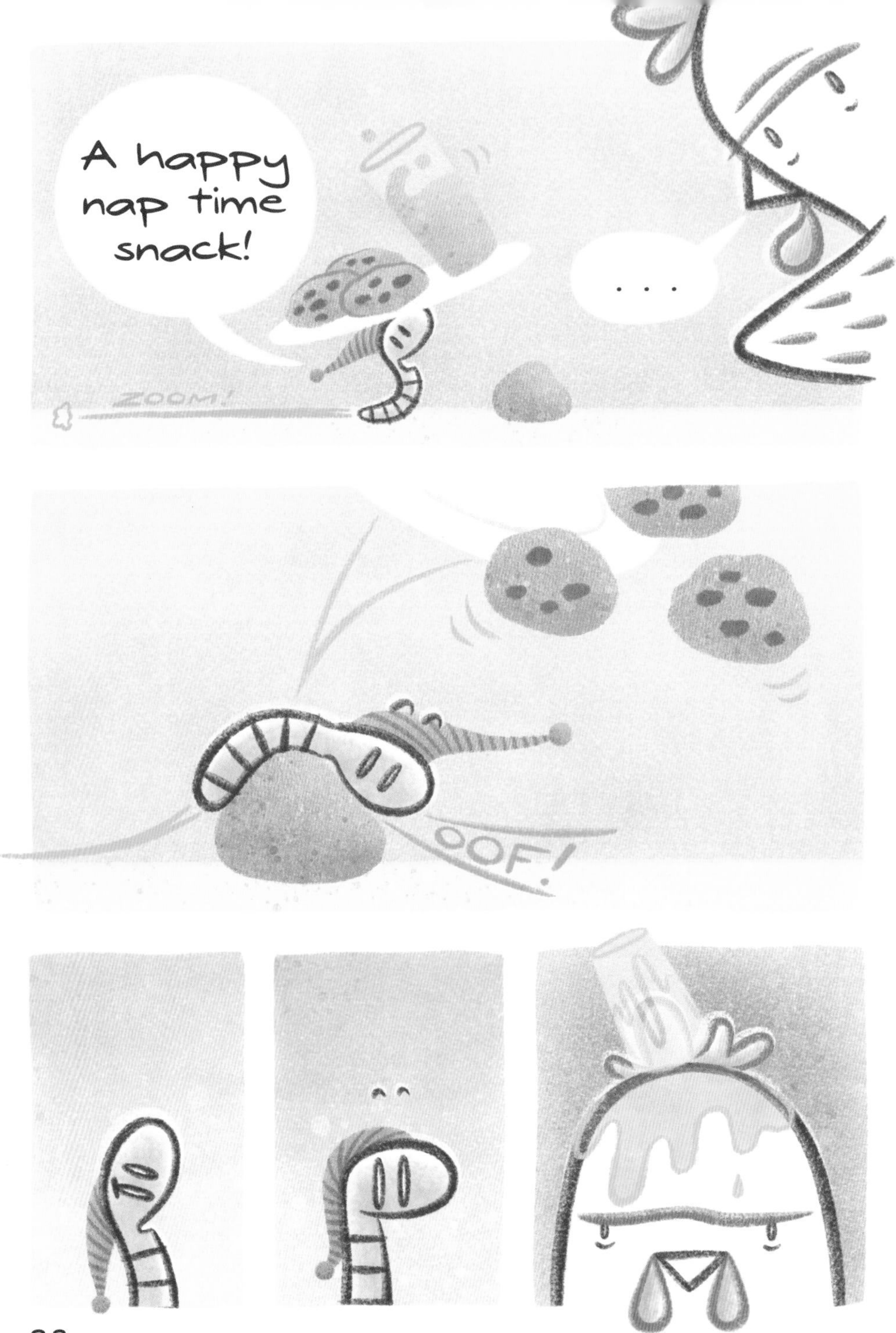

A happy nap time snack!

ZOOM!

. . .

OOF!

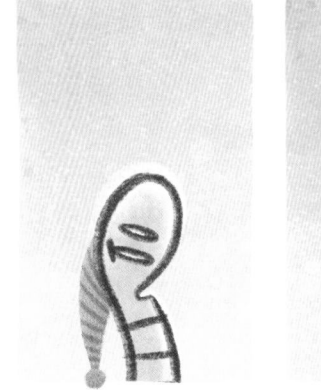

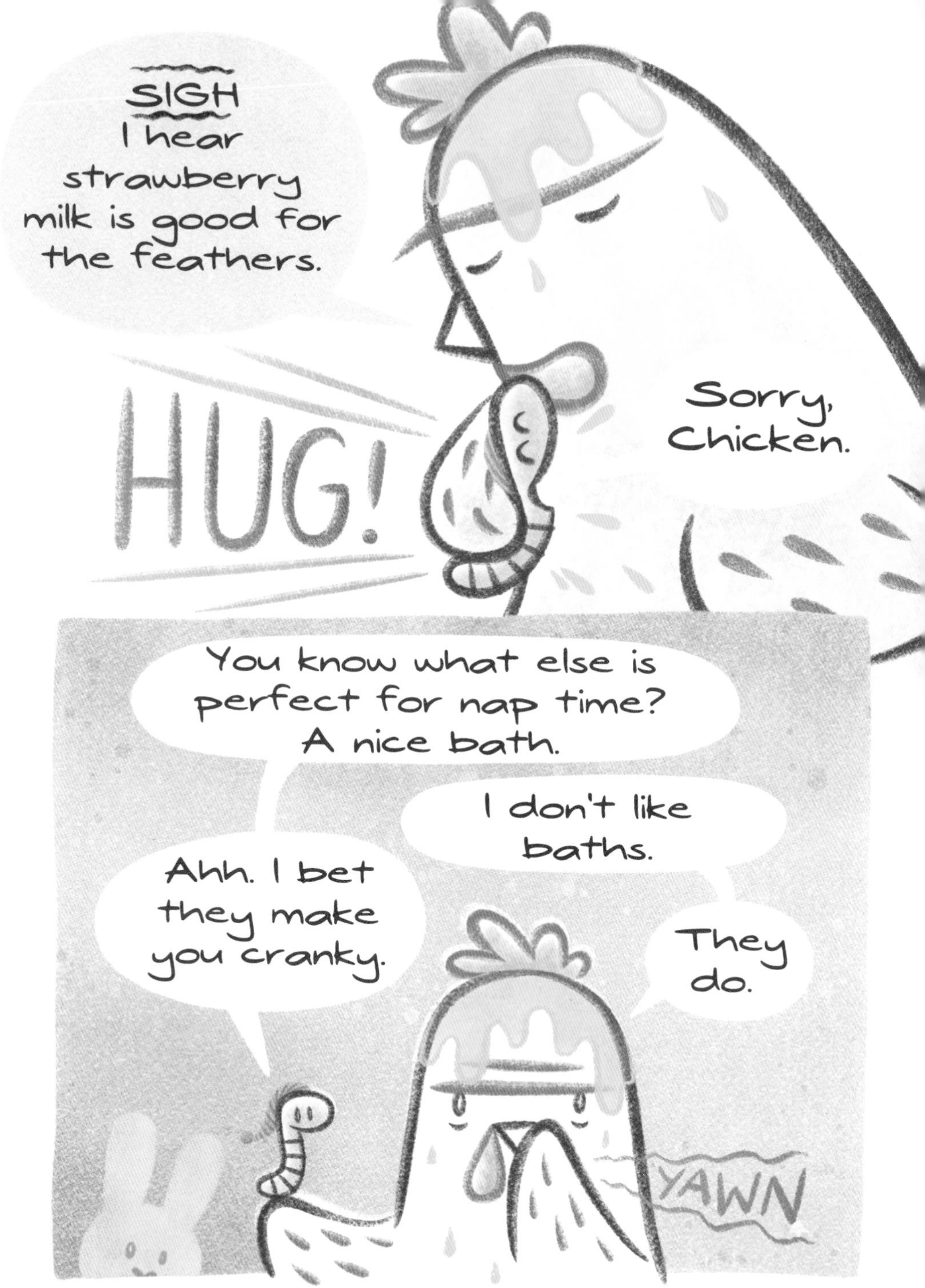
SIGH I hear strawberry milk is good for the feathers.
HUG!
Sorry, Chicken.
You know what else is perfect for nap time? A nice bath.
I don't like baths.
Ahh. I bet they make you cranky.
They do.
YAWN

Why Baths Make Cranky Chicken Cranky

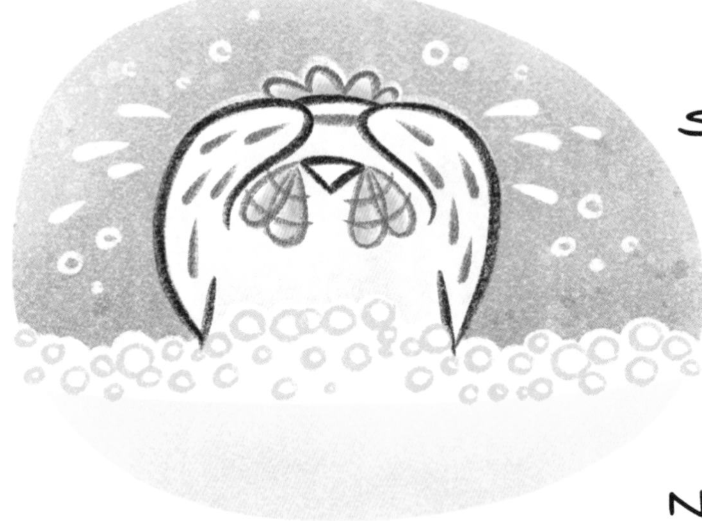

Soap gets in eyes

No room for rubber ducky collection

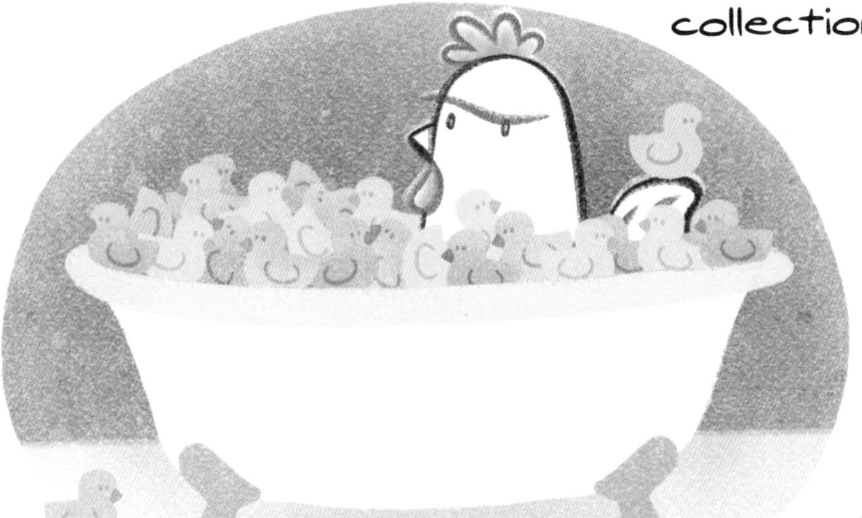

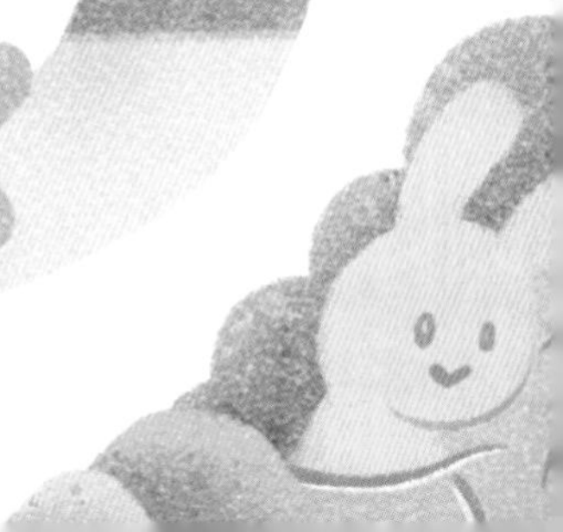

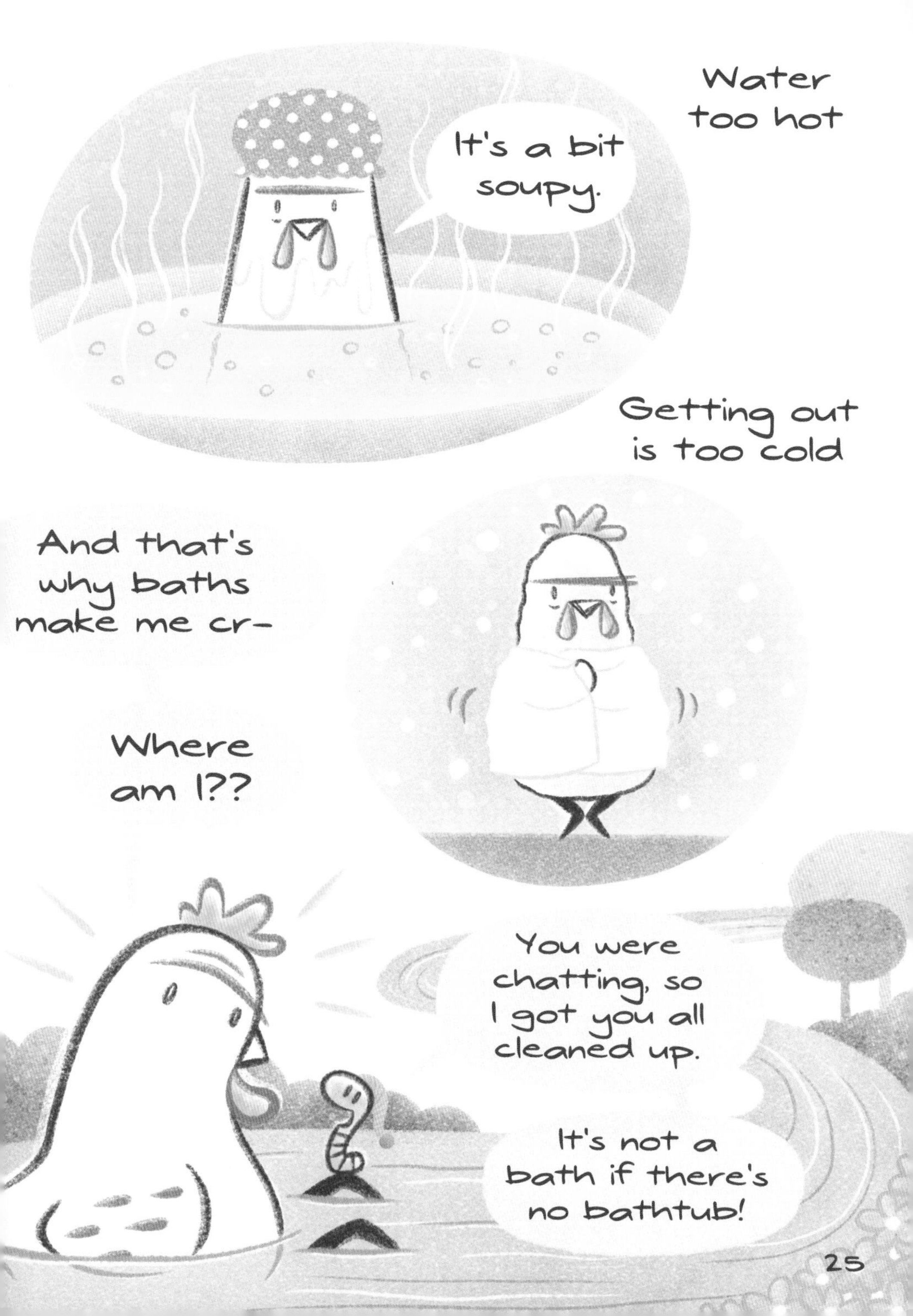

Water too hot
It's a bit soupy.
Getting out is too cold
And that's why baths make me cr-
Where am I??
You were chatting, so I got you all cleaned up.
It's not a bath if there's no bathtub!

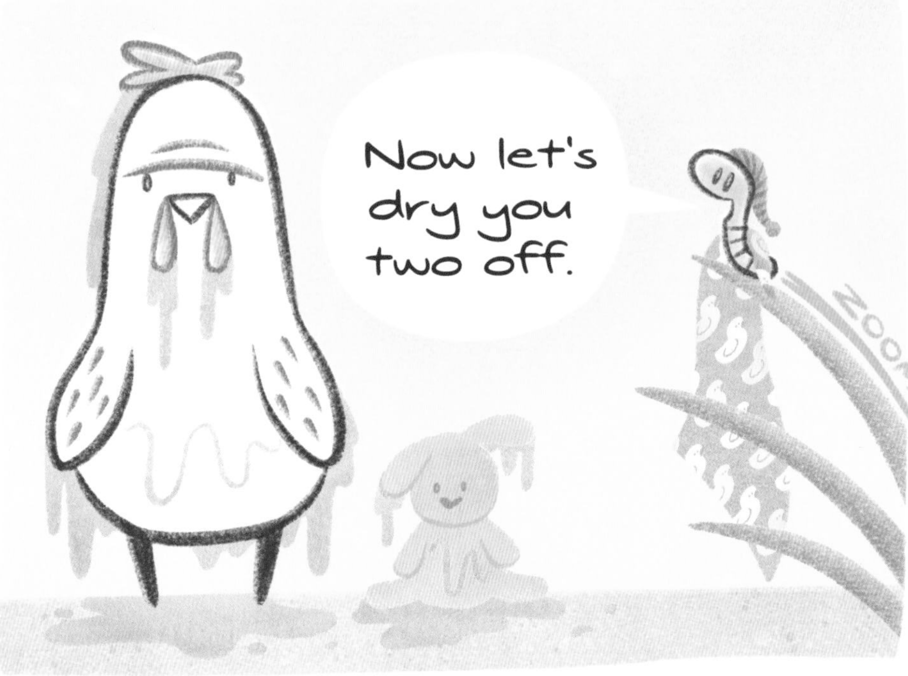
Now let's dry you two off.
ZOOM!

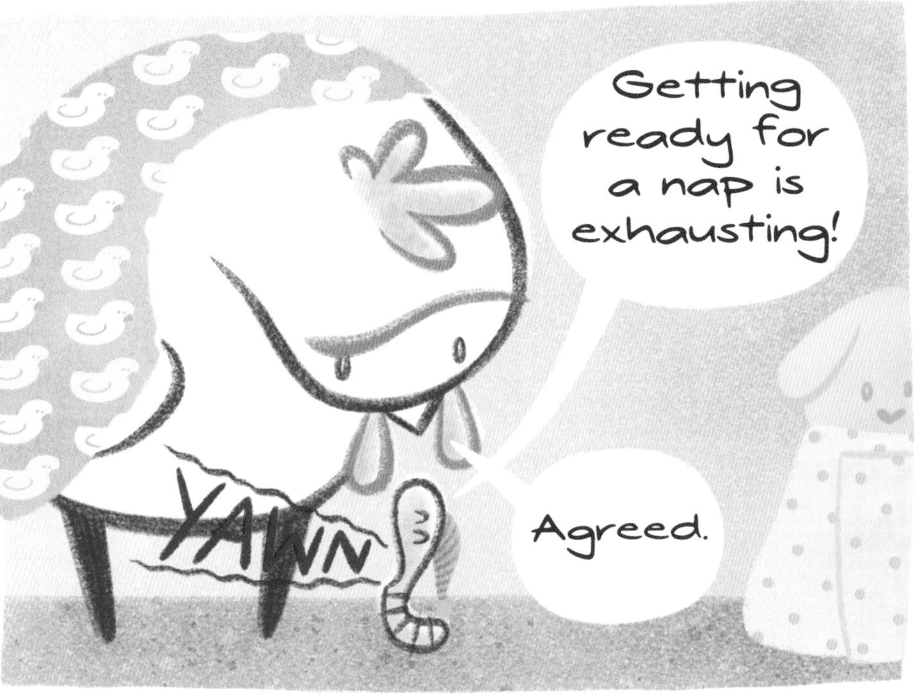
Getting ready for a nap is exhausting!
YAWN
Agreed.

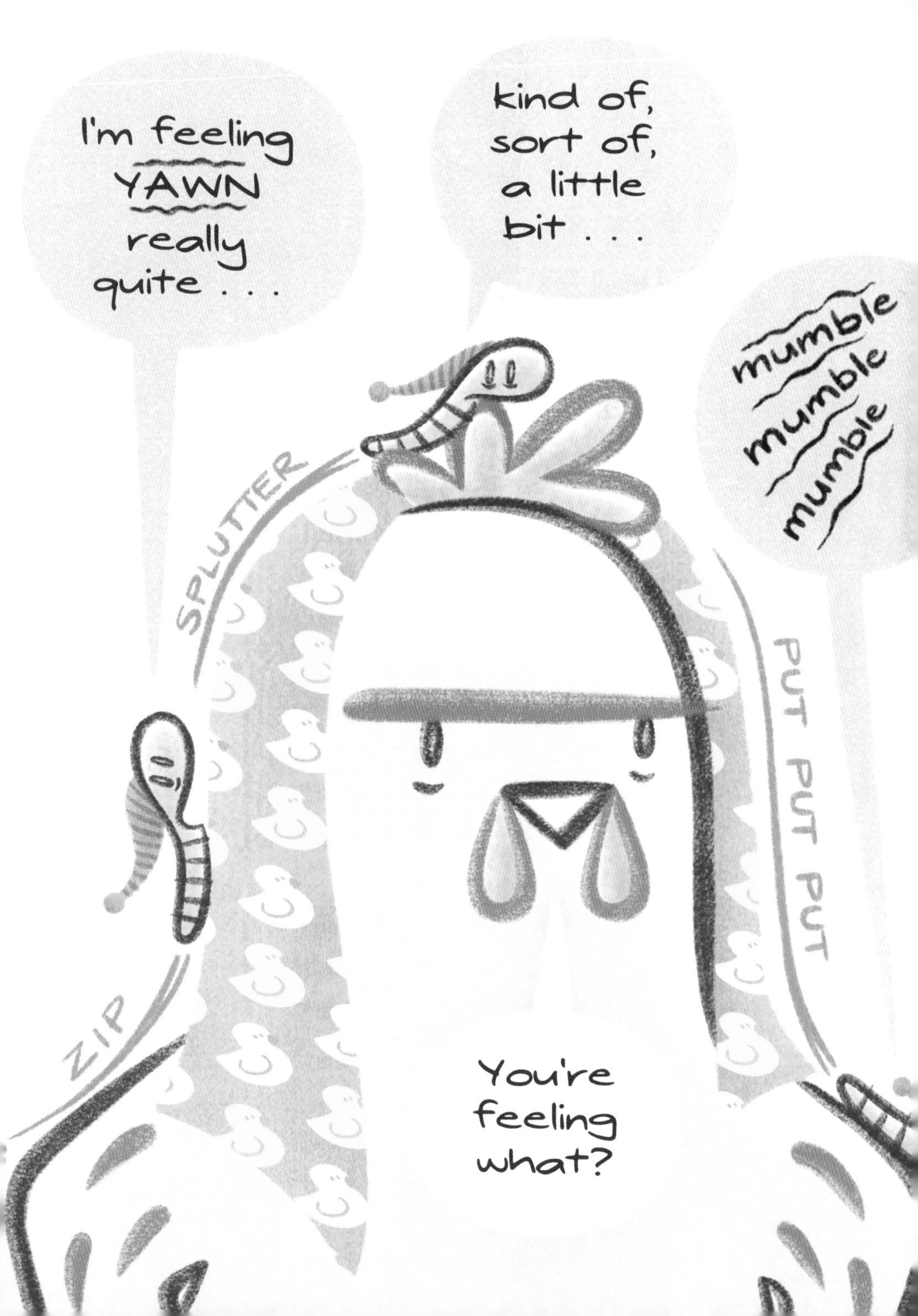
I'm feeling YAWN really quite . . .
kind of, sort of, a little bit . . .
mumble mumble mumble
SPLUTTER
PUT PUT PUT
ZIP
You're feeling what?

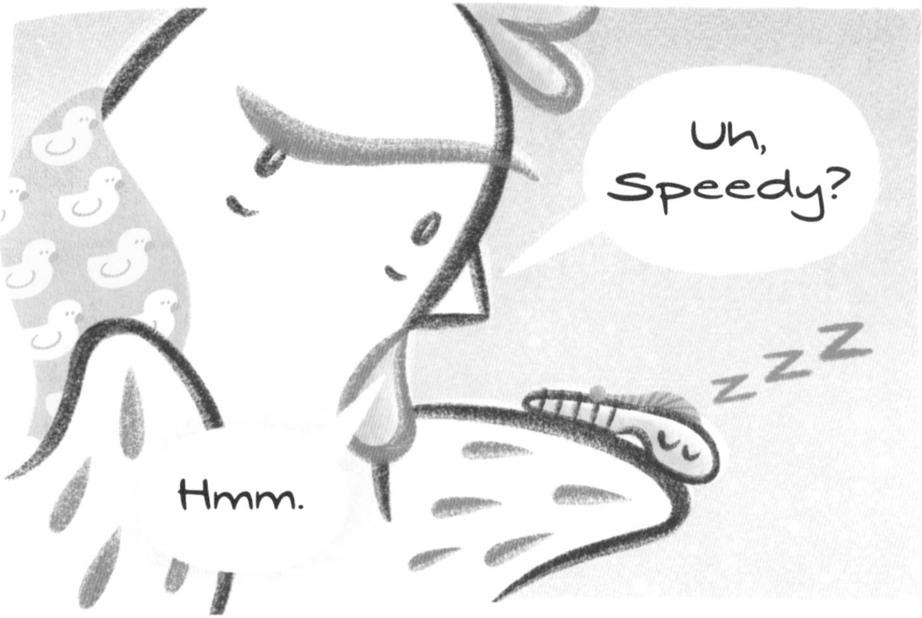
Uh, Speedy?
ZZZ
Hmm.

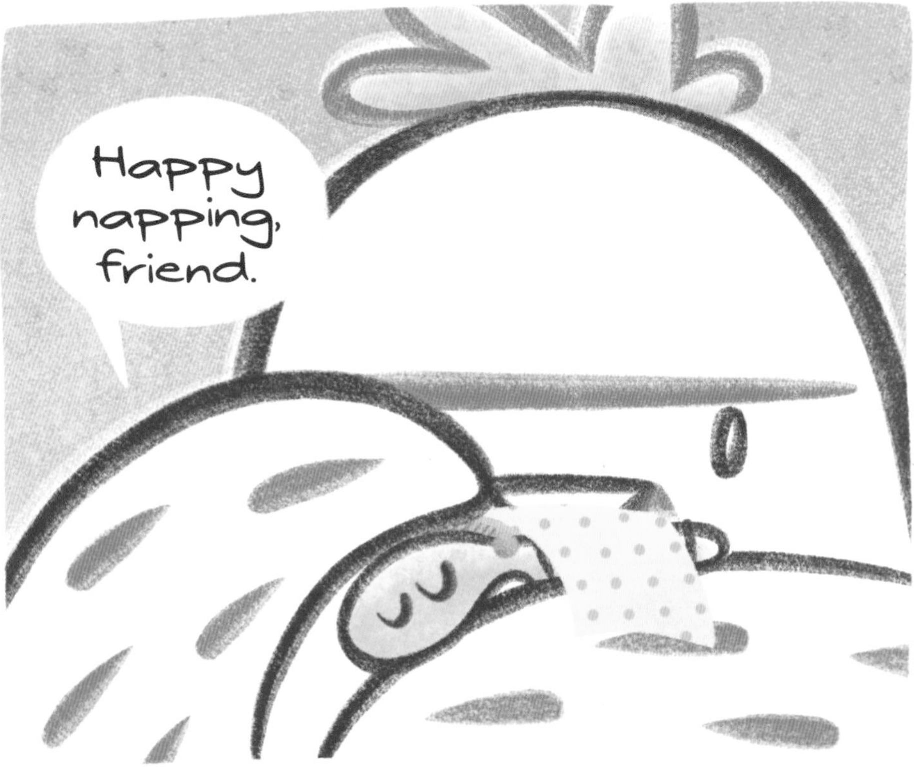
Happy napping, friend.

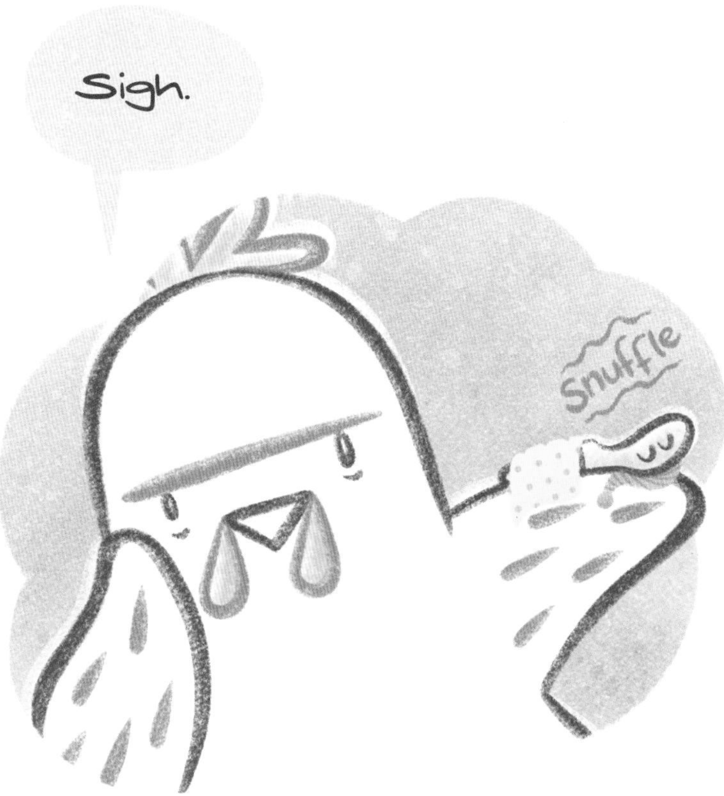
Sigh.
Snuffle

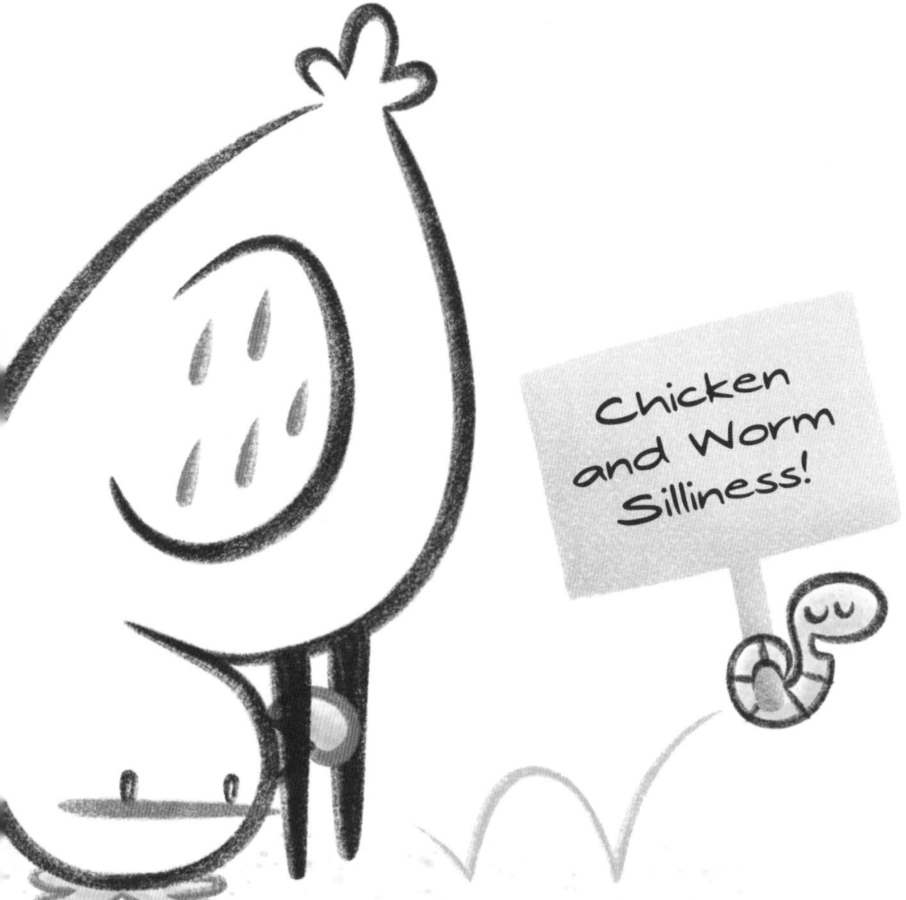
Chicken
and Worm
Silliness!

Chicken and Speedy's Favorite Costumes

Flower Power

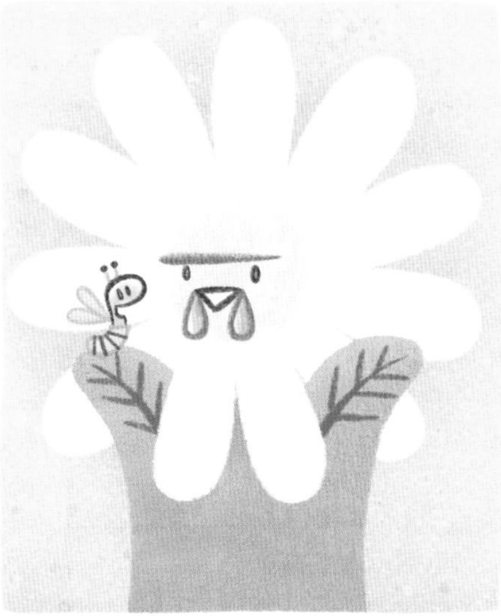

Space Heroes

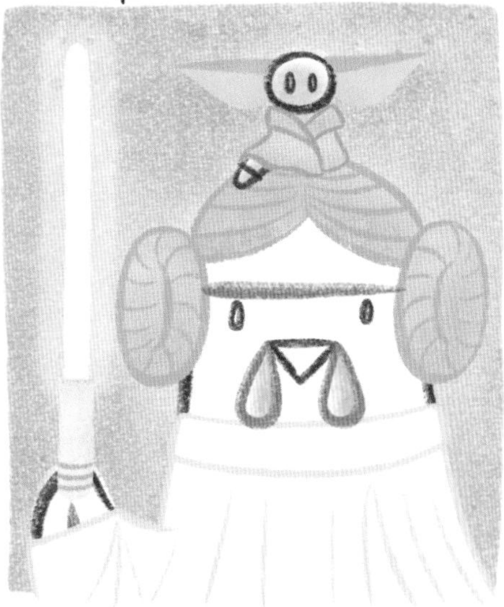

Stripy Lost Guy

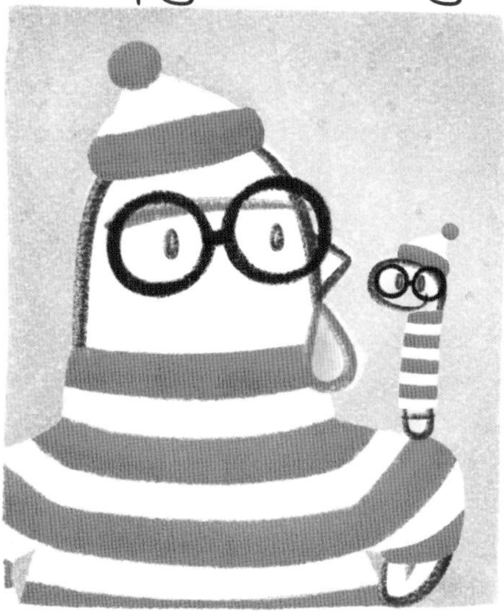

Chicken and Worm

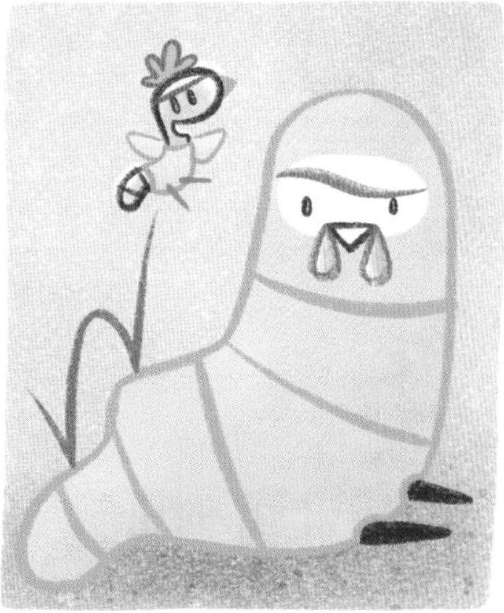

Things That Make Chicken Cranky

Crowds

Trampolines

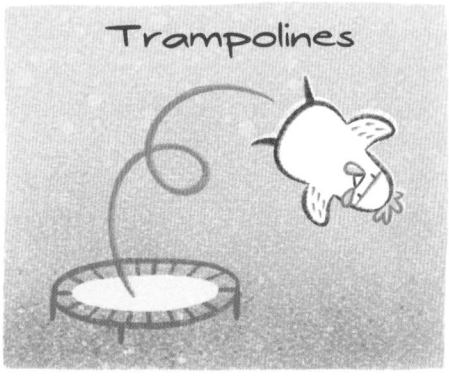

Humid summers

Dry winters

Baths

Skipping naps

Things That DON'T Make Chicken Cranky

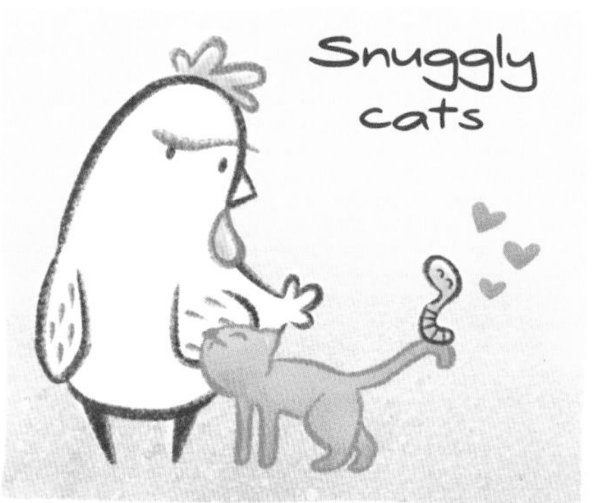
Snuggly cats

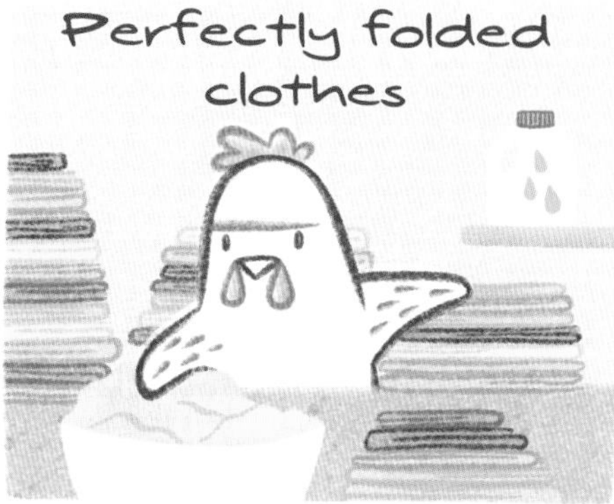
Perfectly folded clothes

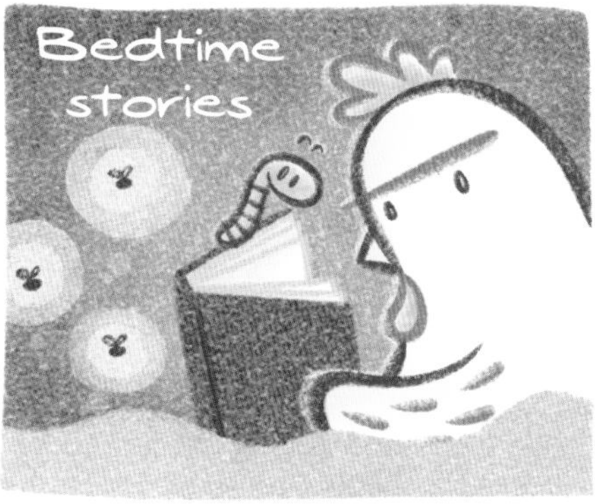
Bedtime stories

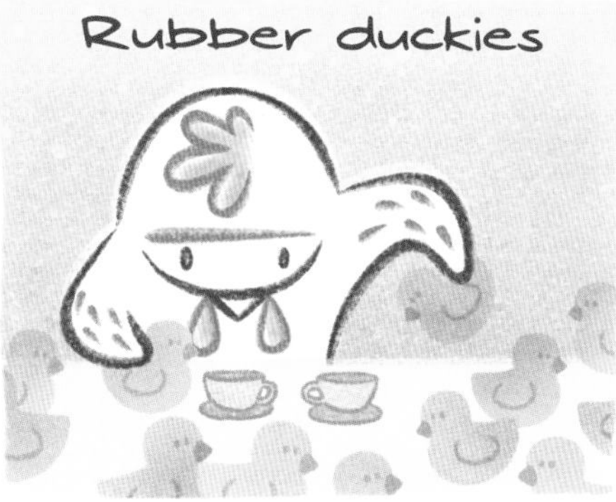
Rubber duckies

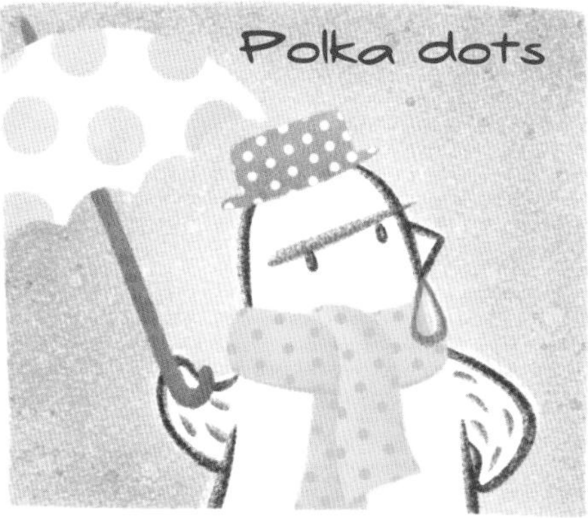
Polka dots

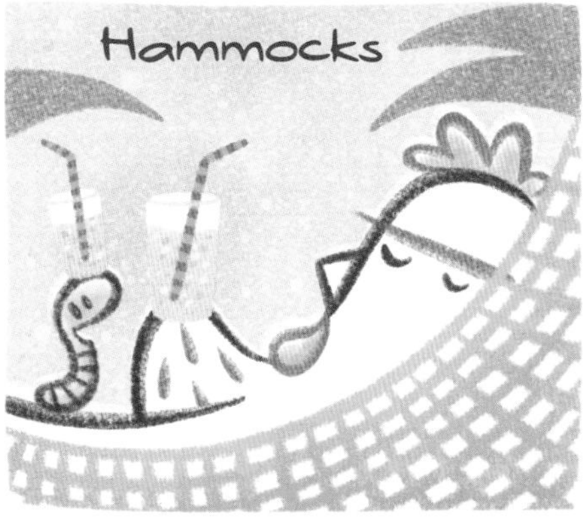
Hammocks

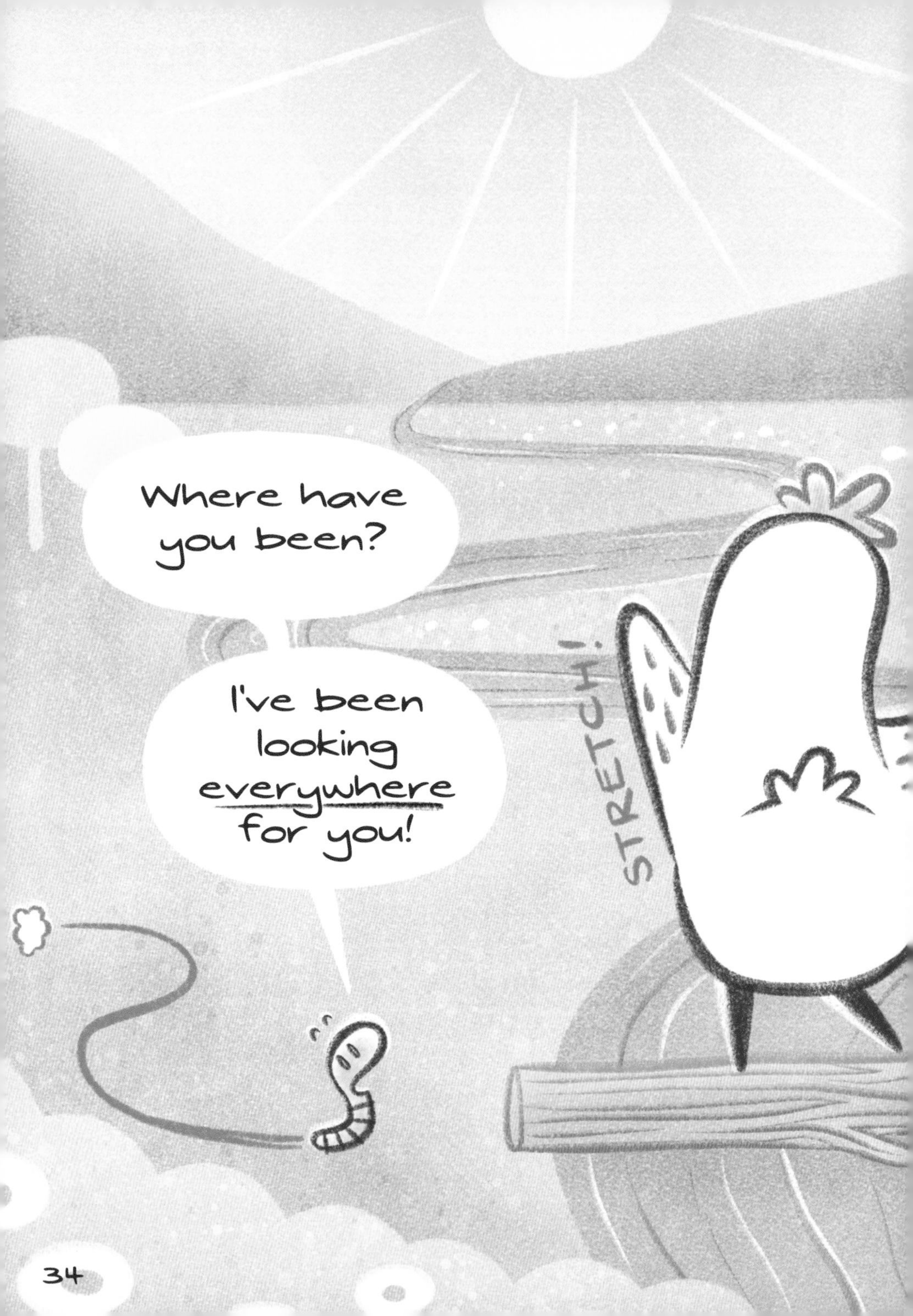
Where have you been?
I've been looking everywhere for you!
STRETCH!

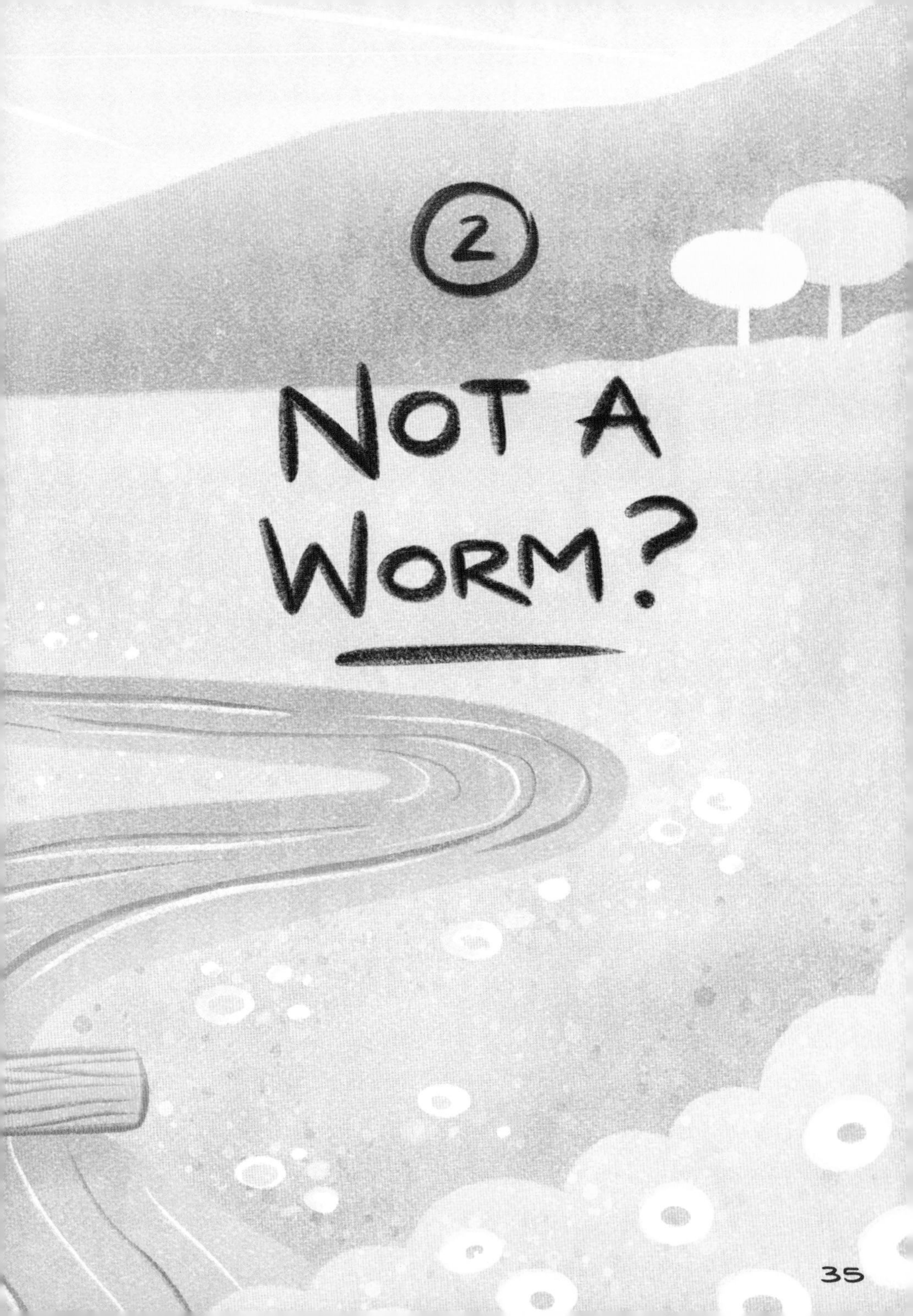

2

Not a Worm?

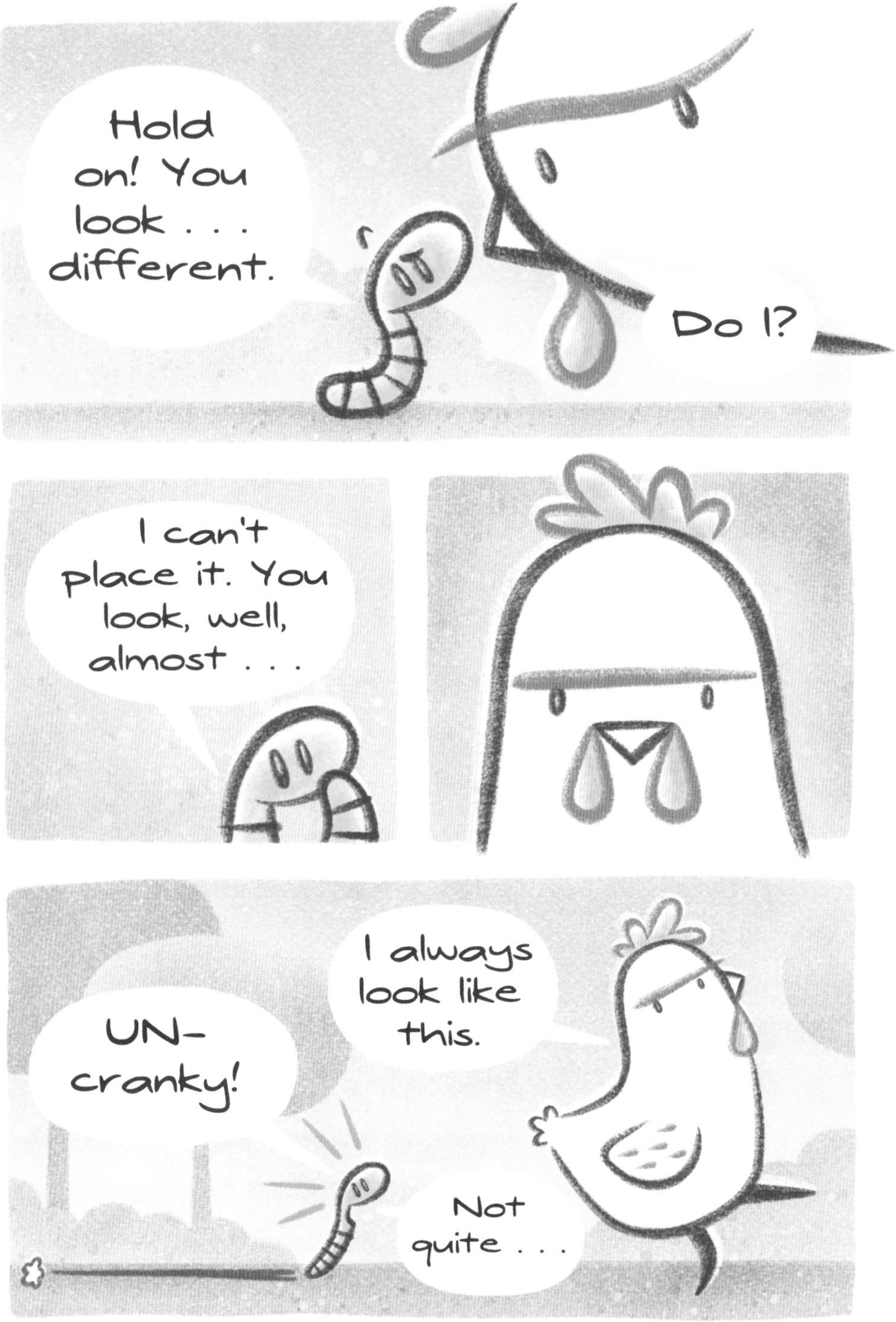
Hold on! You look . . . different.
Do I?
I can't place it. You look, well, almost . . .
I always look like this.
UN-cranky!
Not quite . . .

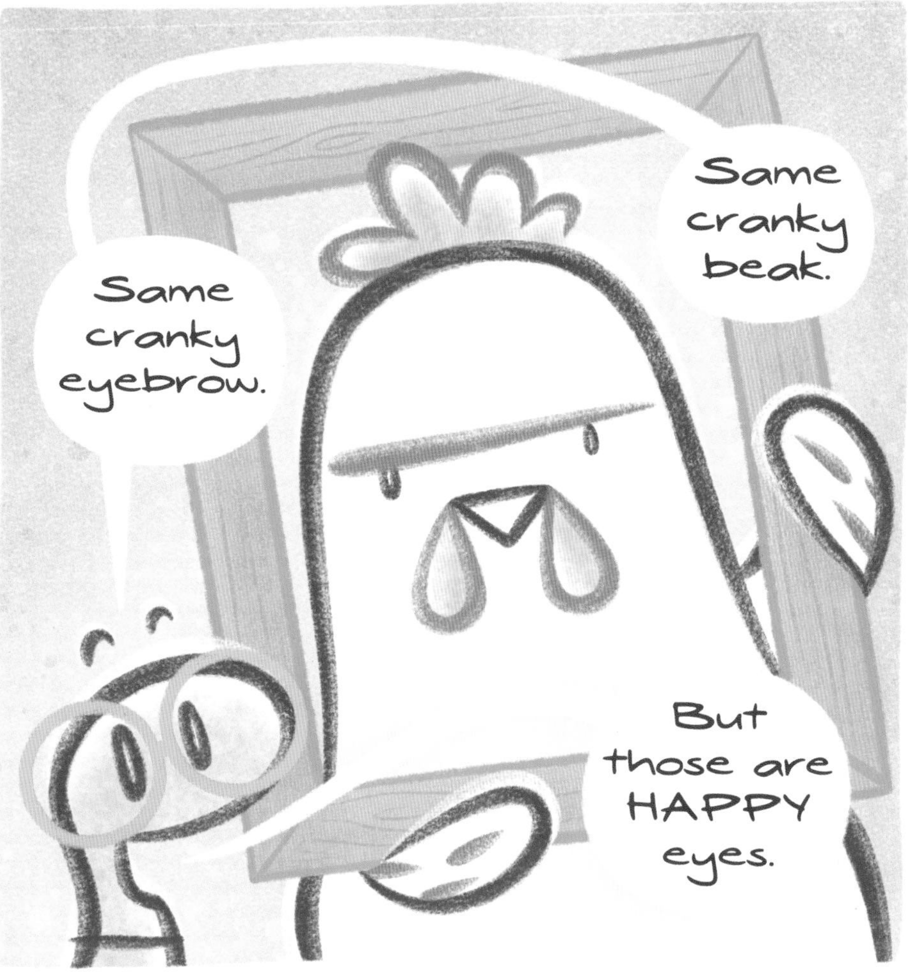
Same cranky eyebrow.
Same cranky beak.
But those are HAPPY eyes.

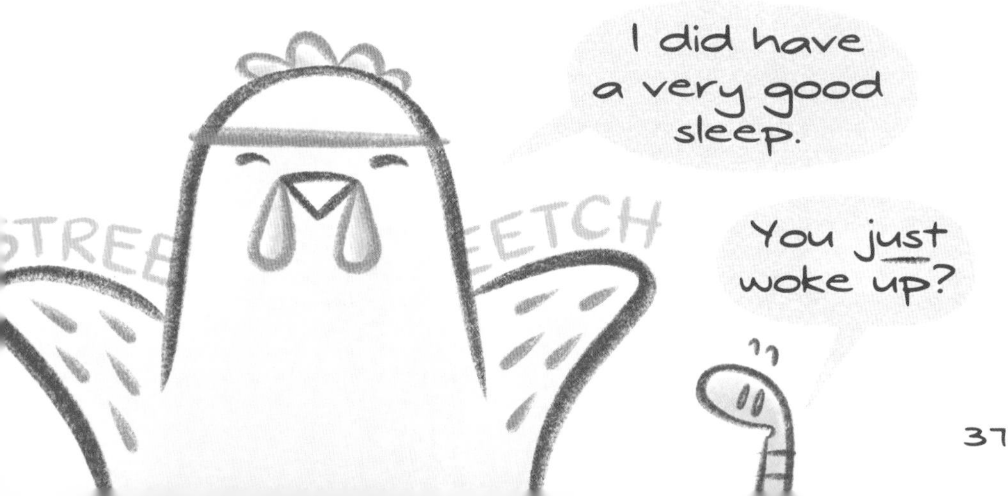
STREEEETCH
I did have a very good sleep.
You just woke up?

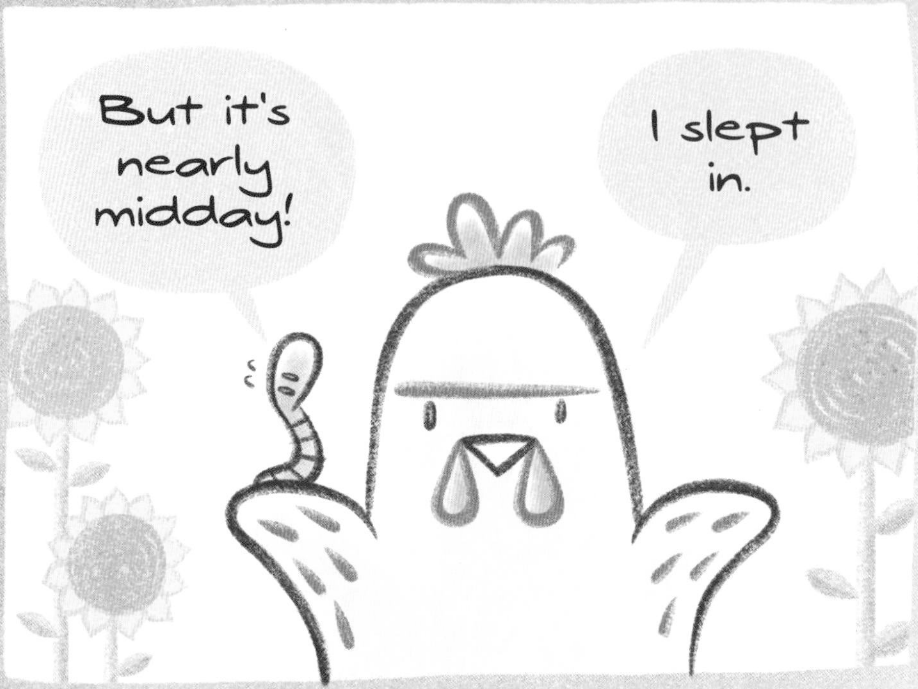
But it's nearly midday!
I slept in.

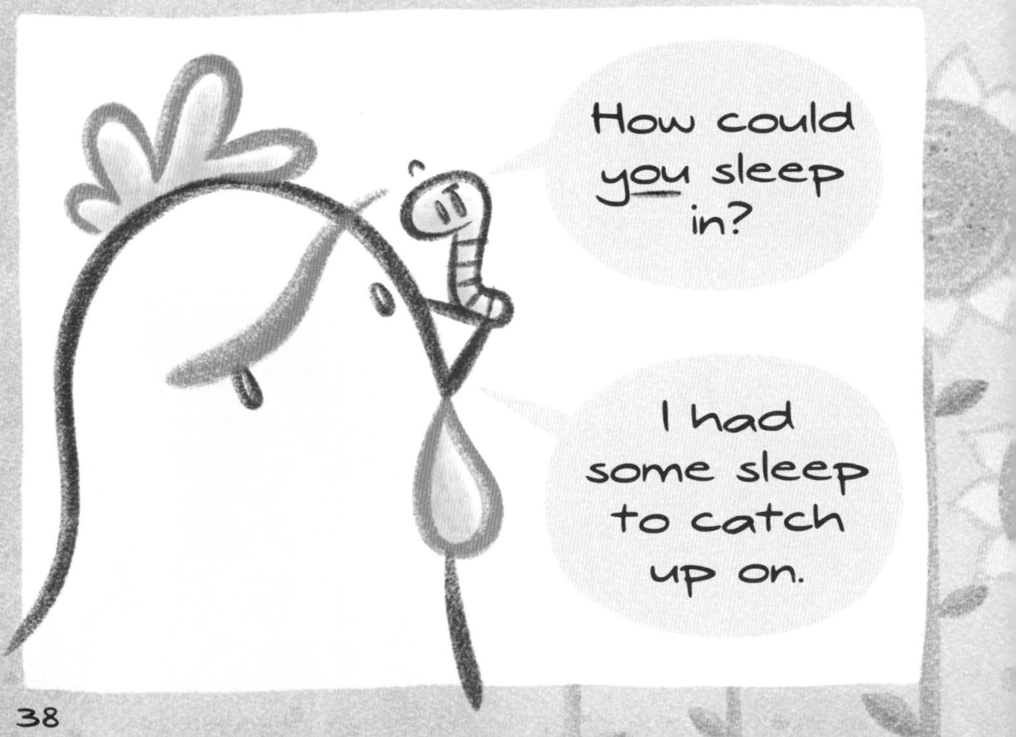
How could you sleep in?
I had some sleep to catch up on.

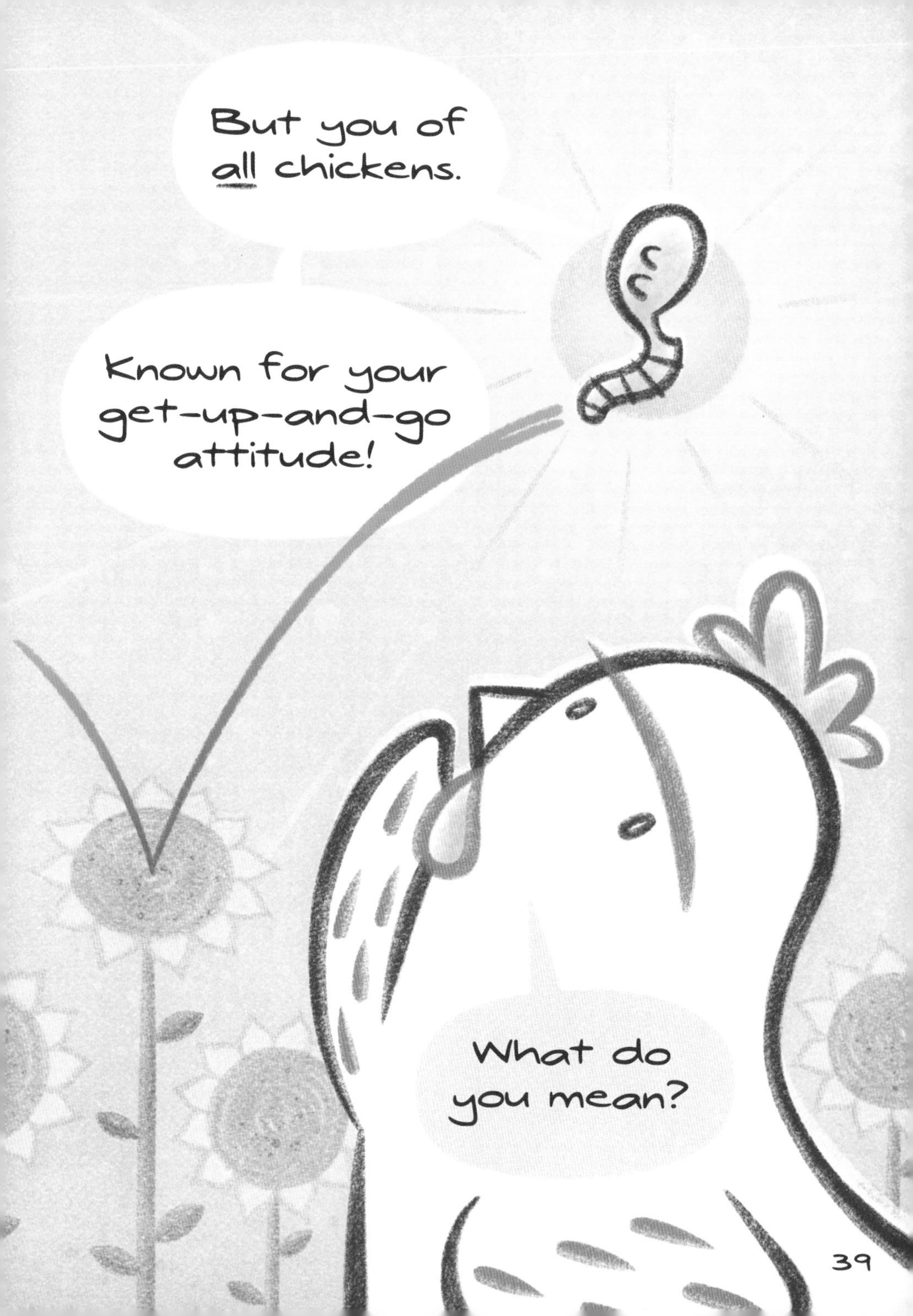
But you of all chickens.
Known for your get-up-and-go attitude!
What do you mean?

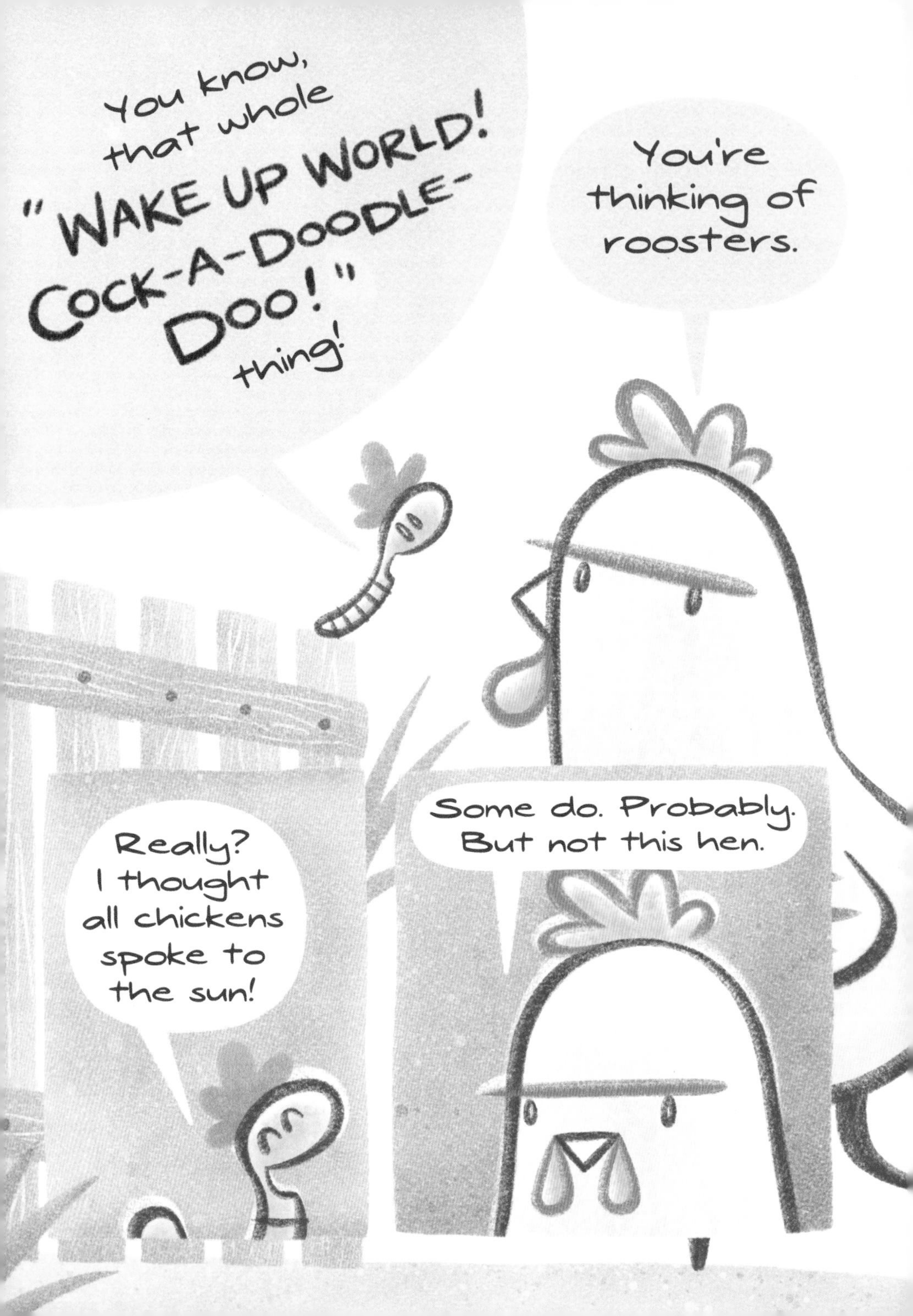
You know, that whole "WAKE UP WORLD! COCK-A-DOODLE-DOO!" thing!
You're thinking of roosters.
Really? I thought all chickens spoke to the sun!
Some do. Probably. But not this hen.

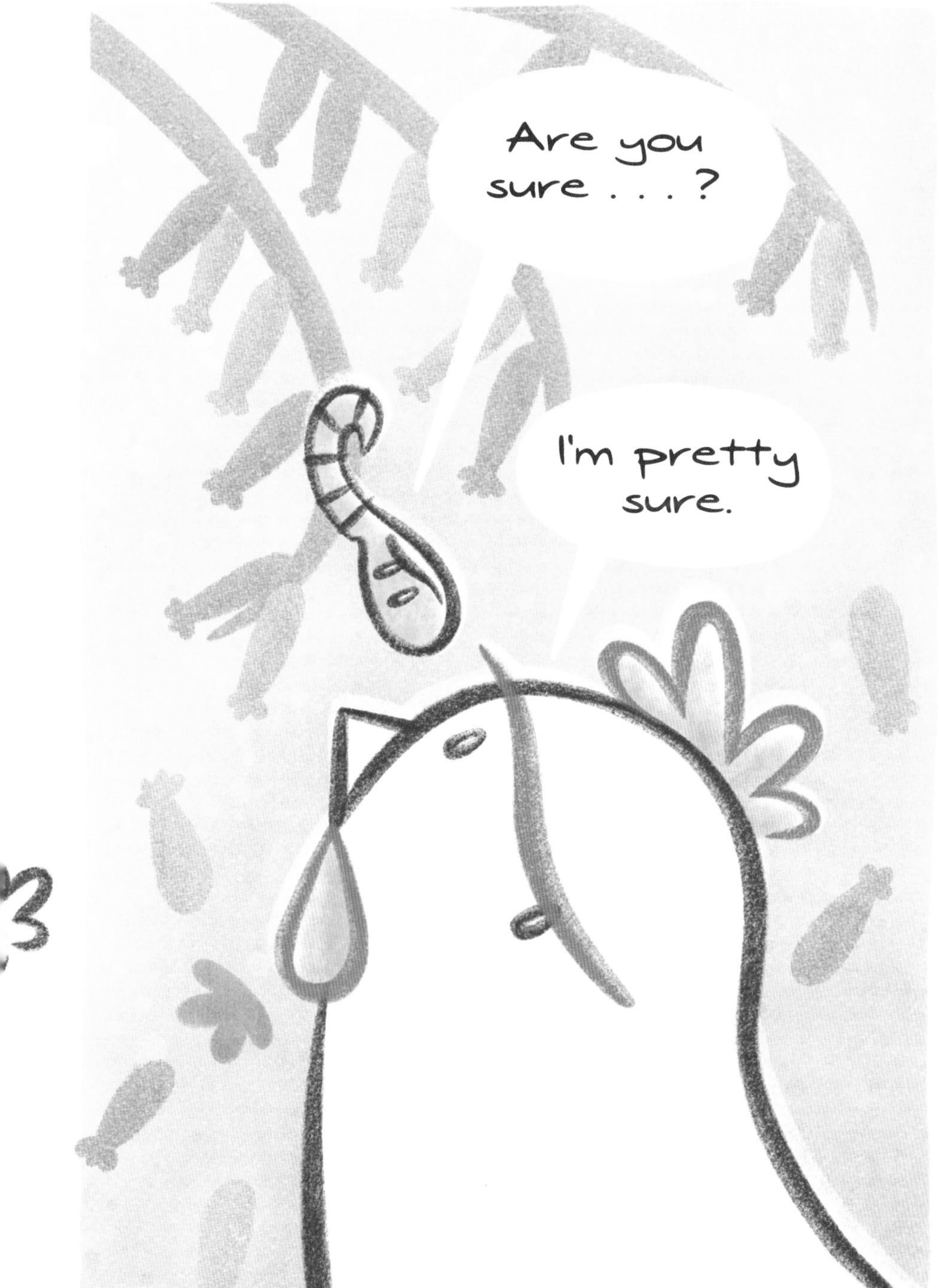
Are you sure . . . ?
I'm pretty sure.

But how do you even know you're a hen?
I just do.
But HOW?
I suppose . . . I feel like a hen.

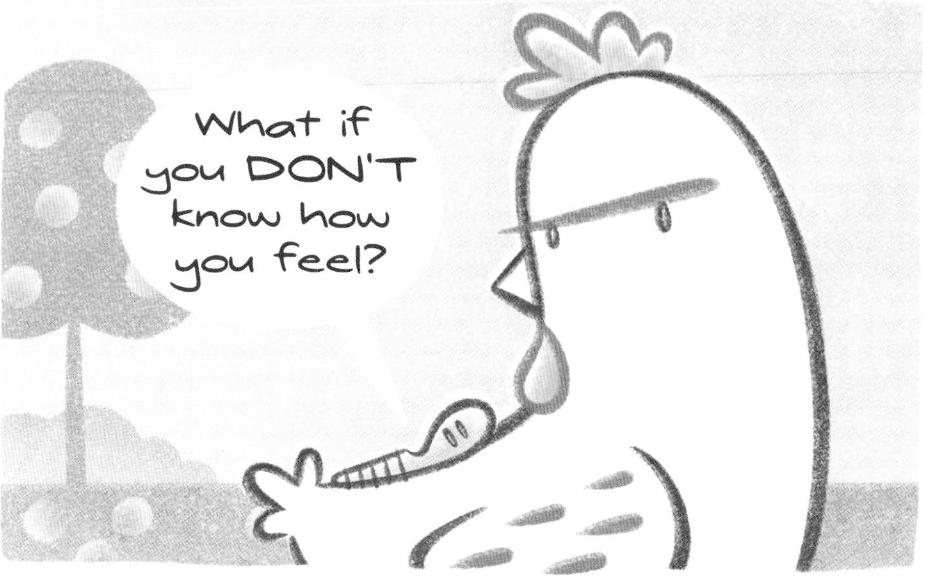
What if you DON'T know how you feel?

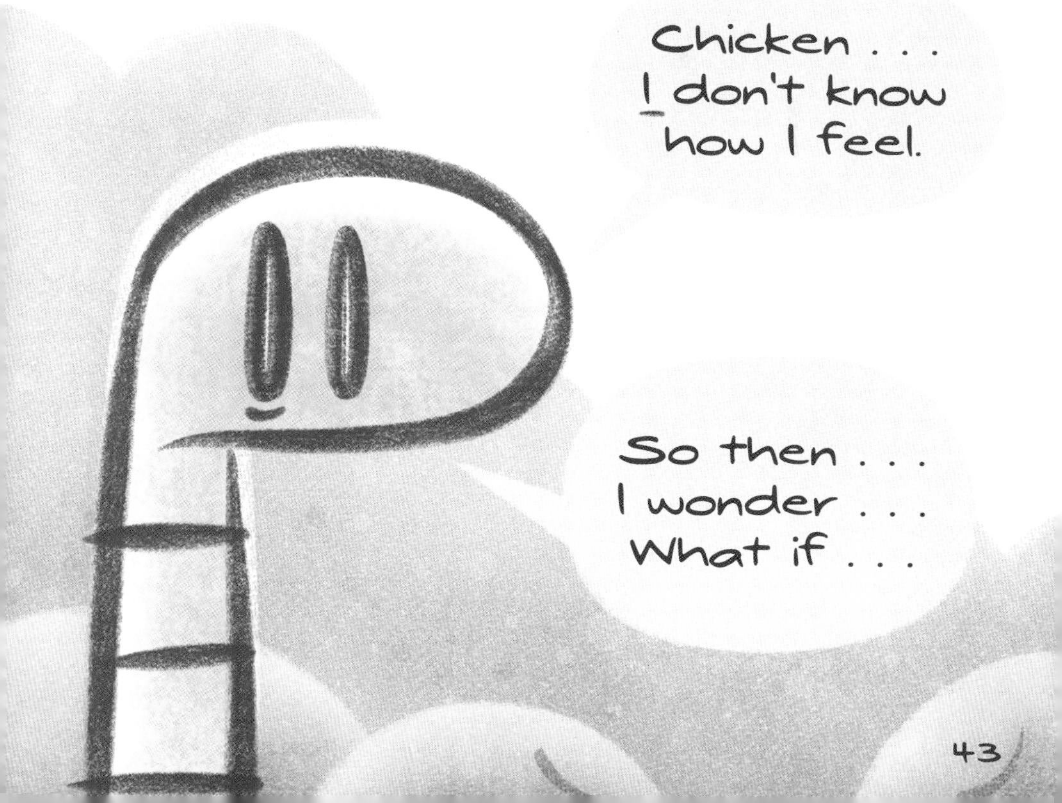
Chicken . . . I don't know how I feel.
So then . . . I wonder . . . What if . . .

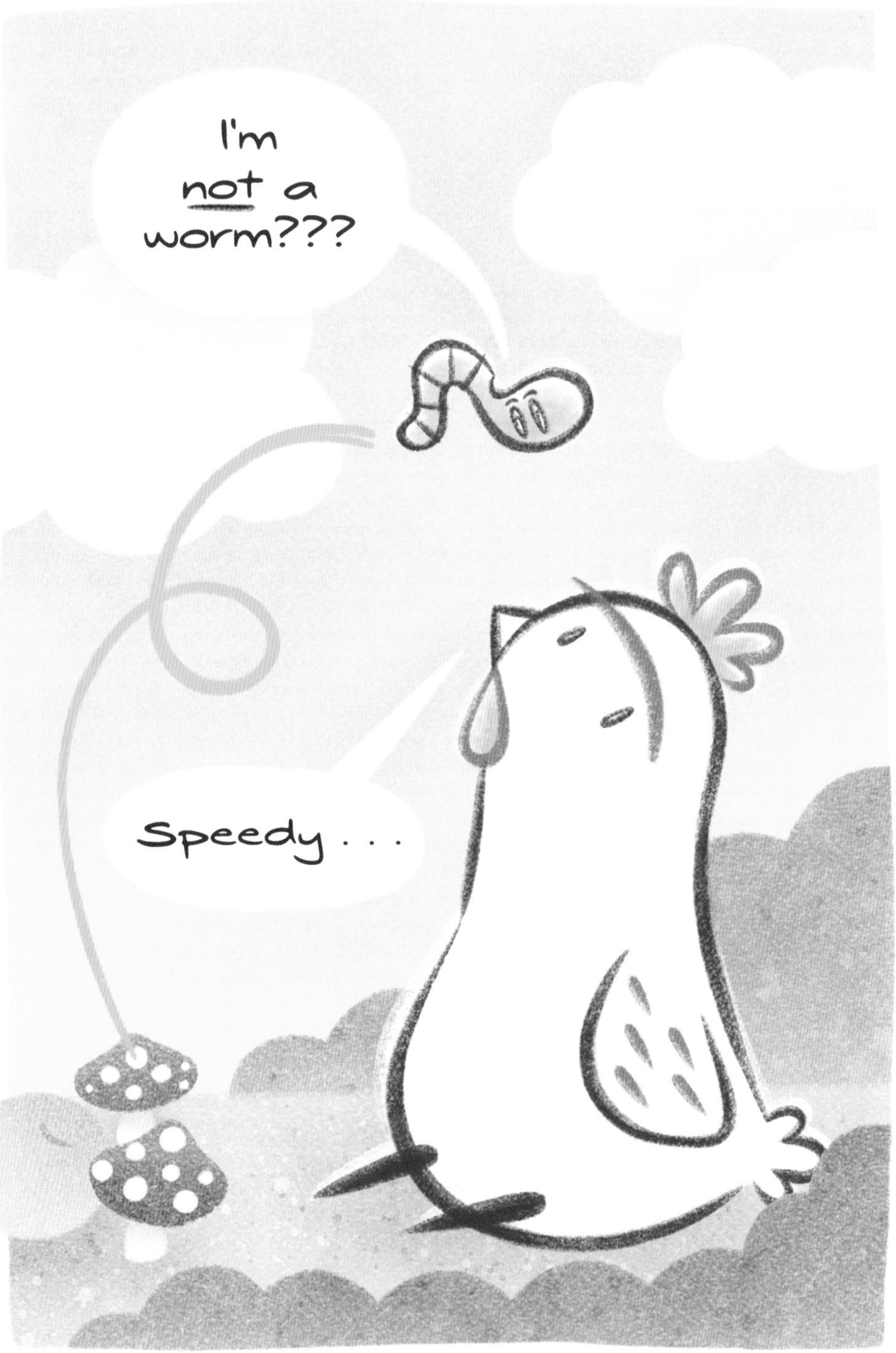
I'm not a worm???
Speedy . . .

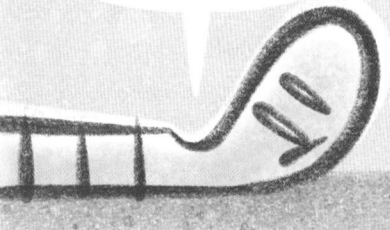

What if I've never been a worm?

All this time, I've been sliding around in the dirt thinking I was just a tiny worm.

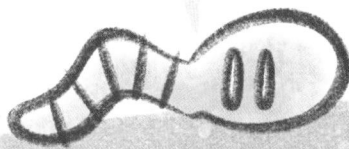

Hmm. I think you're having an identity . . . wobble.

No, no. What if I'm really a . . . a . . .

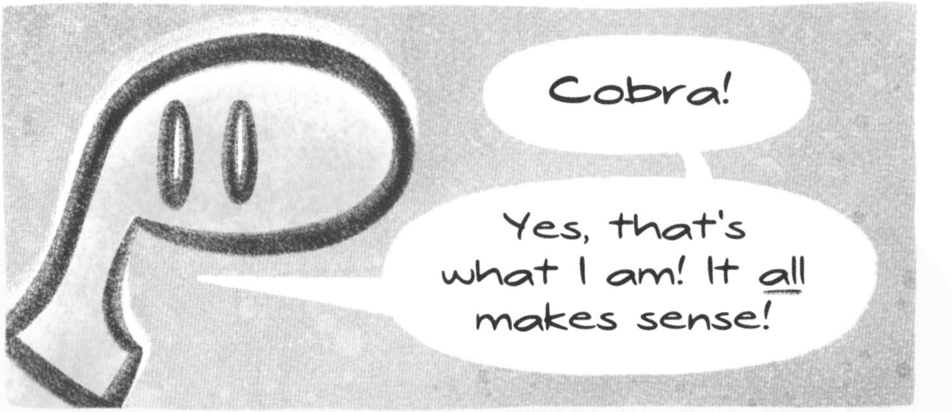
Cobra!
Yes, that's what I am! It all makes sense!

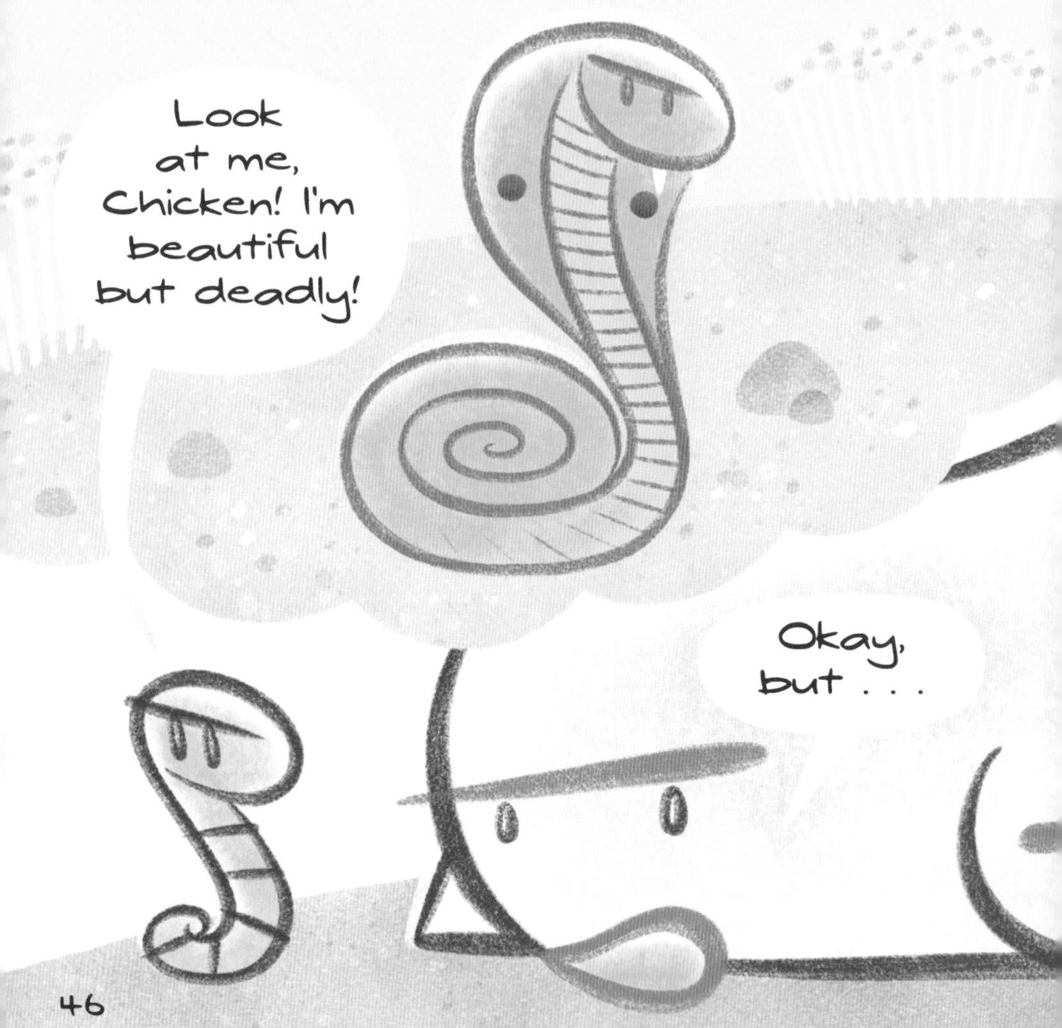
Look at me, Chicken! I'm beautiful but deadly!
Okay, but . . .

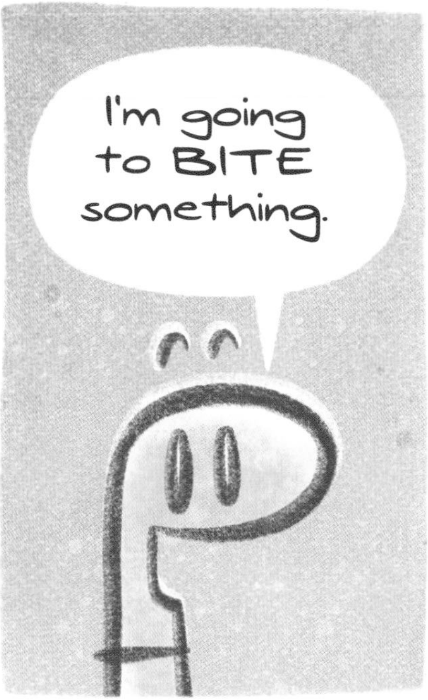
I'm going to BITE something.

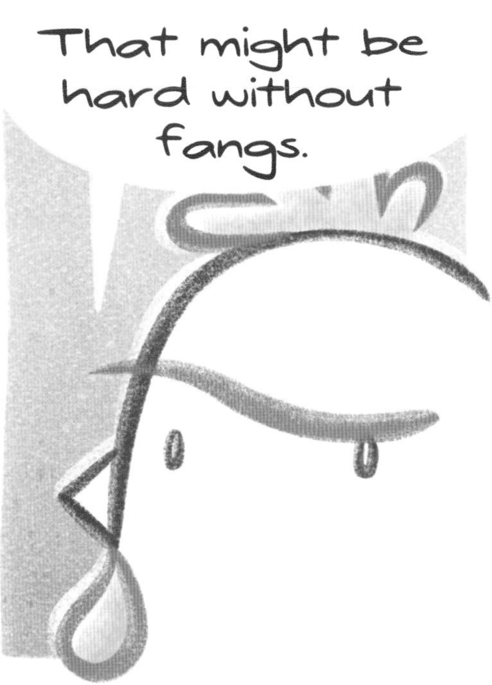
That might be hard without fangs.

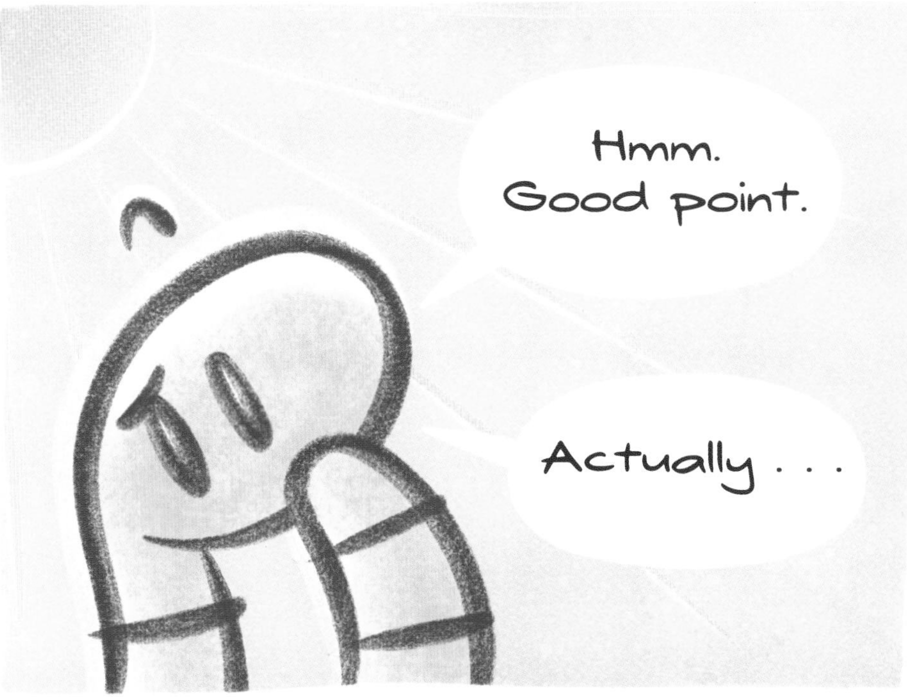
Hmm. Good point.
Actually . . .

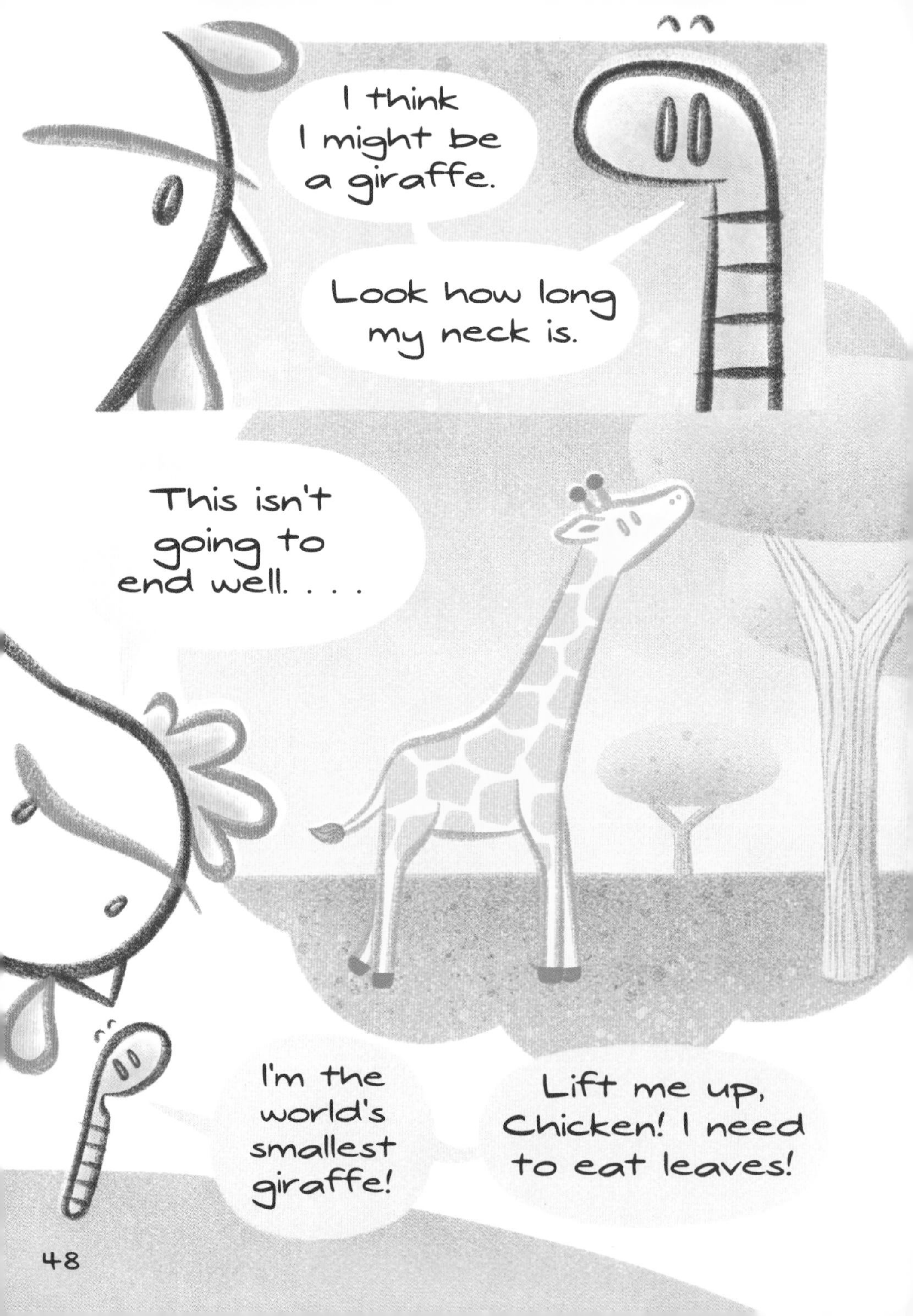
I think I might be a giraffe.
Look how long my neck is.
This isn't going to end well. . . .
I'm the world's smallest giraffe!
Lift me up, Chicken! I need to eat leaves!

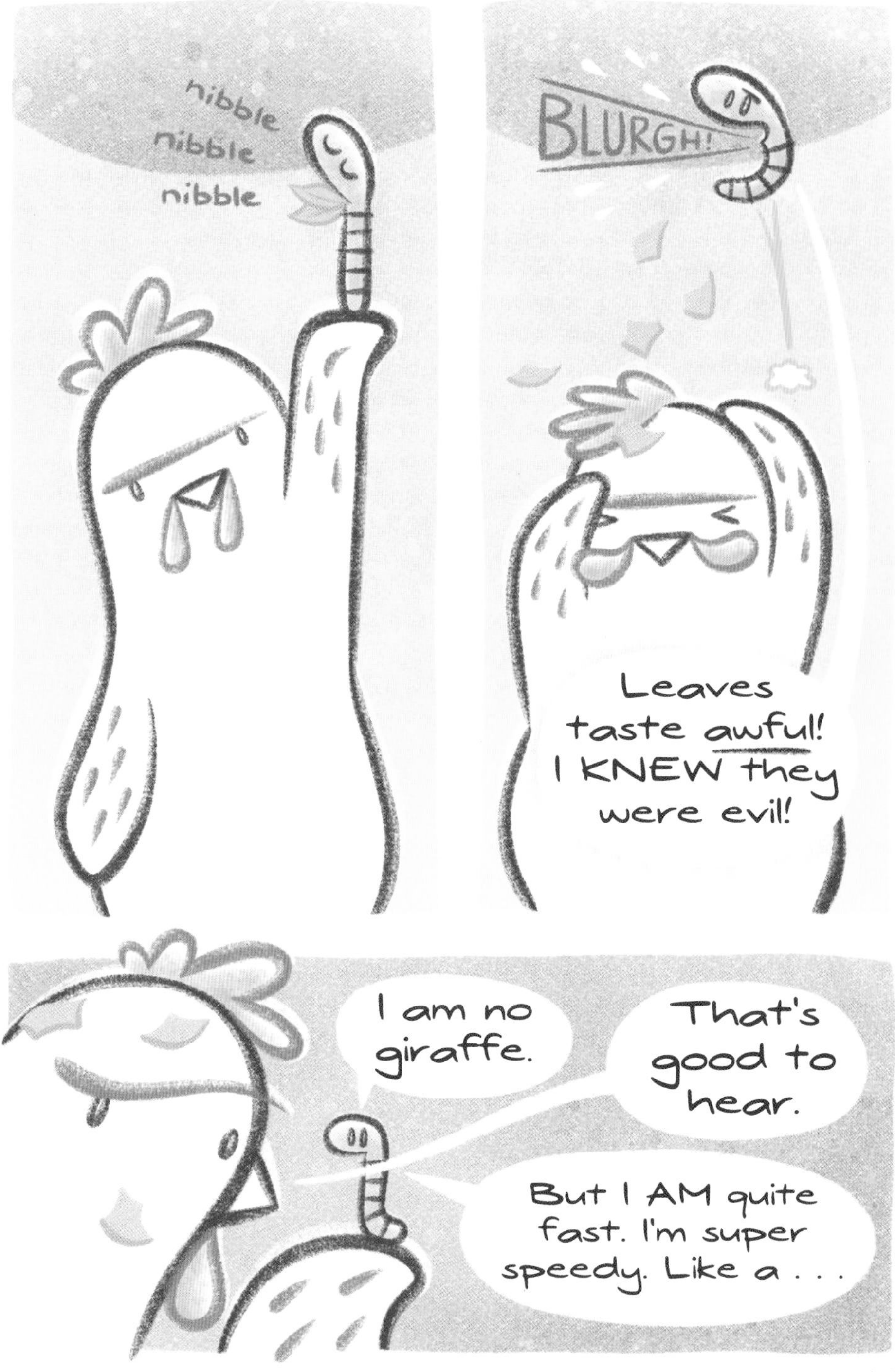
nibble
nibble
nibble
BLURGH!
Leaves taste awful! I KNEW they were evil!
I am no giraffe.
That's good to hear.
But I AM quite fast. I'm super speedy. Like a . . .

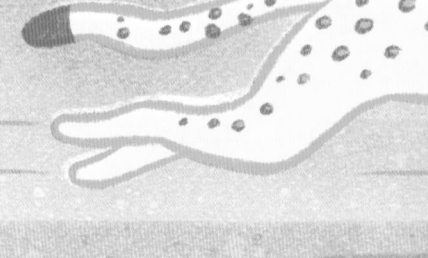

Cheetah!

You'd be the world's first stripy cheetah.

Oh yeah, where are my spots?

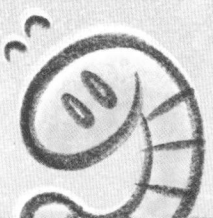

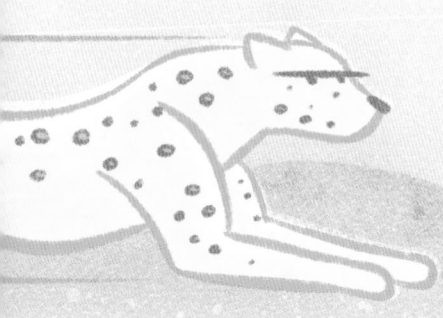

Zooming wild and free across the savanna!

Look at me go!

ZOOM!

I am *quite* wiggly, though.

Ooh, maybe I'm a . . .

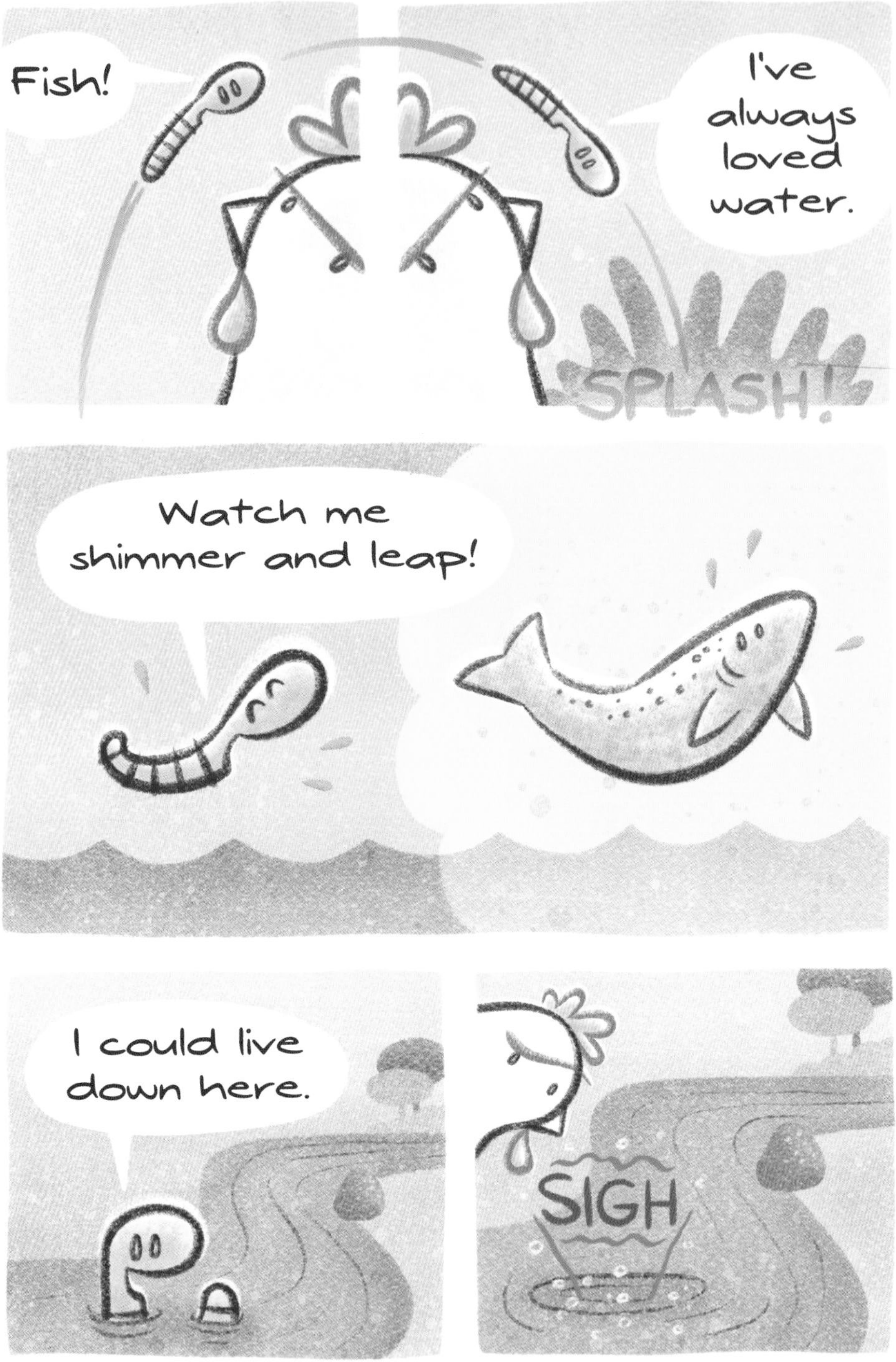
Fish!
I've always loved water.
SPLASH!
Watch me shimmer and leap!
I could live down here.
SIGH

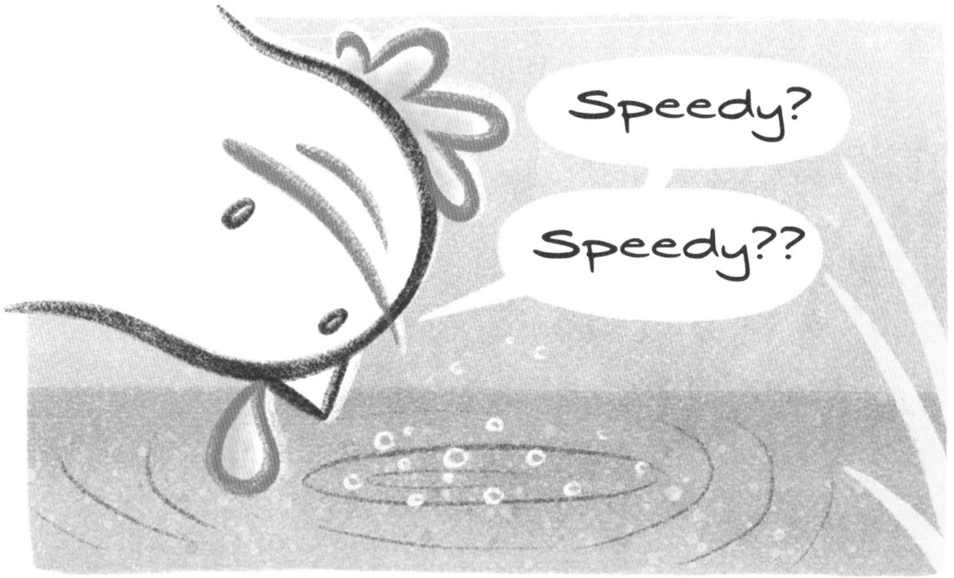
Speedy?
Speedy??

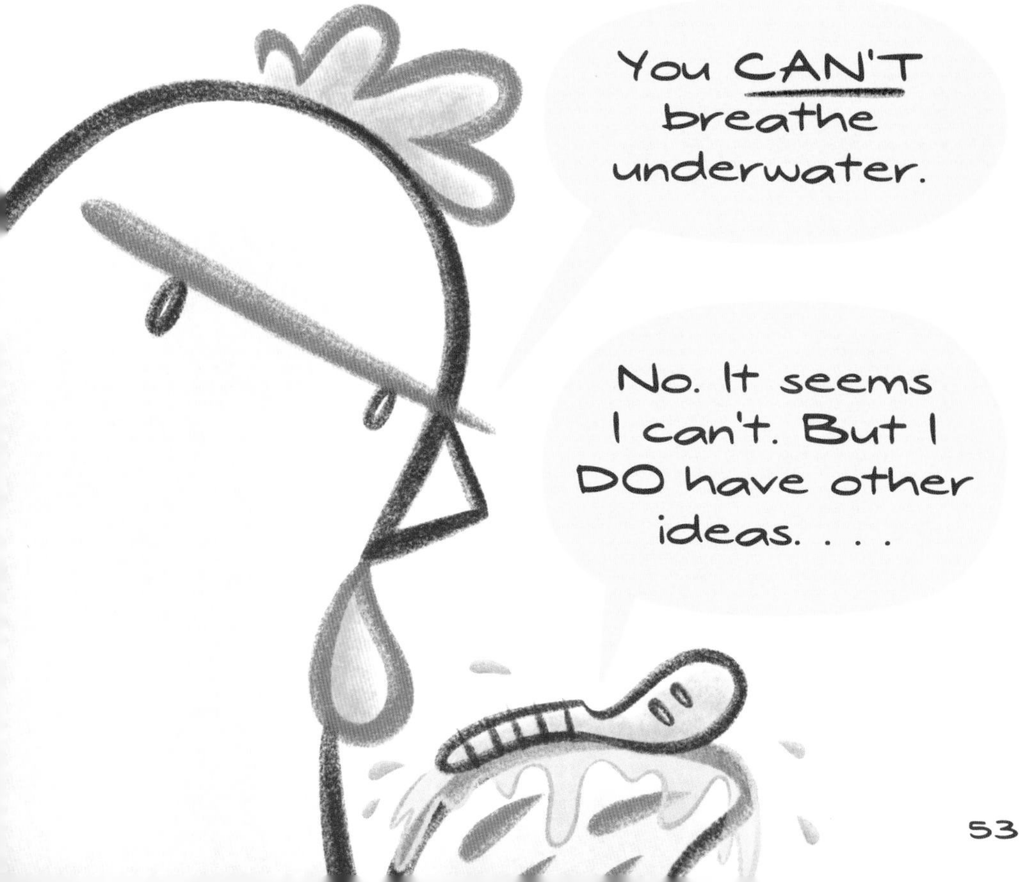
You CAN'T breathe underwater.
No. It seems I can't. But I DO have other ideas. . . .

Maybe
I'm a . . .

flamingo!

Legless skink!

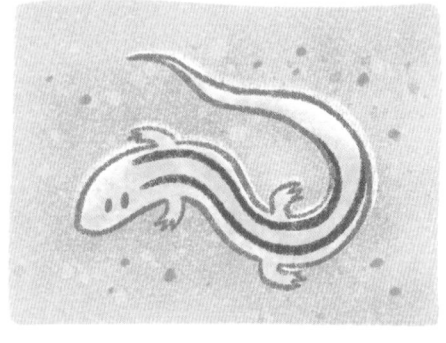

Wingless
butterfly!

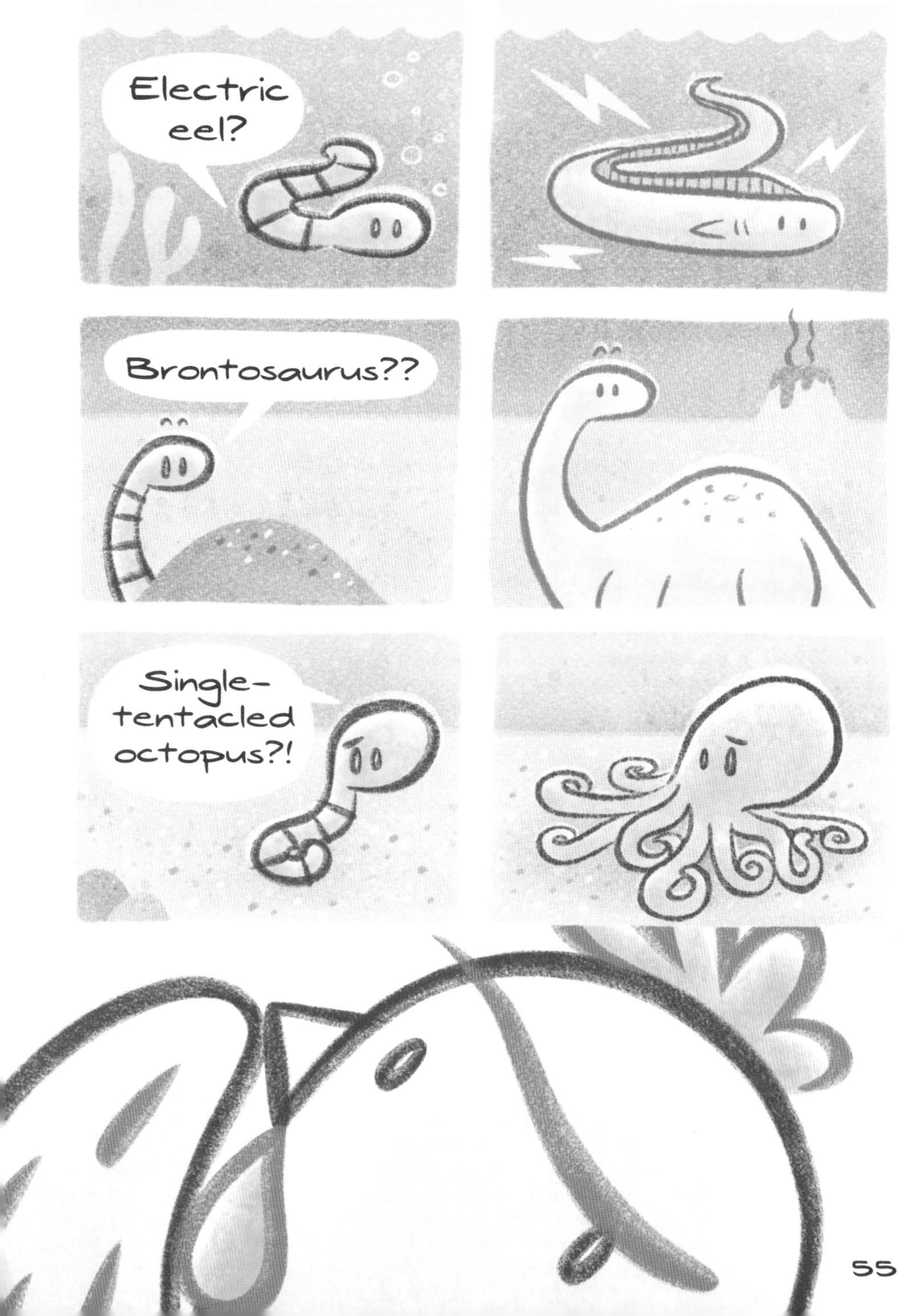
Electric eel?
Brontosaurus??
Single-tentacled octopus?!

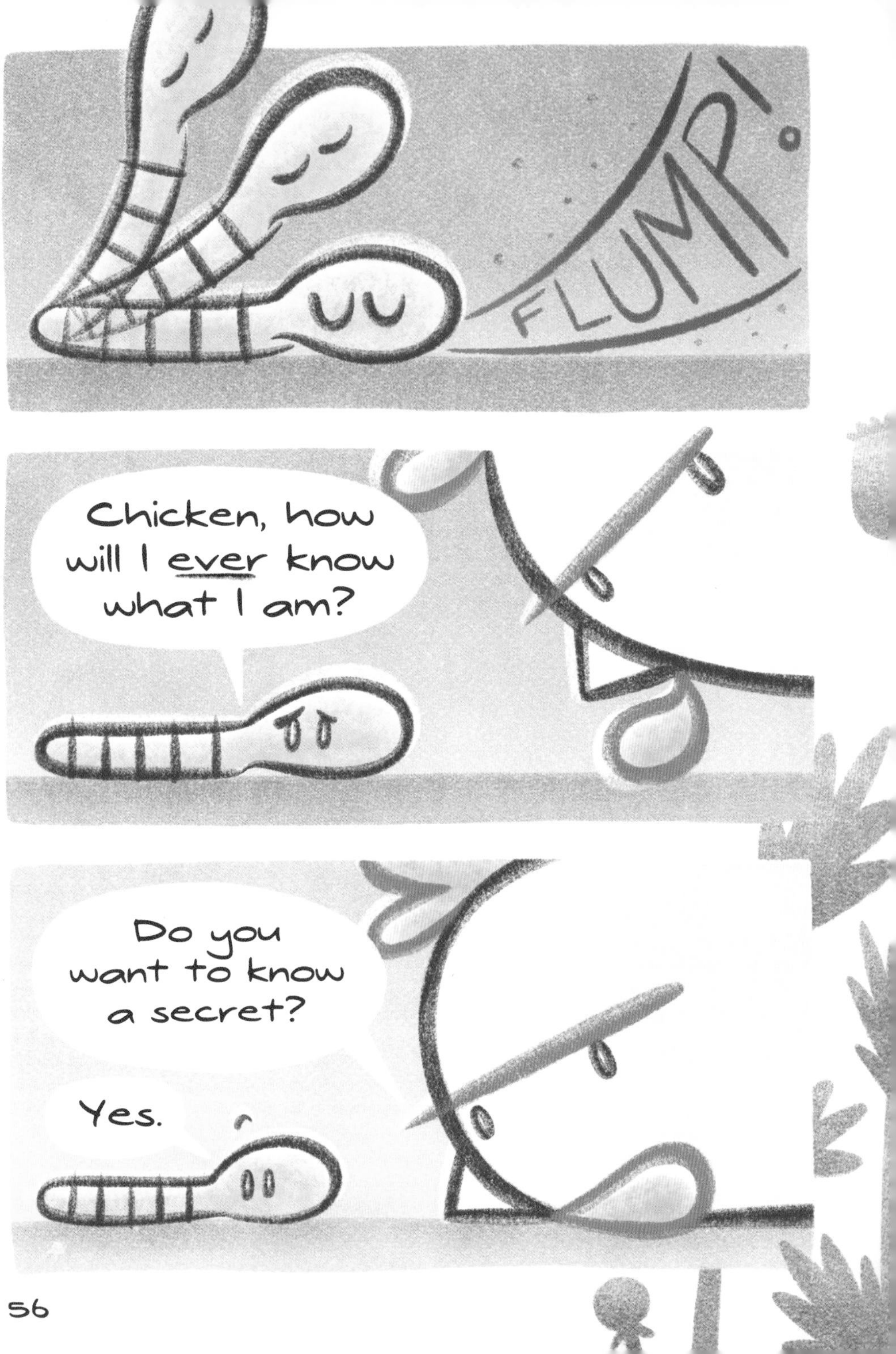
FLUMP!
Chicken, how will I ever know what I am?
Do you want to know a secret?
Yes.

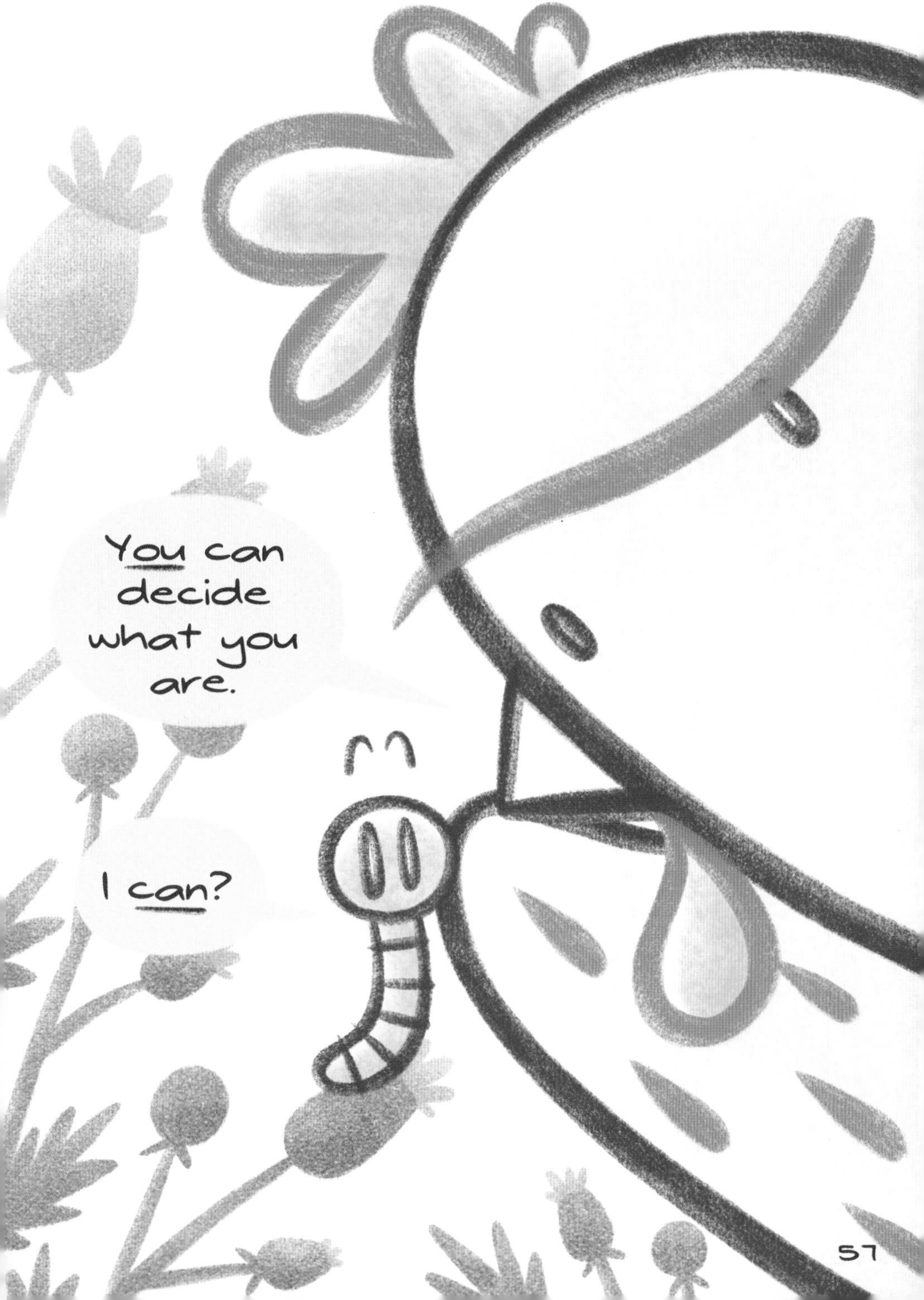
You can decide what you are.
I can?

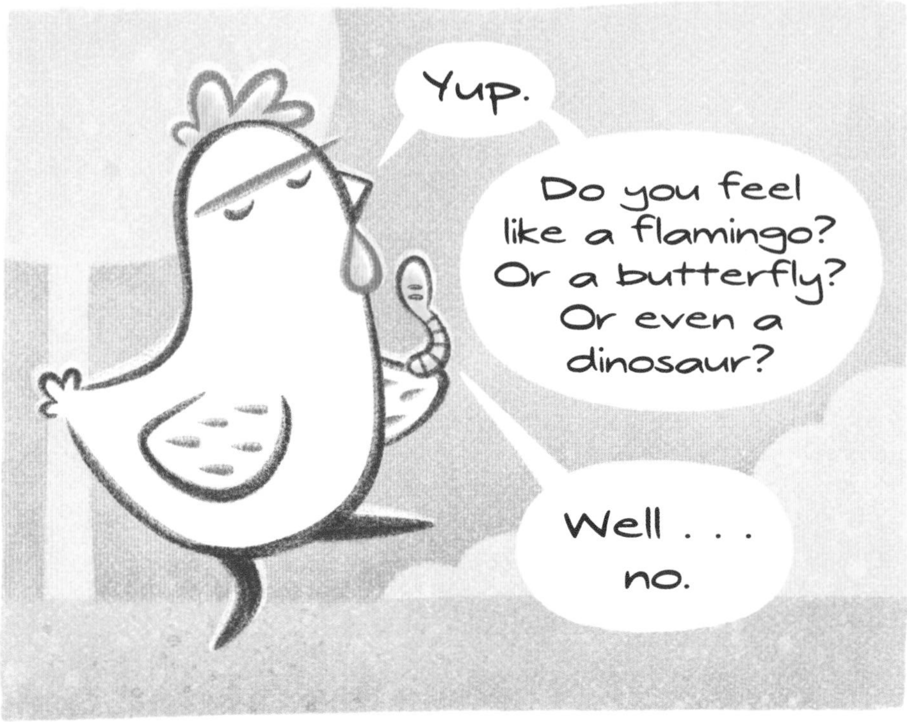
Yup.
Do you feel like a flamingo? Or a butterfly? Or even a dinosaur?
Well . . . no.

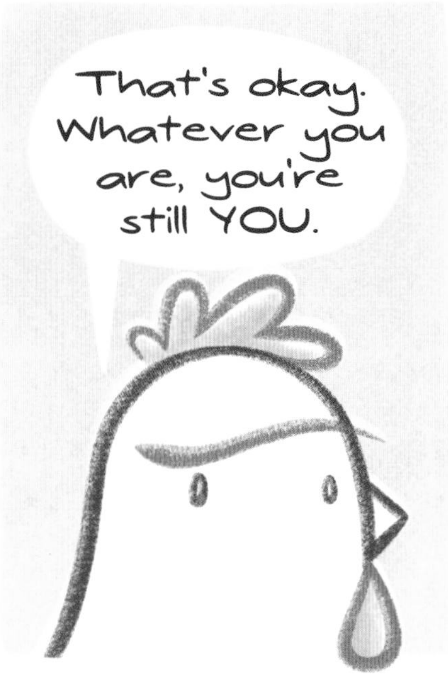
That's okay. Whatever you are, you're still YOU.

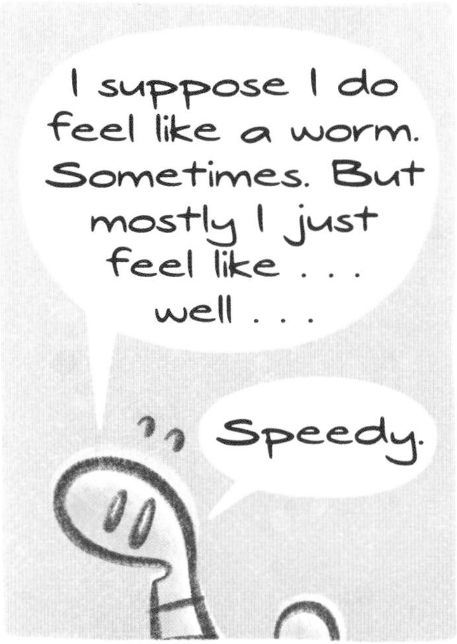
I suppose I do feel like a worm. Sometimes. But mostly I just feel like . . . well . . .
Speedy.

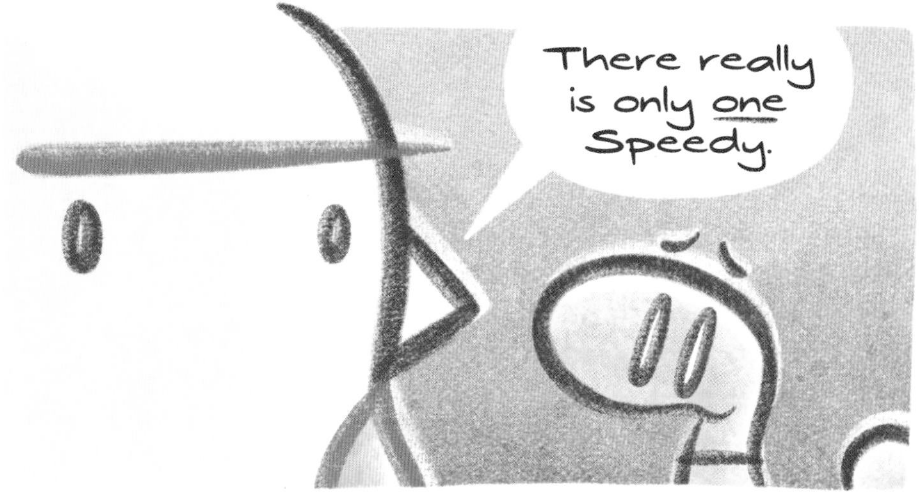
There really is only one Speedy.

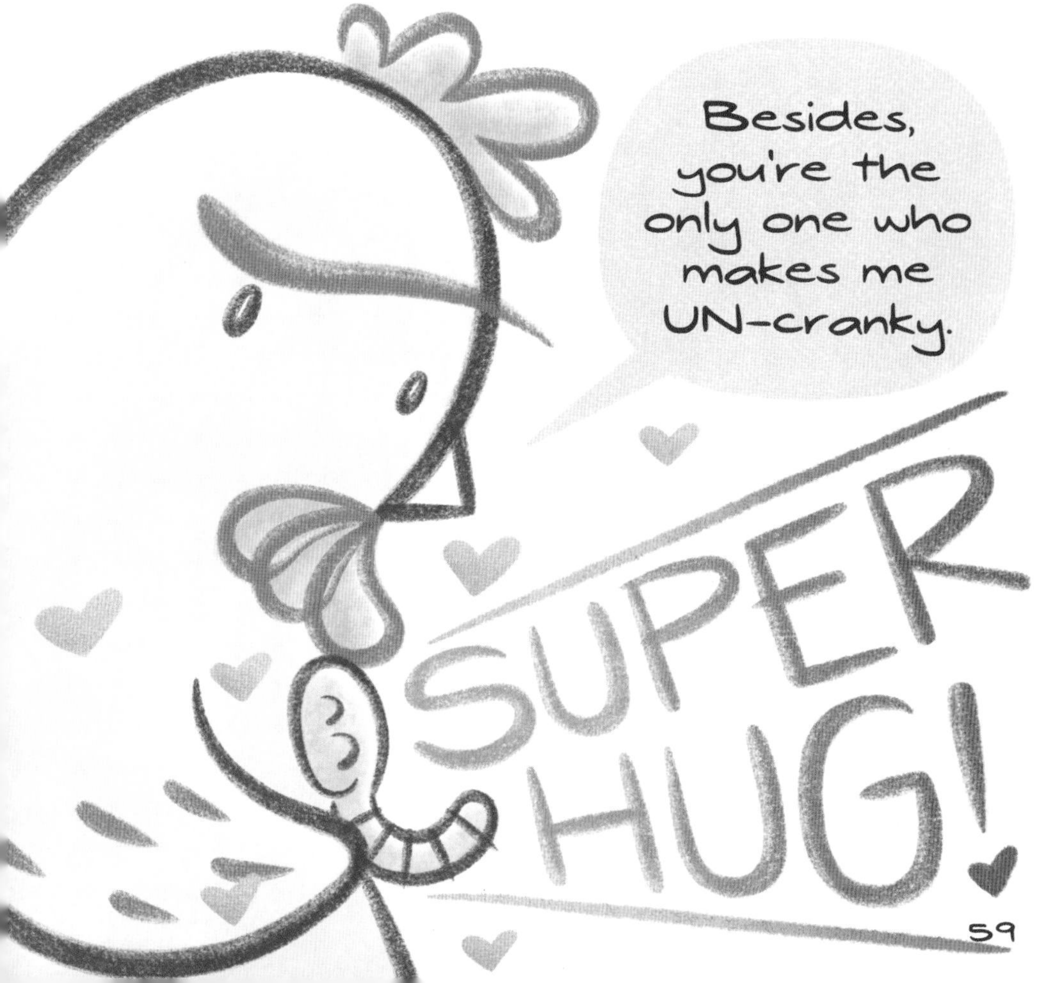
Besides, you're the only one who makes me UN-cranky.
SUPER HUG!

WHY SPEEDY WORM MAKES CRANKY CHICKEN UN-CRANKY

Loves to snack

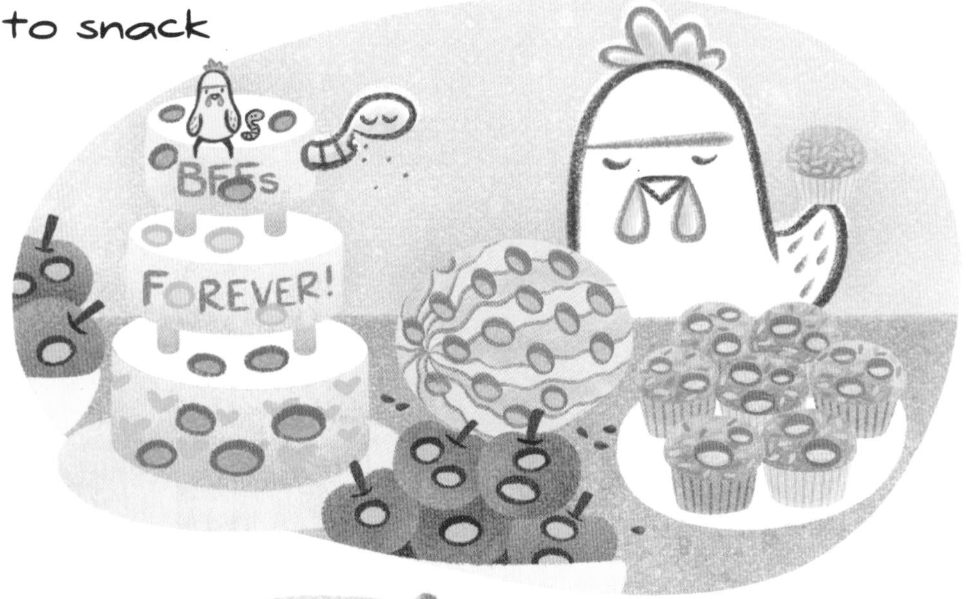
BFFs
FOREVER!

Tiny and tickly

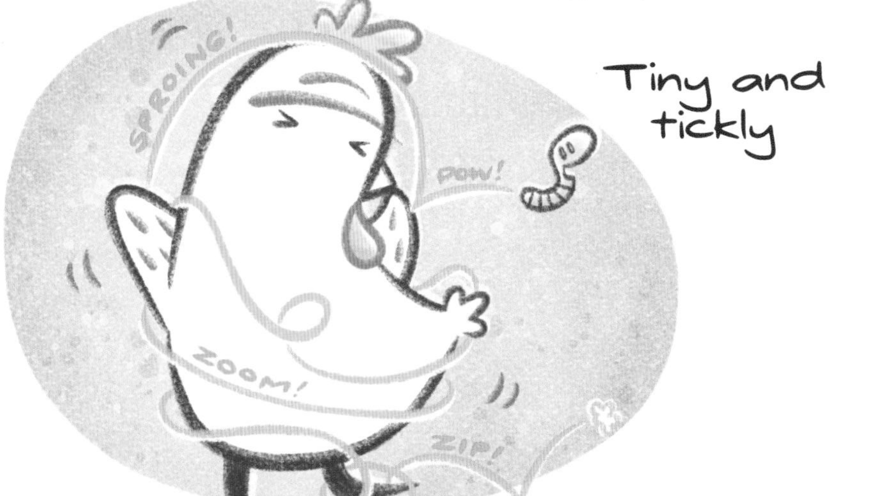
SPROING!
POW!
ZOOM!
ZIP!

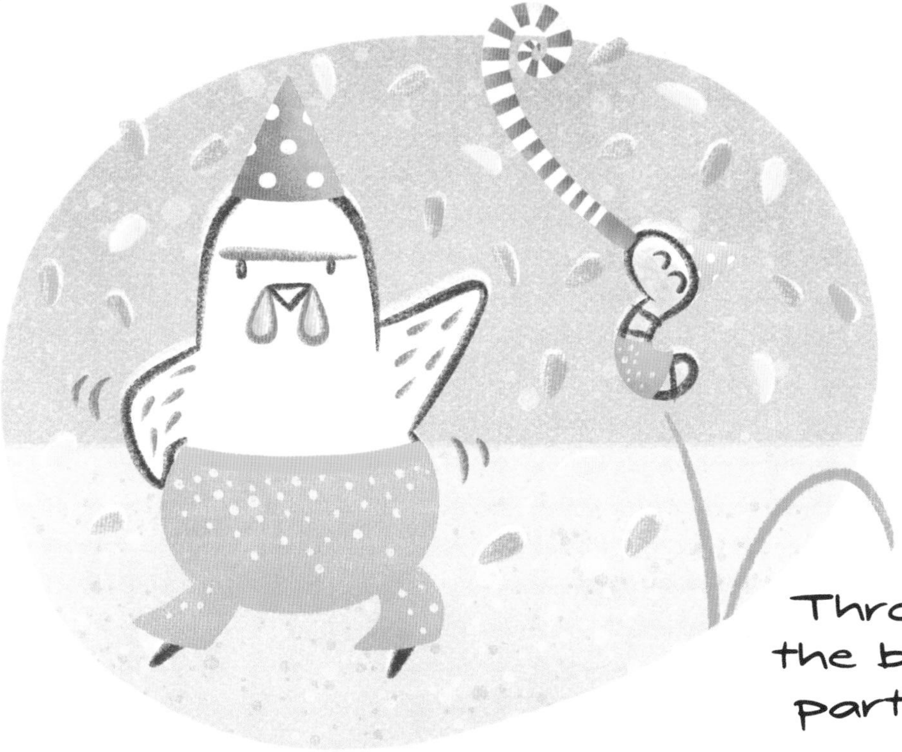

Throws
the best
parties

Likes Chicken
for exactly
who she is

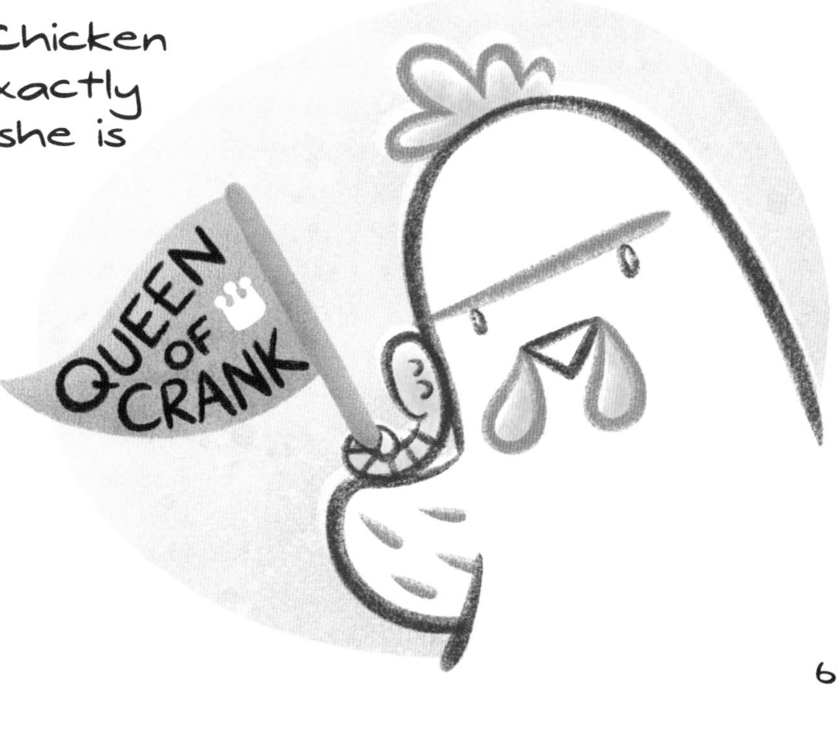
QUEEN OF CRANK

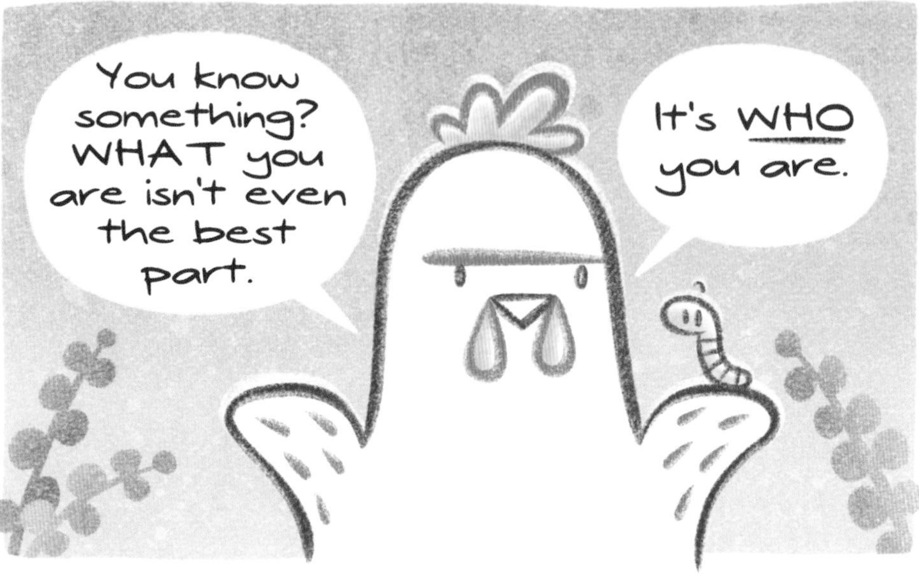
You know something? WHAT you are isn't even the best part.
It's WHO you are.

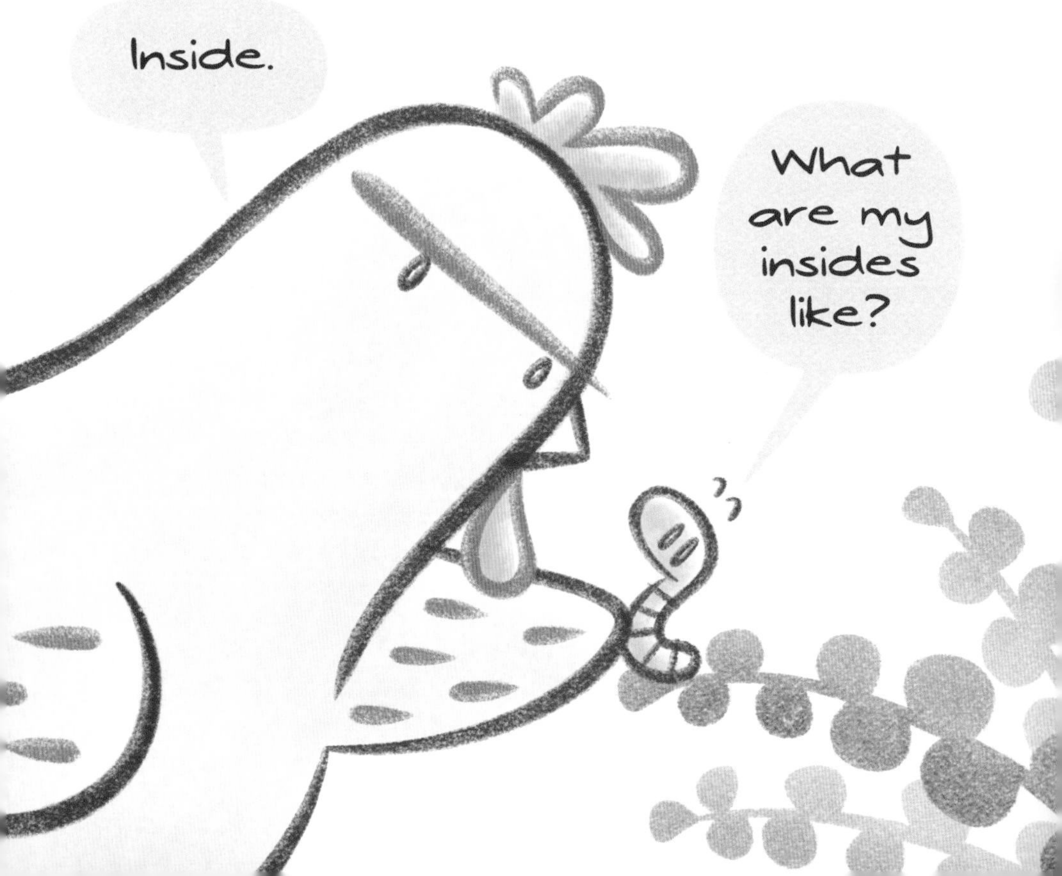
Inside.
What are my insides like?

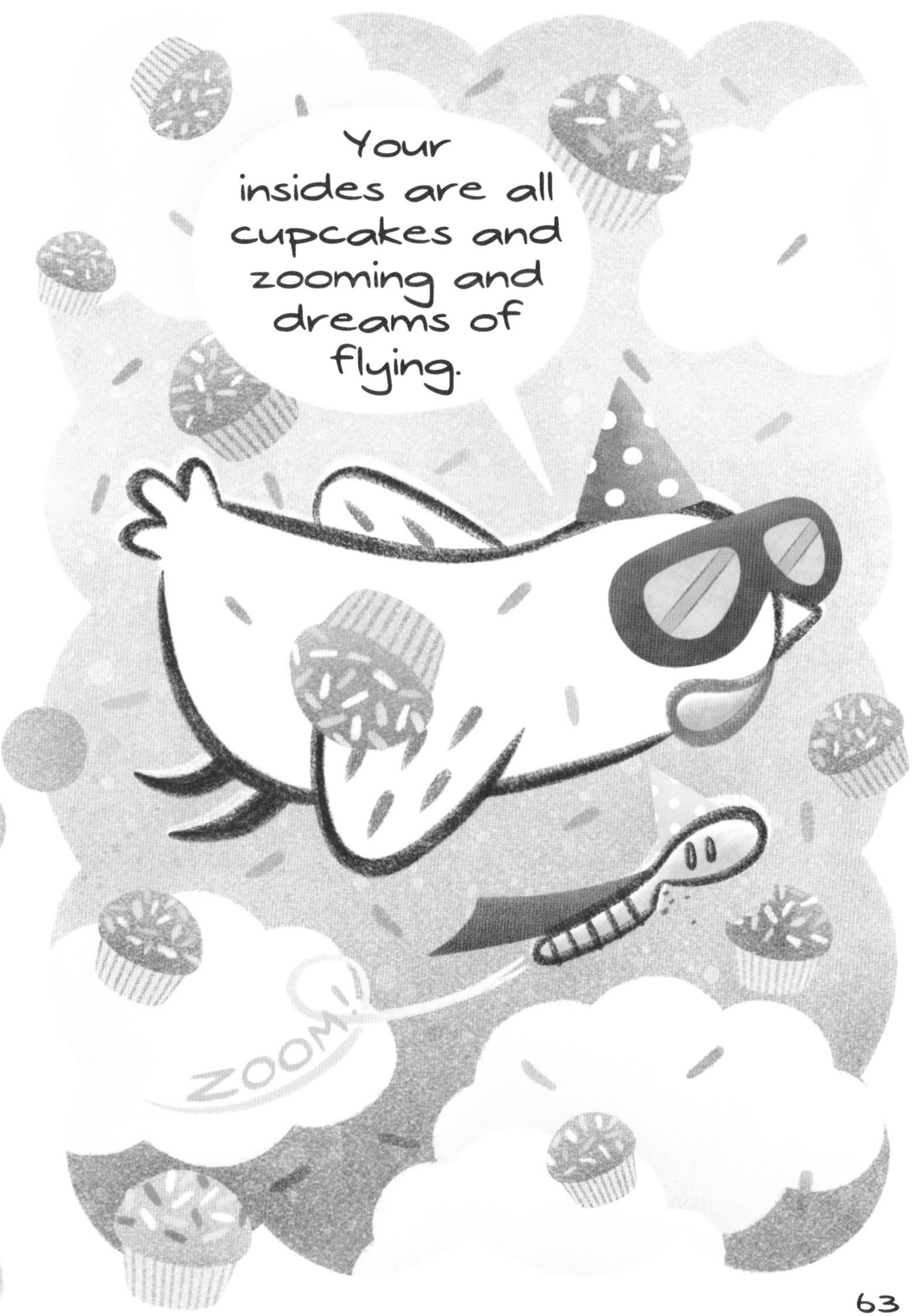
Your insides are all cupcakes and zooming and dreams of flying.
ZOOM!

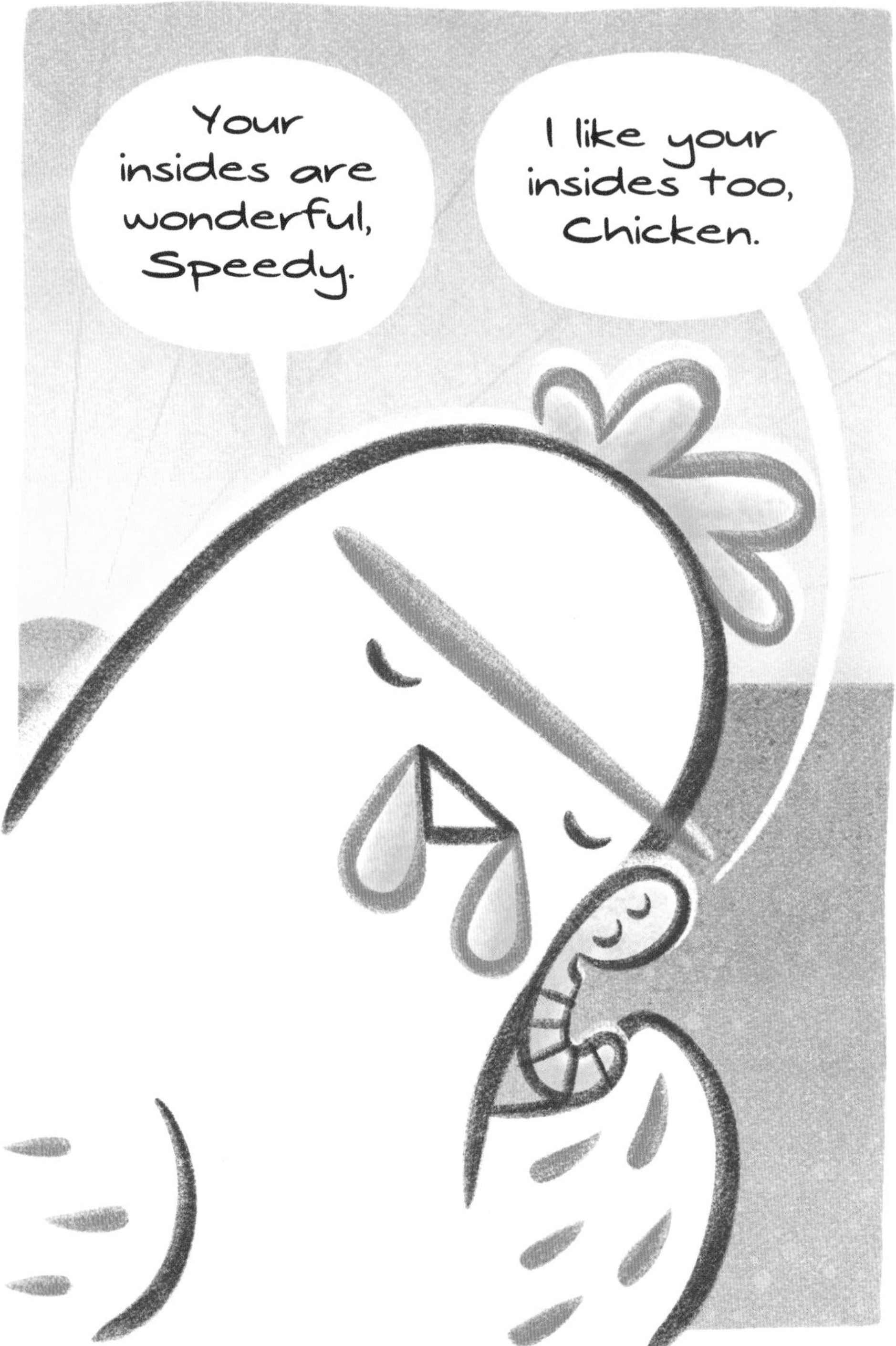
Your insides are wonderful, Speedy.
I like your insides too, Chicken.

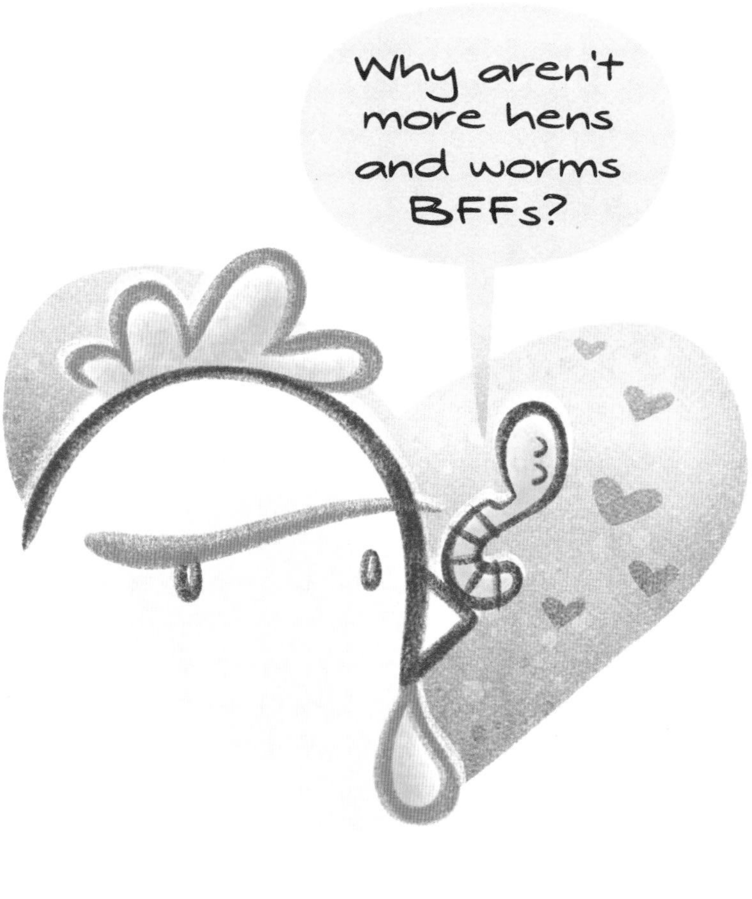
Why aren't more hens and worms BFFs?

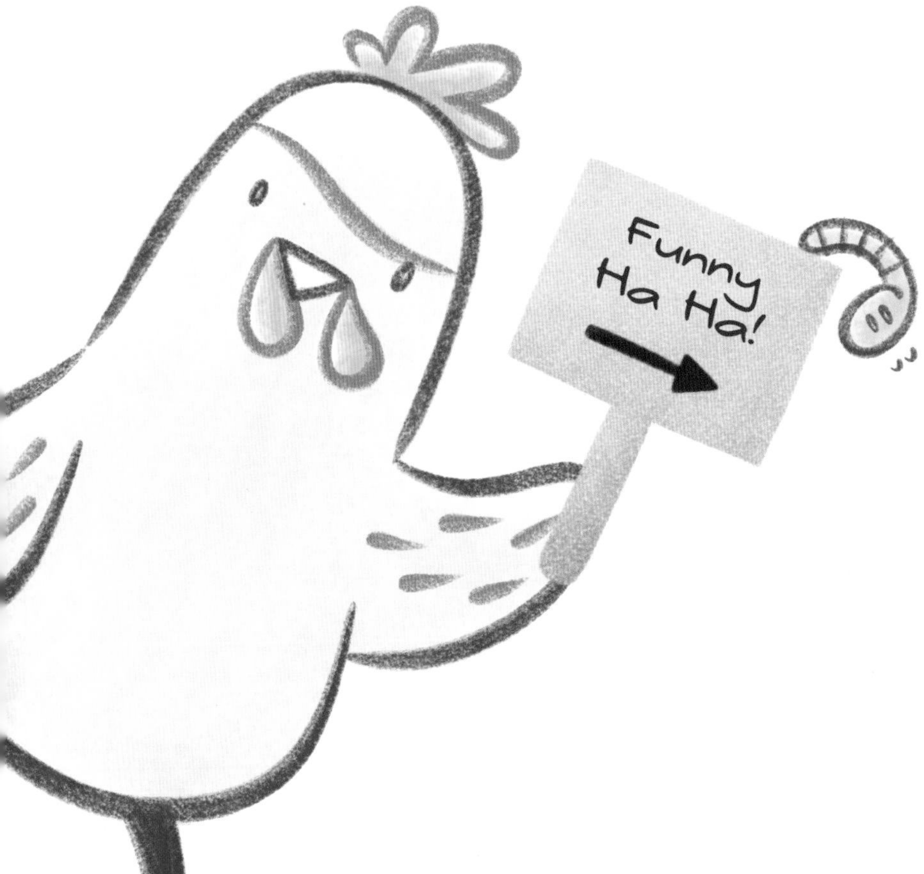
Funny
Ha Ha!

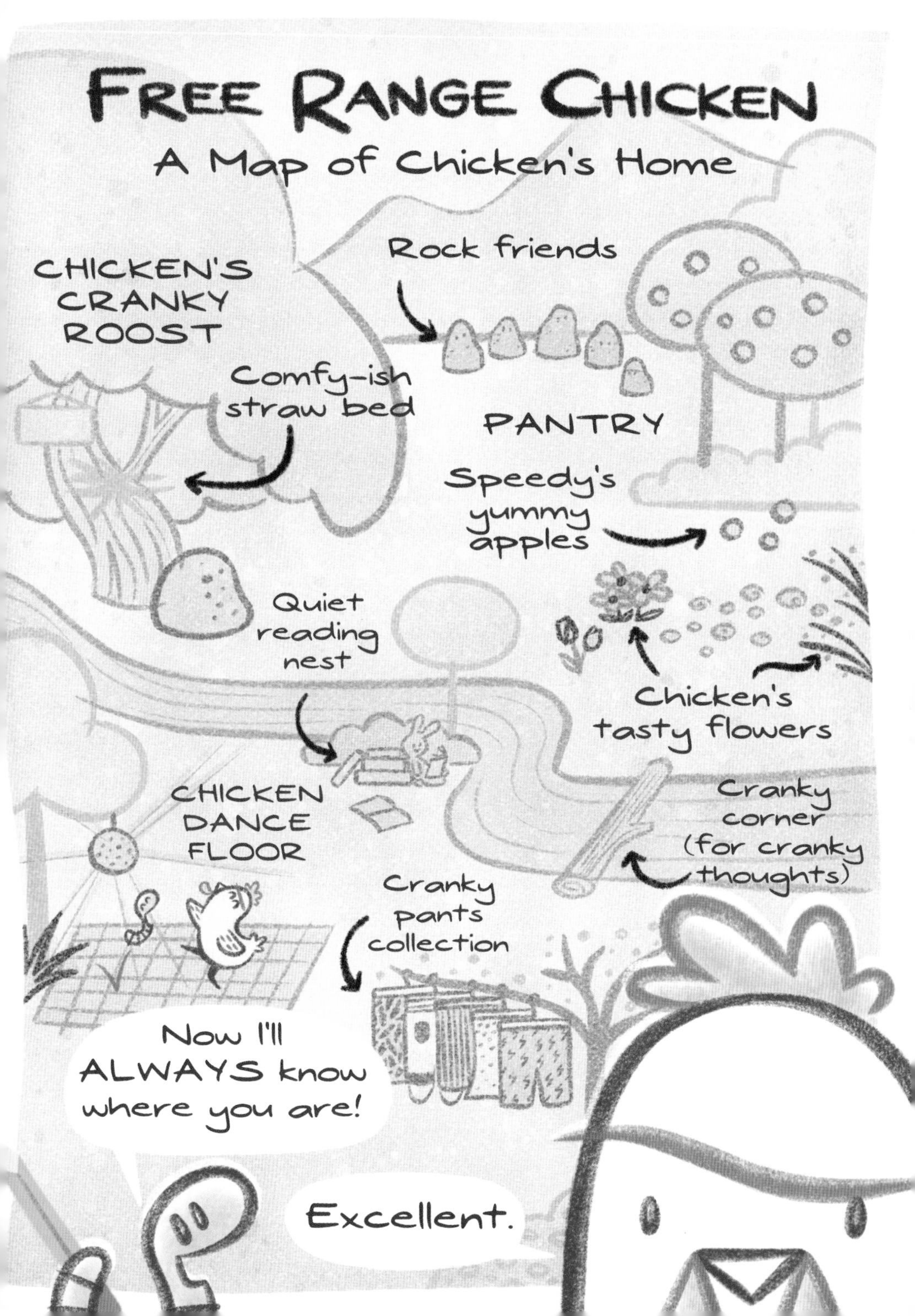

FREE RANGE CHICKEN
A Map of Chicken's Home
CHICKEN'S CRANKY ROOST
Rock friends
Comfy-ish straw bed
PANTRY
Speedy's yummy apples
Quiet reading nest
Chicken's tasty flowers
CHICKEN DANCE FLOOR
Cranky corner (for cranky thoughts)
Cranky pants collection
Now I'll ALWAYS know where you are!
Excellent.

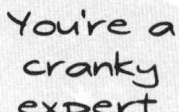

You're a cranky expert.

Things That Make Speedy Cranky

Thanks to you!

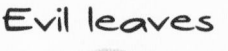

Evil leaves

Dirt

Speeding tickets

ZIP!
ZAP!
ZOOM!

Empty fridges

Missing friends

Chicken?

The Cranky Club

Speedy's Famous Dirt Drawings

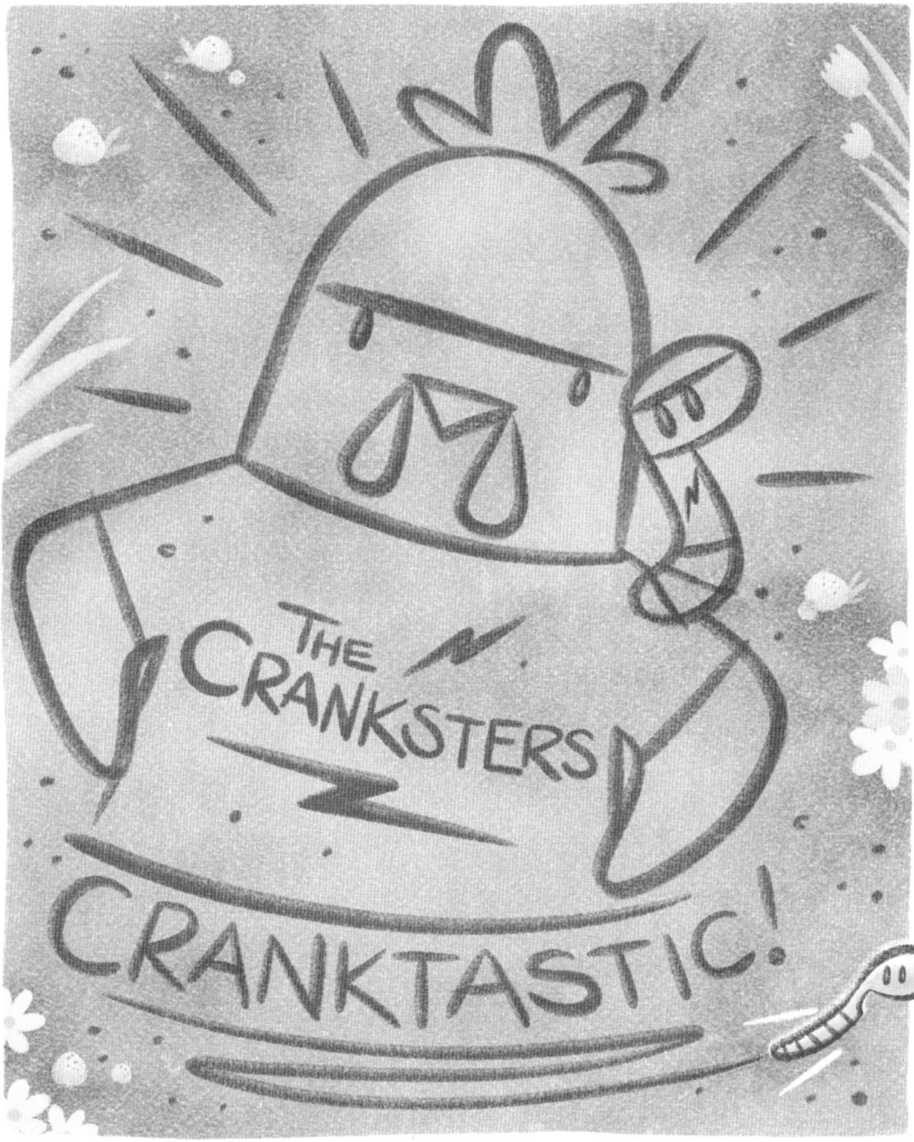
THE CRANKSTERS
CRANKTASTIC!

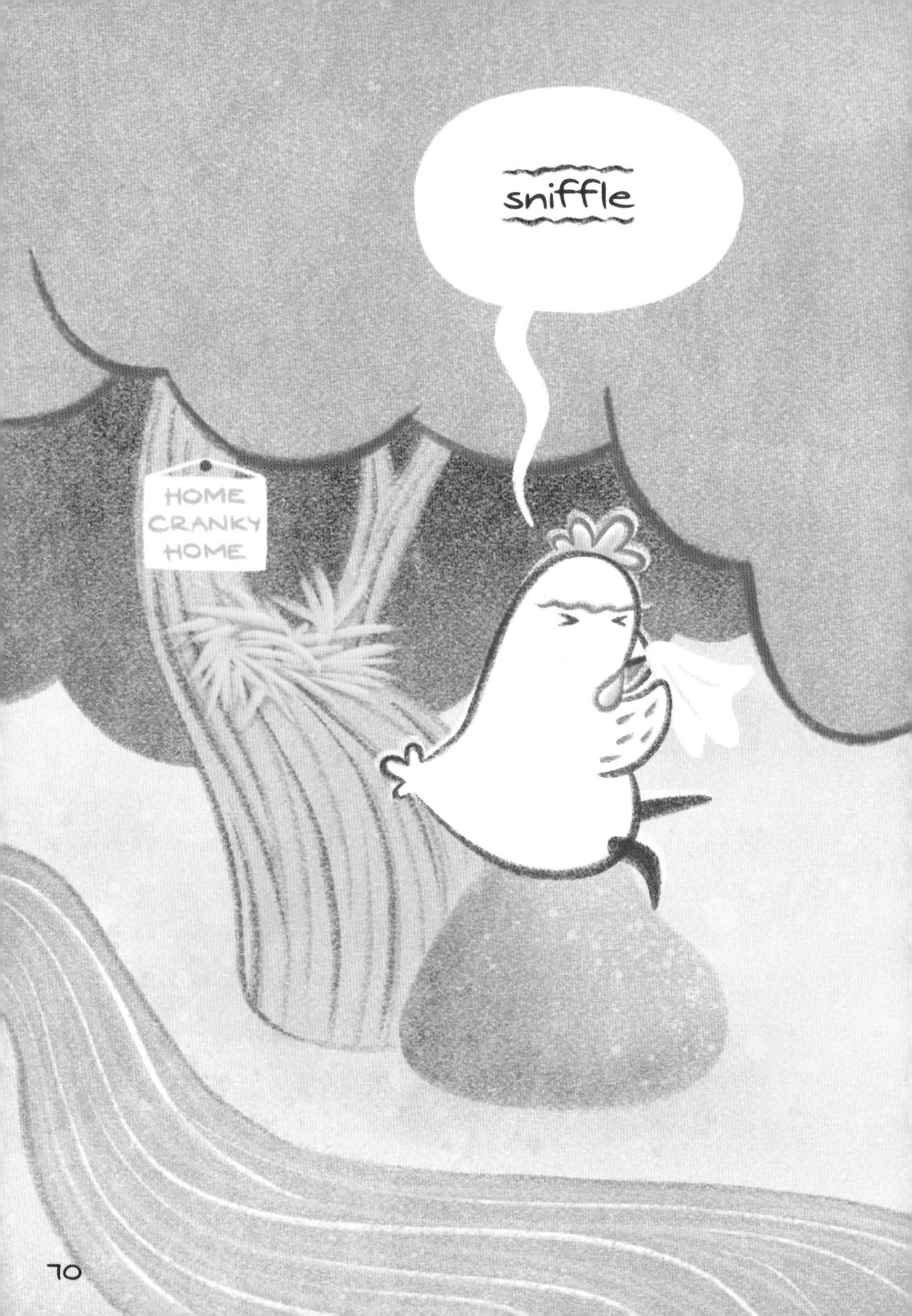
sniffle
HOME
CRANKY
HOME

3

BEST FEATHERED FAMILY

Uh-oh. Are you sick?

ZIP!

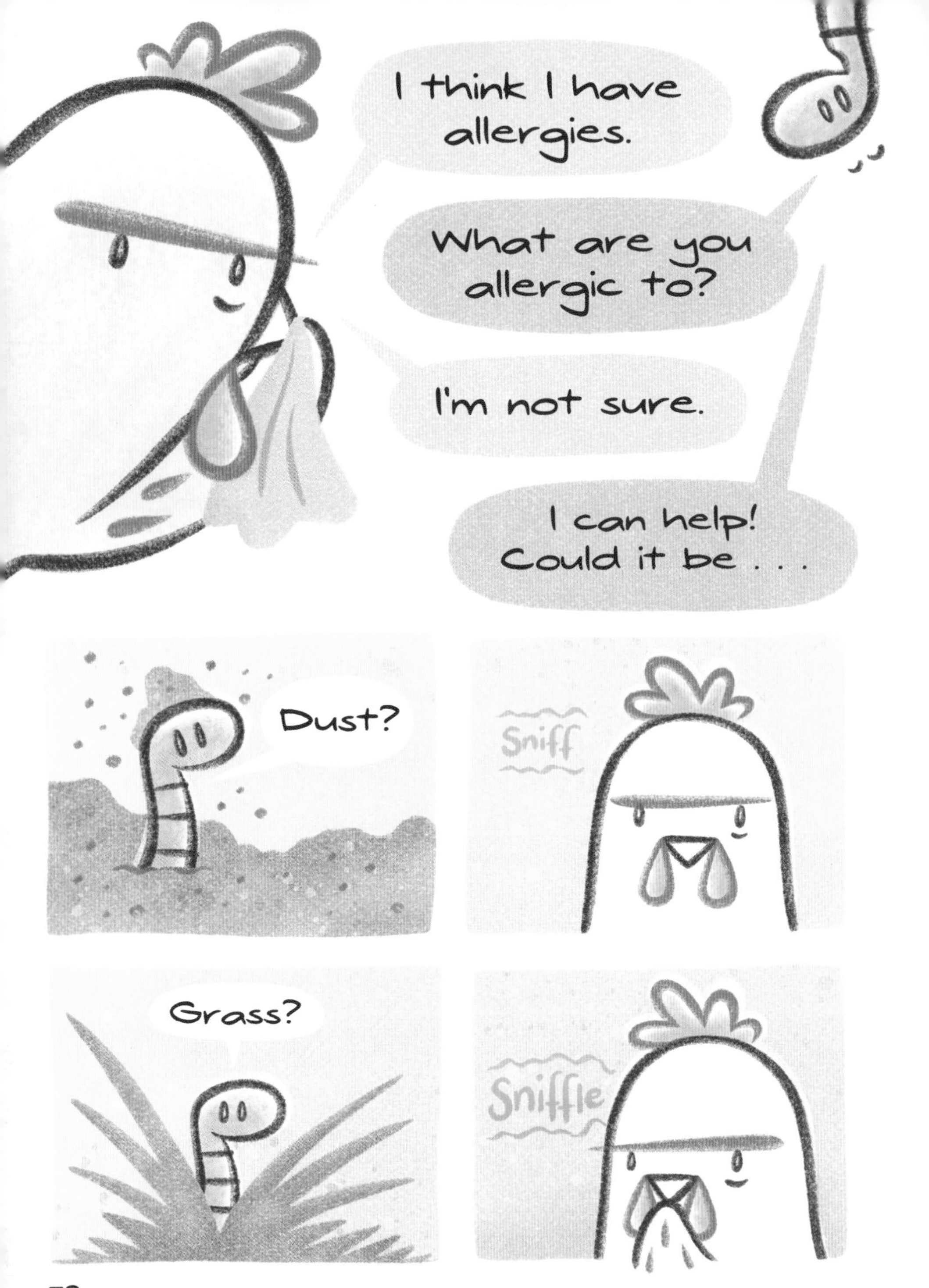
I think I have allergies.
What are you allergic to?
I'm not sure.
I can help! Could it be . . .
Dust?
Sniff
Grass?
Sniffle

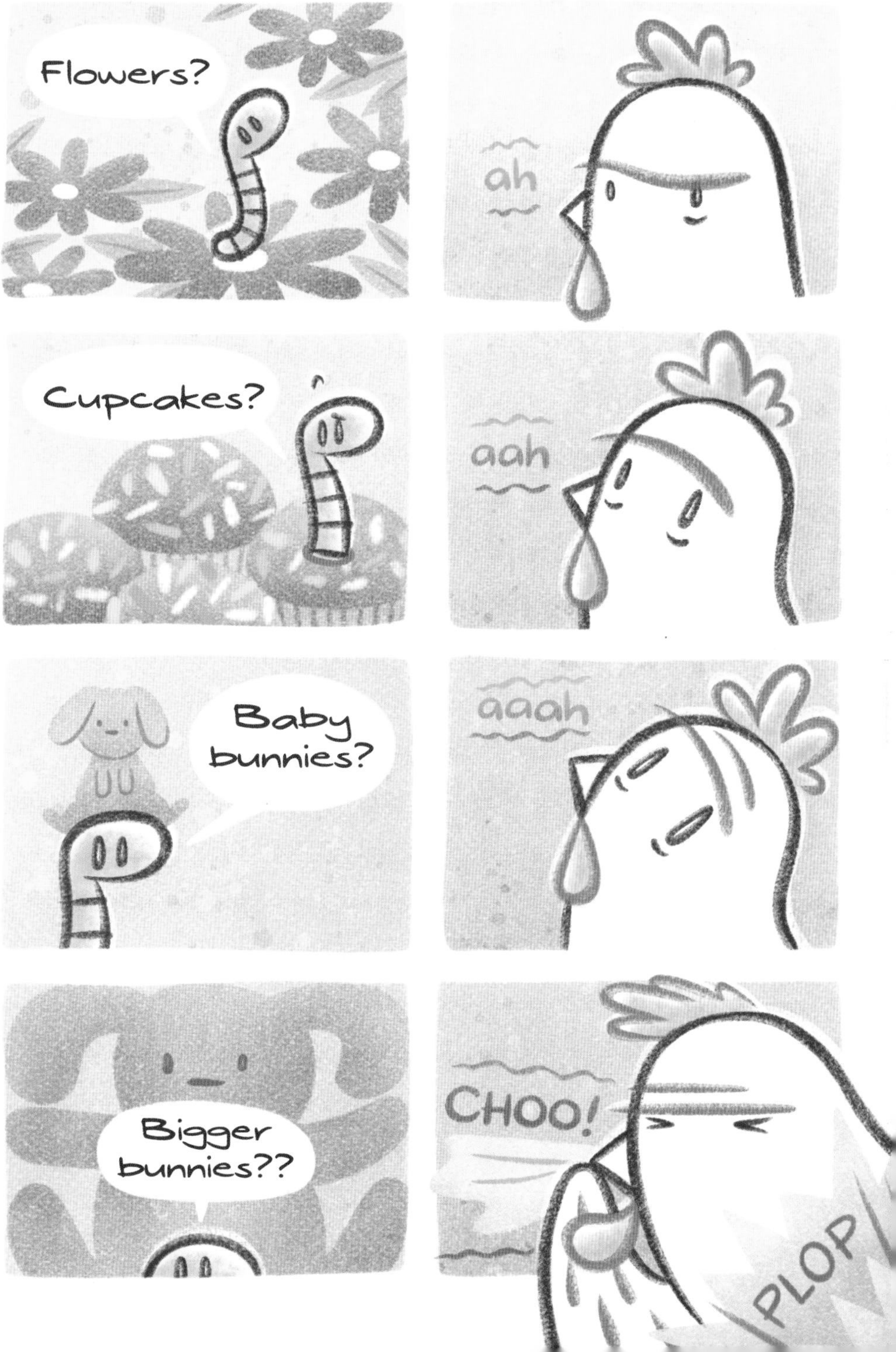
Flowers?
ah
Cupcakes?
aah
Baby bunnies?
aaah
Bigger bunnies??
CHOO!
PLOP

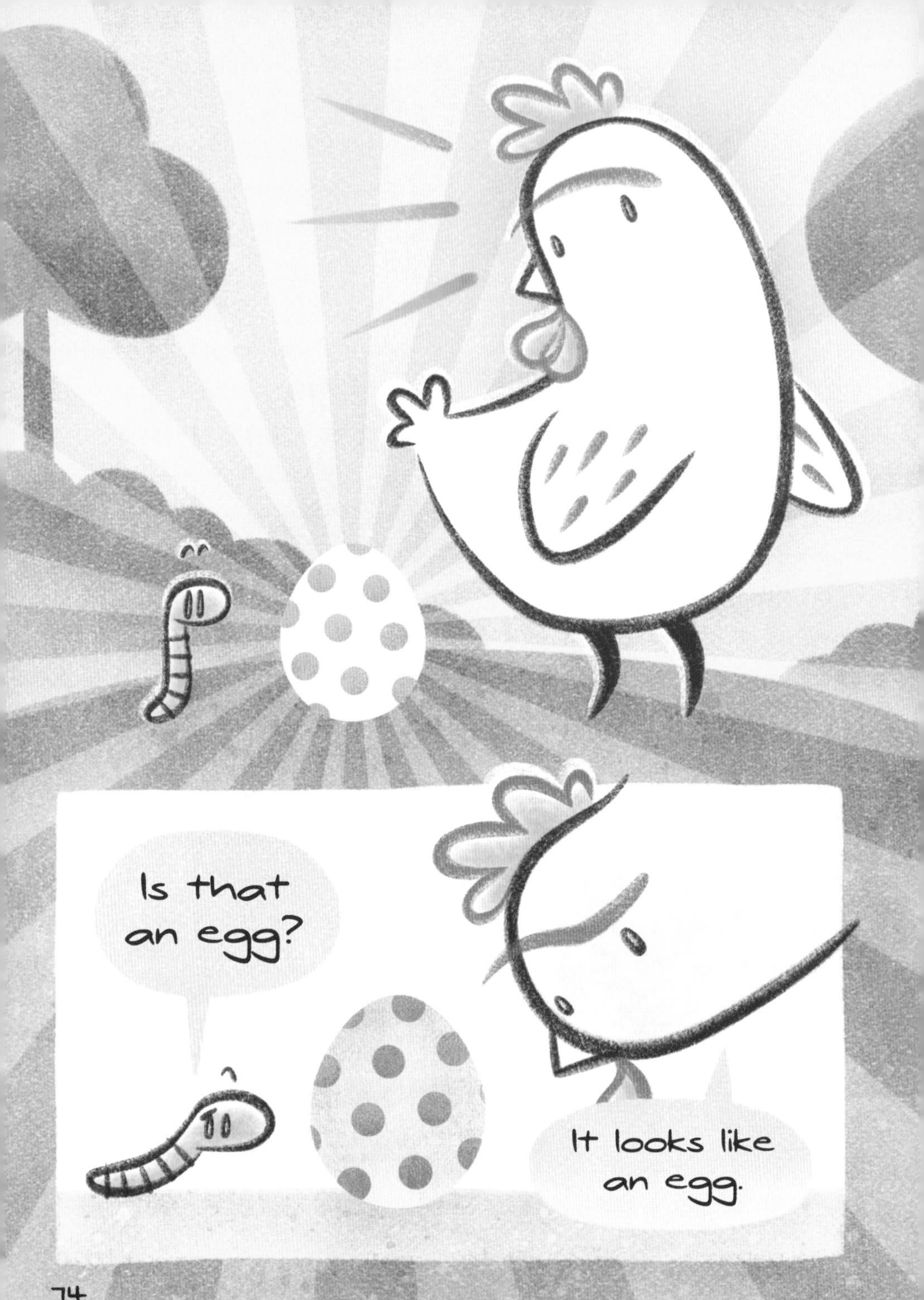

Is that an egg?
It looks like an egg.

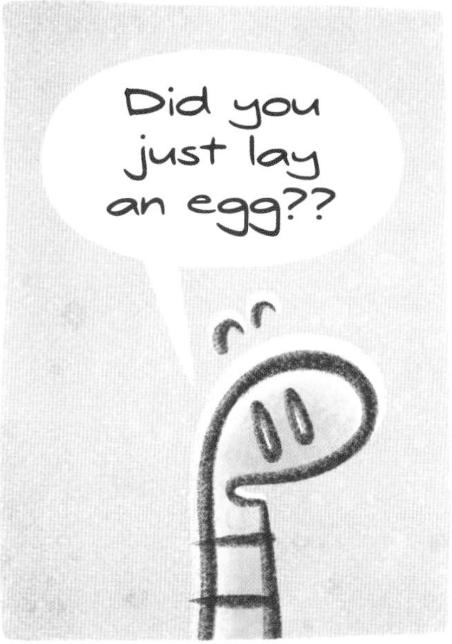
Did you just lay an egg??

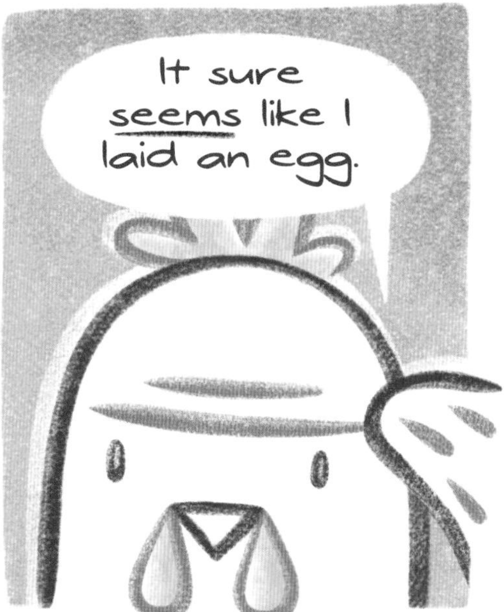
It sure seems like I laid an egg.

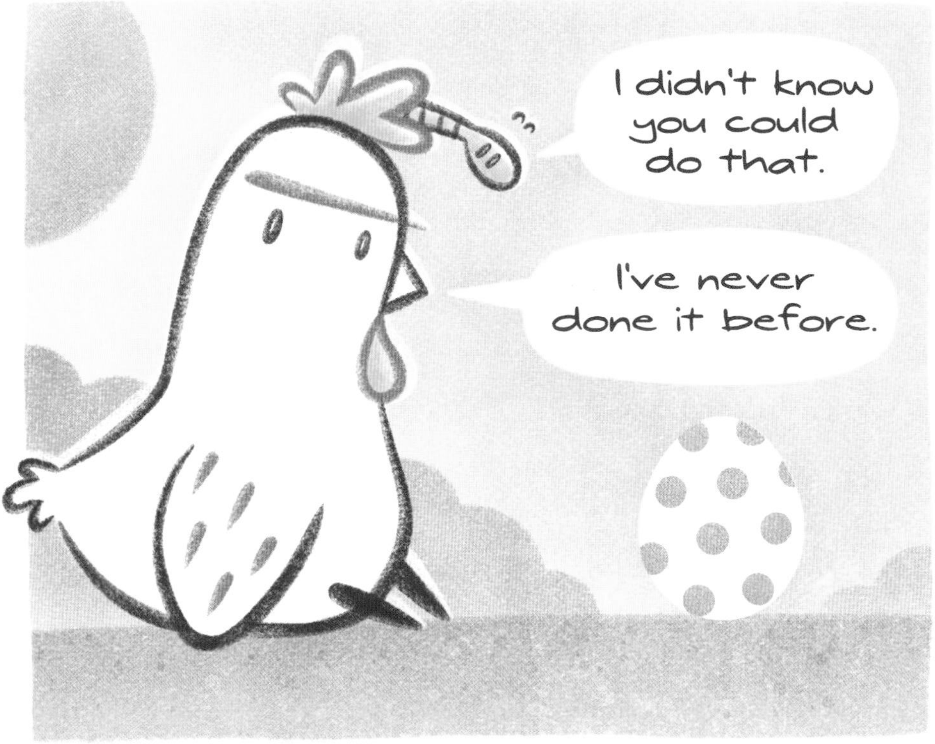
I didn't know you could do that.
I've never done it before.

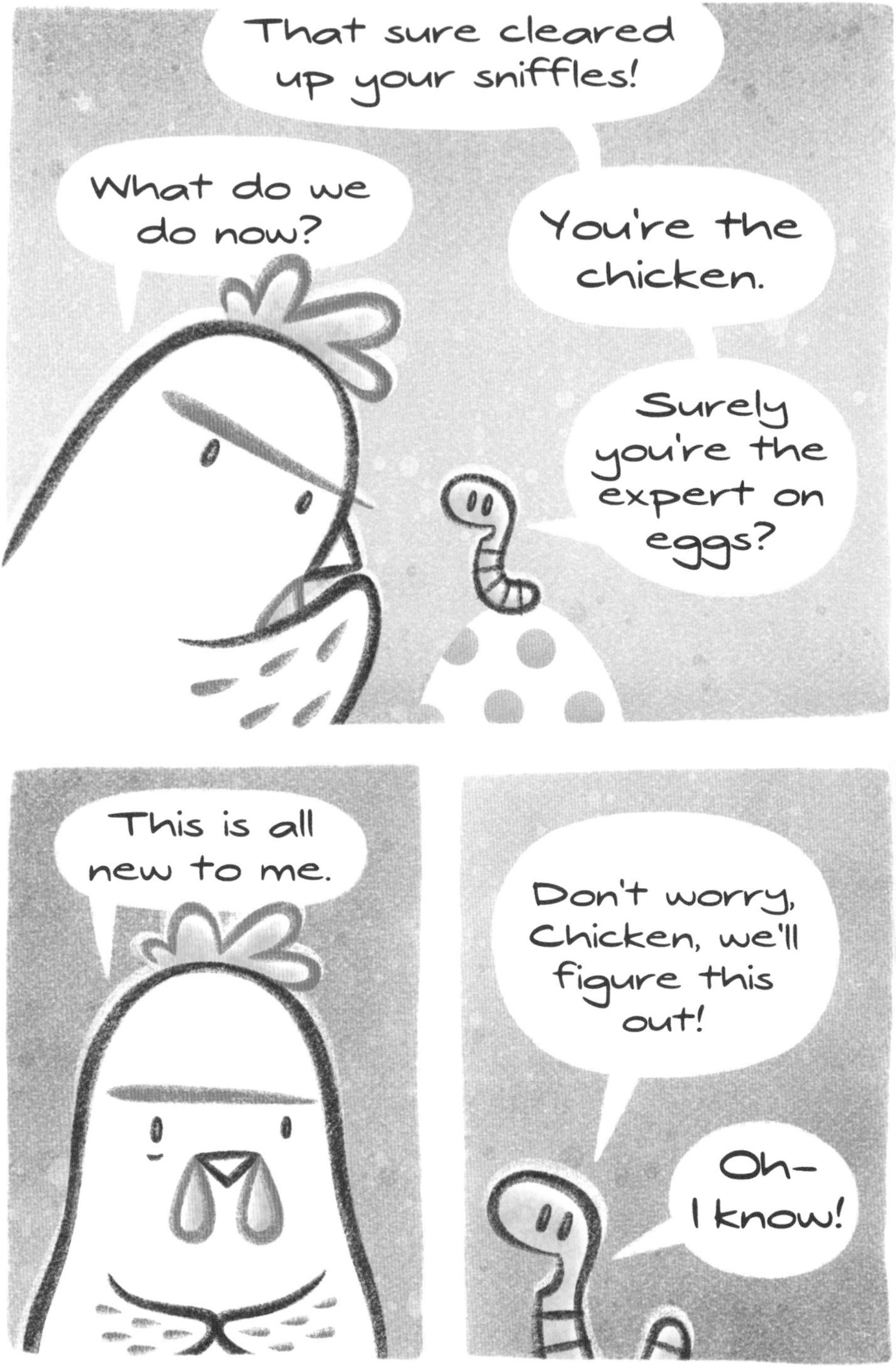
That sure cleared up your sniffles!
What do we do now?
You're the chicken.
Surely you're the expert on eggs?
This is all new to me.
Don't worry, Chicken, we'll figure this out!
Oh- I know!

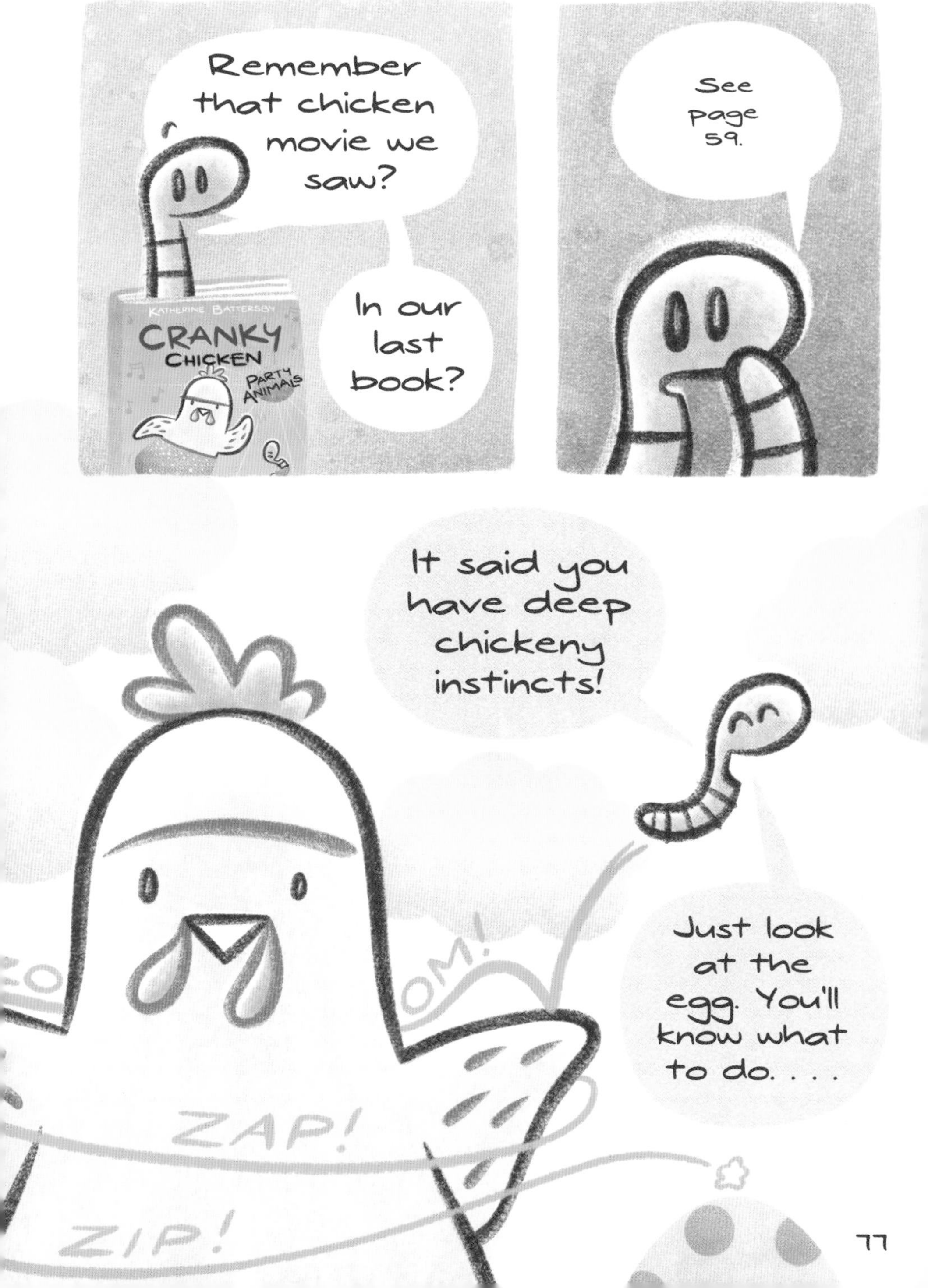
Remember that chicken movie we saw?
Katherine Battersby
CRANKY CHICKEN
PARTY ANIMALS
In our last book?
See page 59.
It said you have deep chickeny instincts!
Just look at the egg. You'll know what to do. . . .
ZAP!
ZIP!

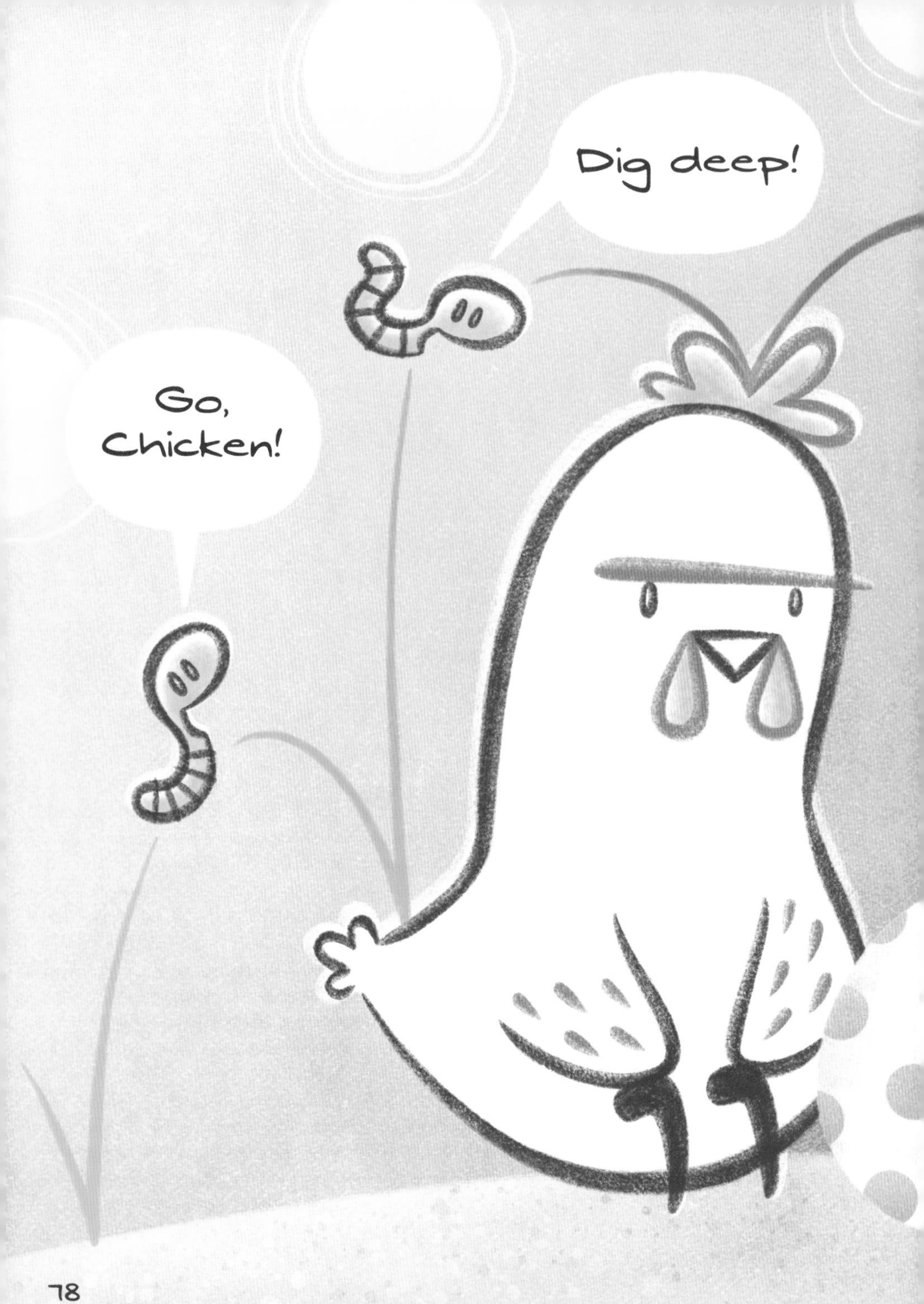
Dig deep!
Go, Chicken!

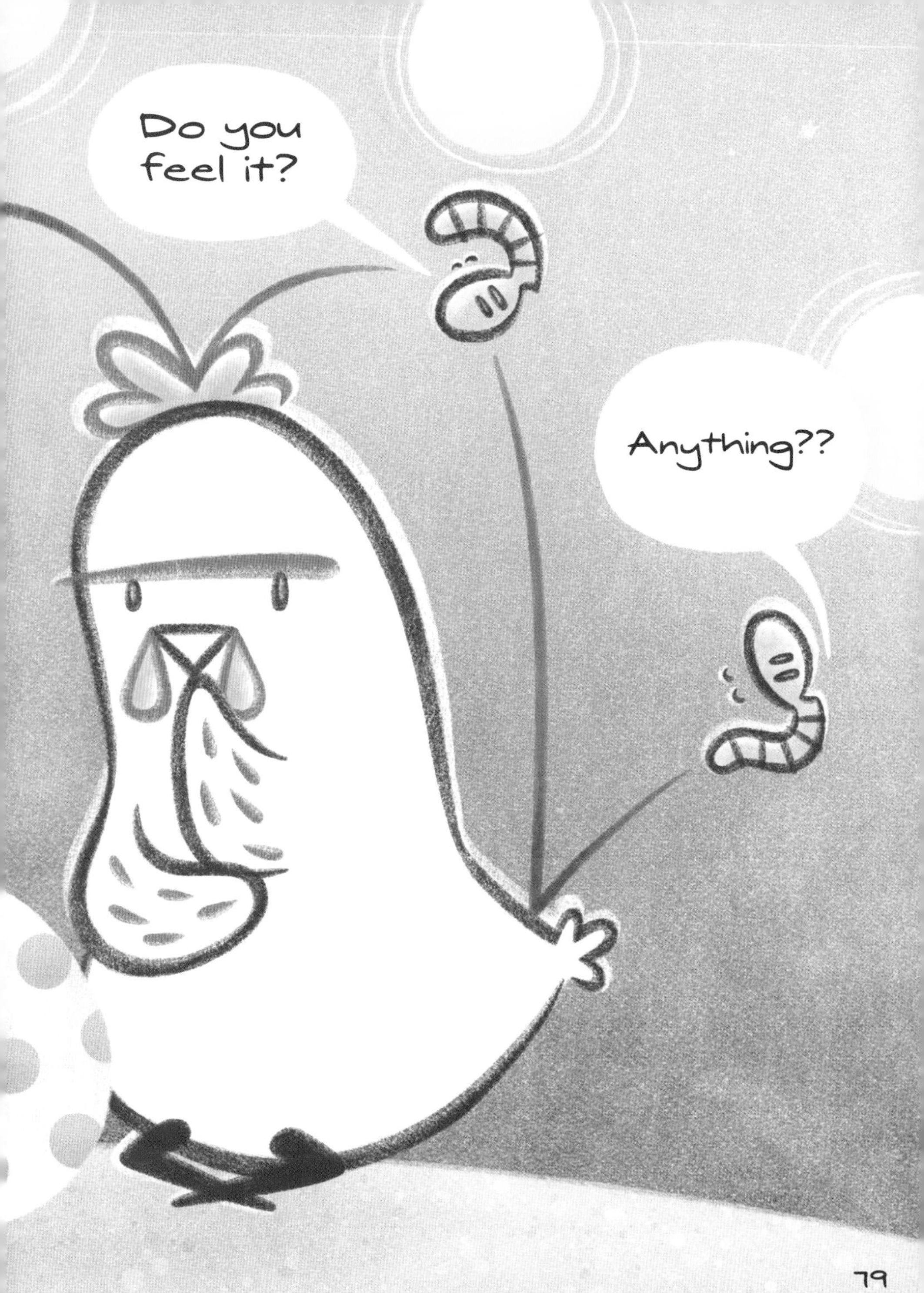
Do you feel it?
Anything??

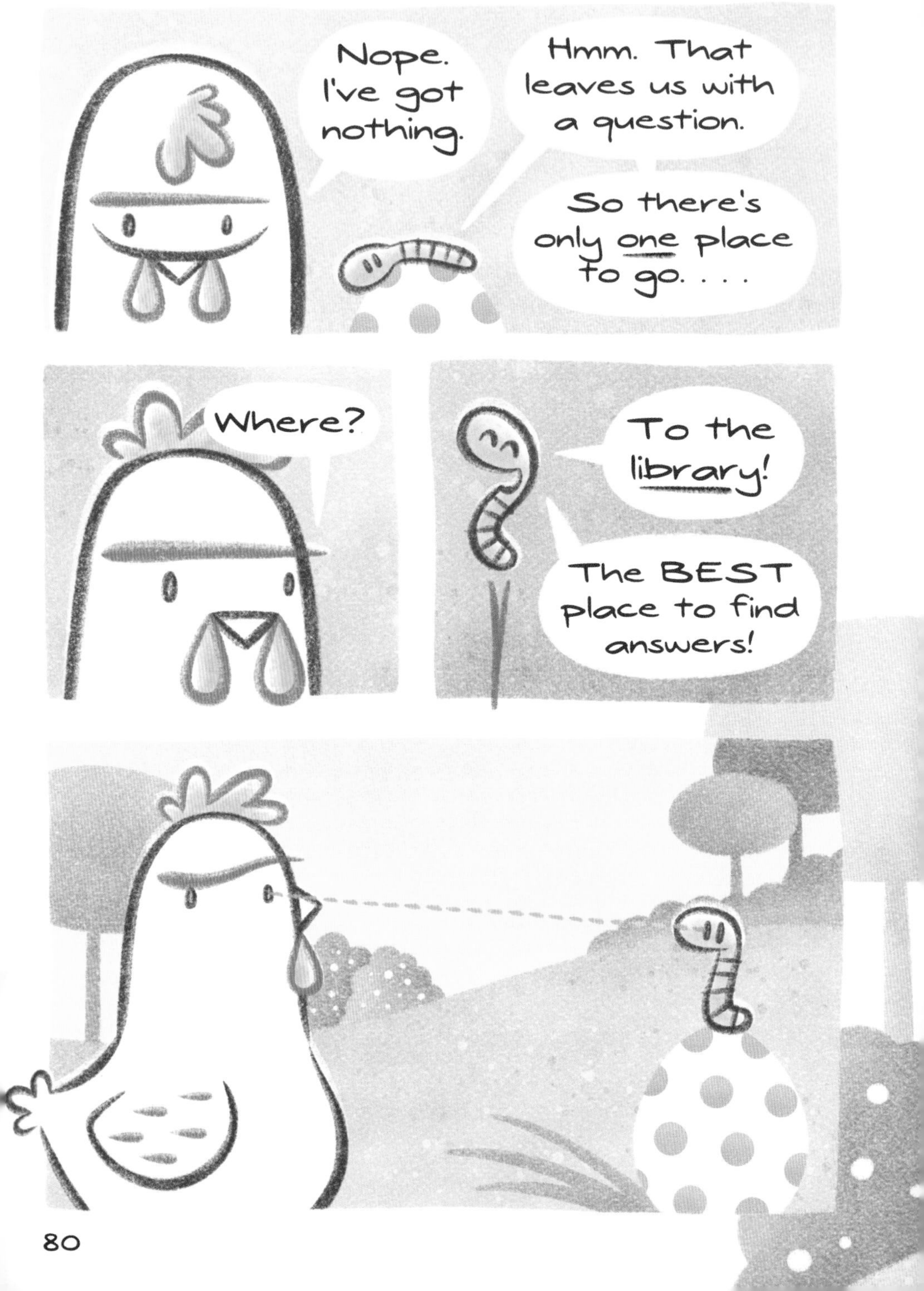
Nope. I've got nothing.
Hmm. That leaves us with a question.
So there's only one place to go. . . .
Where?
To the library!
The BEST place to find answers!

Don't you have something to say?

Like what?

Like "grumble grumble, libraries make me cranky."

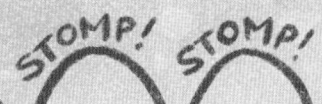

STOMP! STOMP!

But I like libraries.

You do?

I like <u>some</u> things.

Why Libraries Don't Make Cranky Chicken Cranky

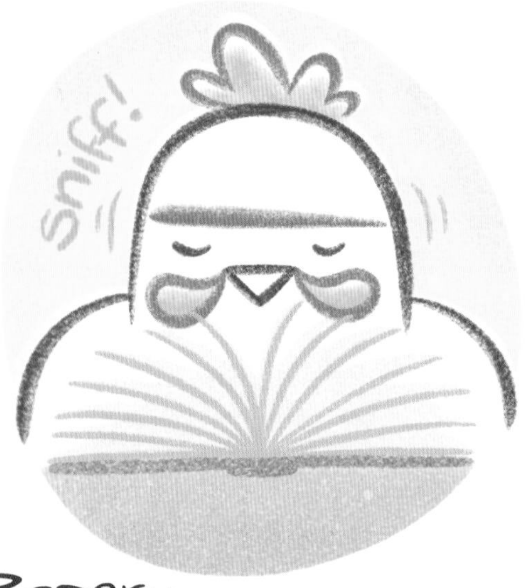
Sniff!

Papery book smell

Comfy chairs

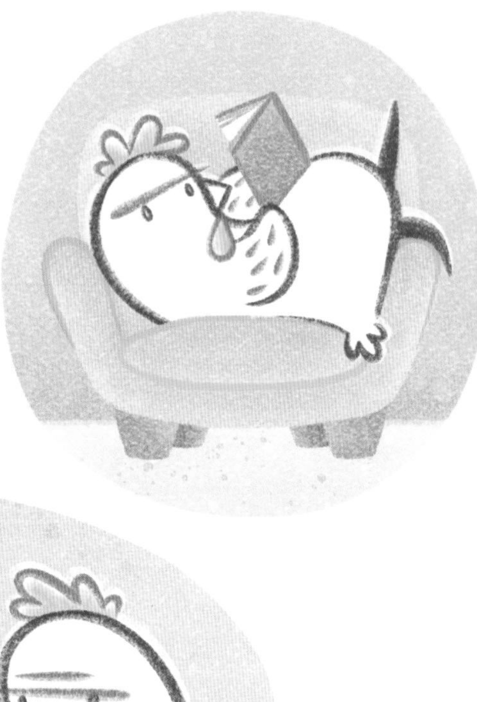

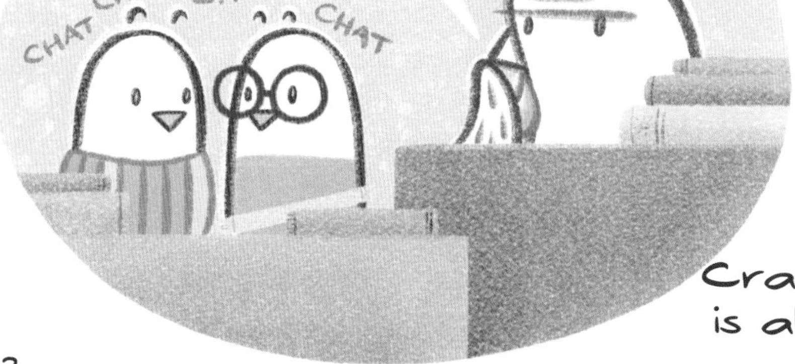
CHAT
CHAT CHAT
CHAT CHAT CHAT
CHAT
CHAT
Shhh...

Crankiness is allowed

Library cats

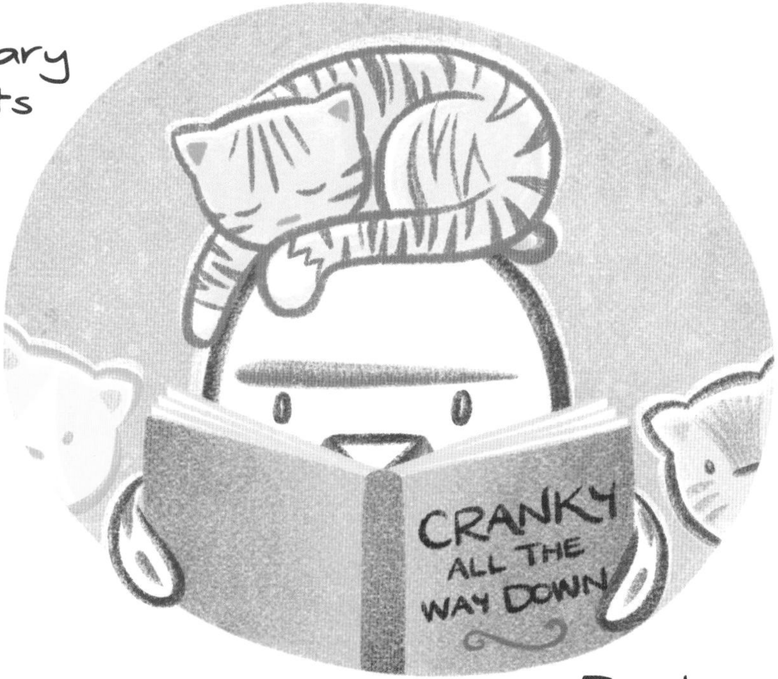
CRANKY ALL THE WAY DOWN

Books and books and books

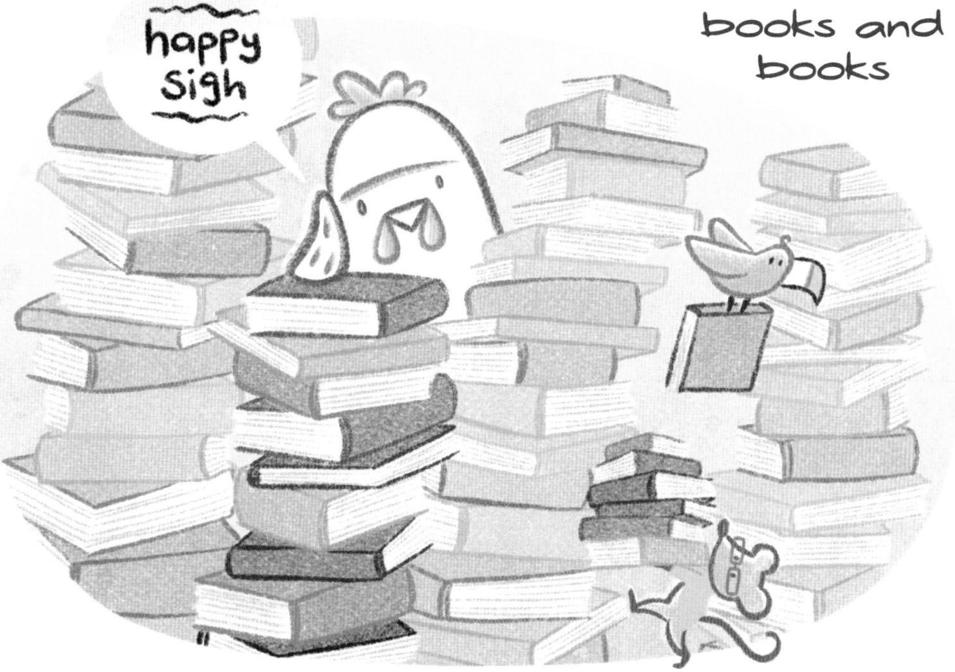
happy sigh

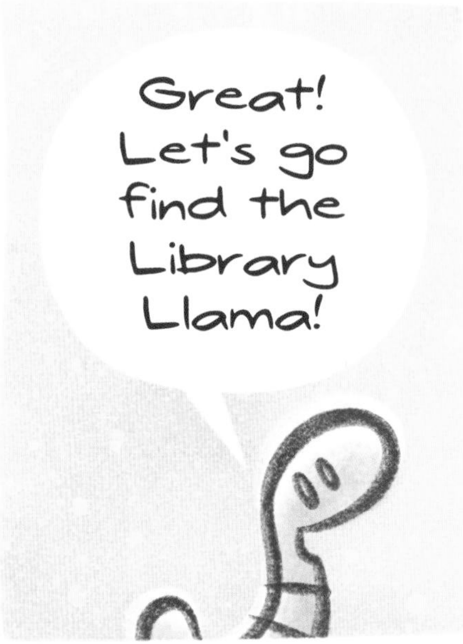
Great! Let's go find the Library Llama!

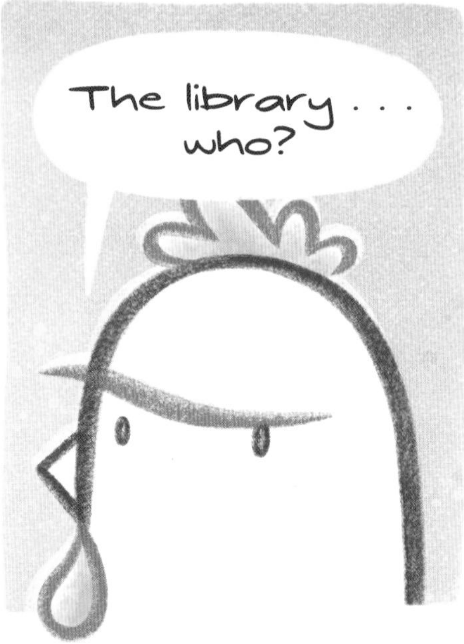
The library . . . who?

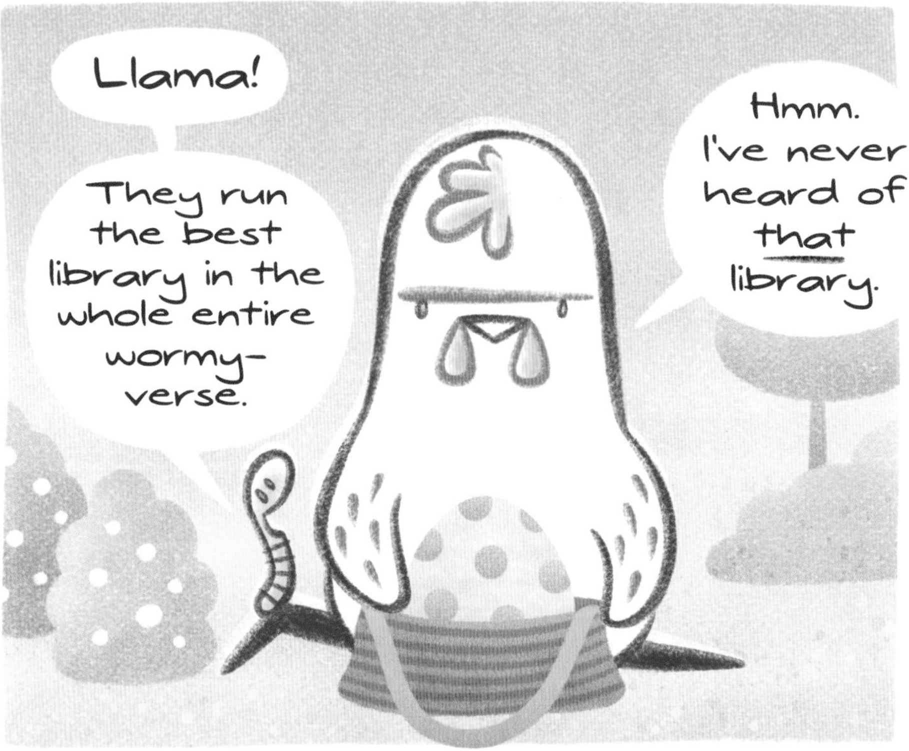
Llama!
They run the best library in the whole entire wormy-verse.
Hmm. I've never heard of that library.

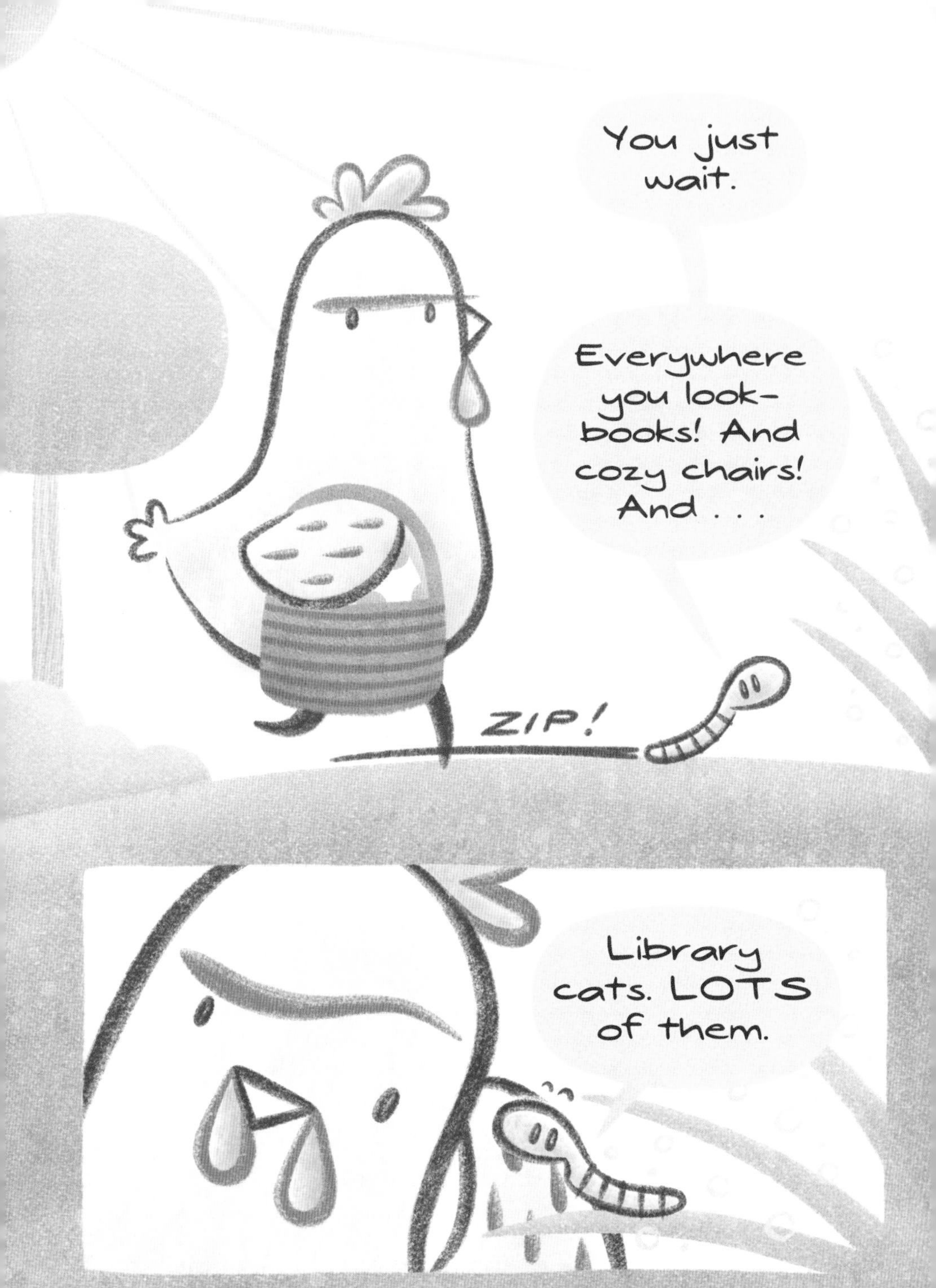
You just wait.
Everywhere you look- books! And cozy chairs! And . . .
ZIP!
Library cats. LOTS of them.

I hope the egg is ok.
It's safe with you.

How much farther?
More than a little, less than a lot.

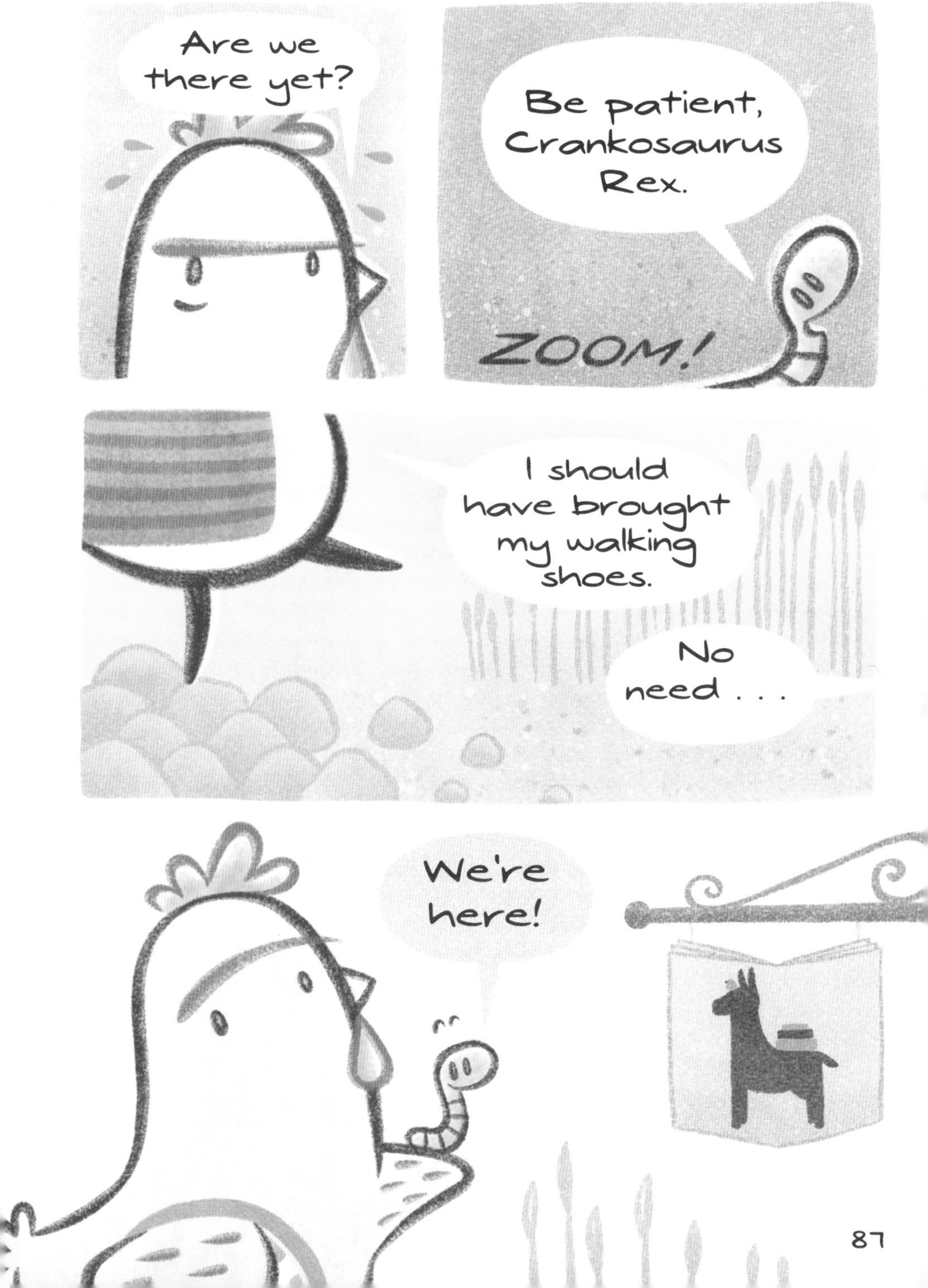
Are we there yet?
Be patient, Crankosaurus Rex.
ZOOM!
I should have brought my walking shoes.
No need . . .
We're here!

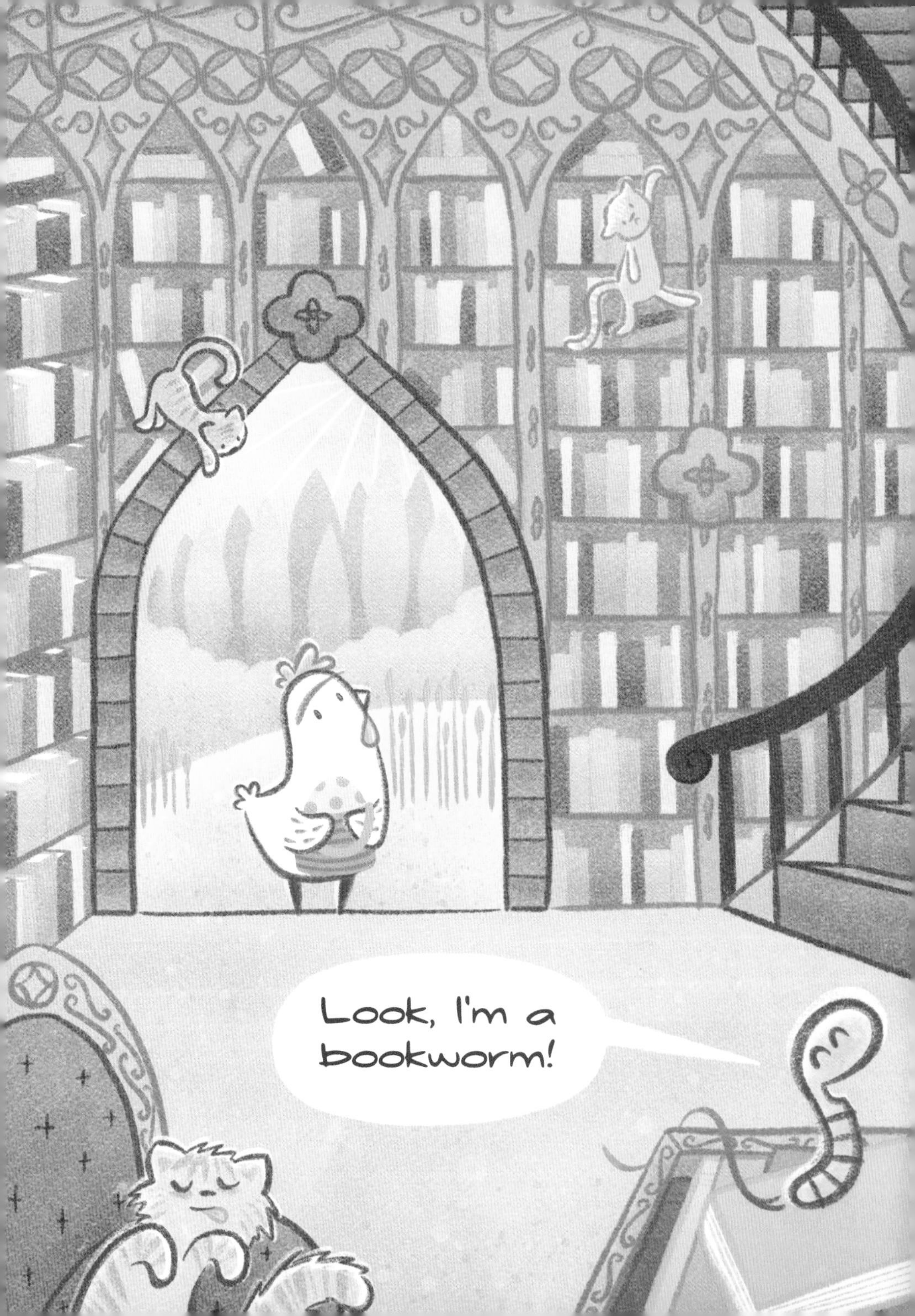
Look, I'm a bookworm!

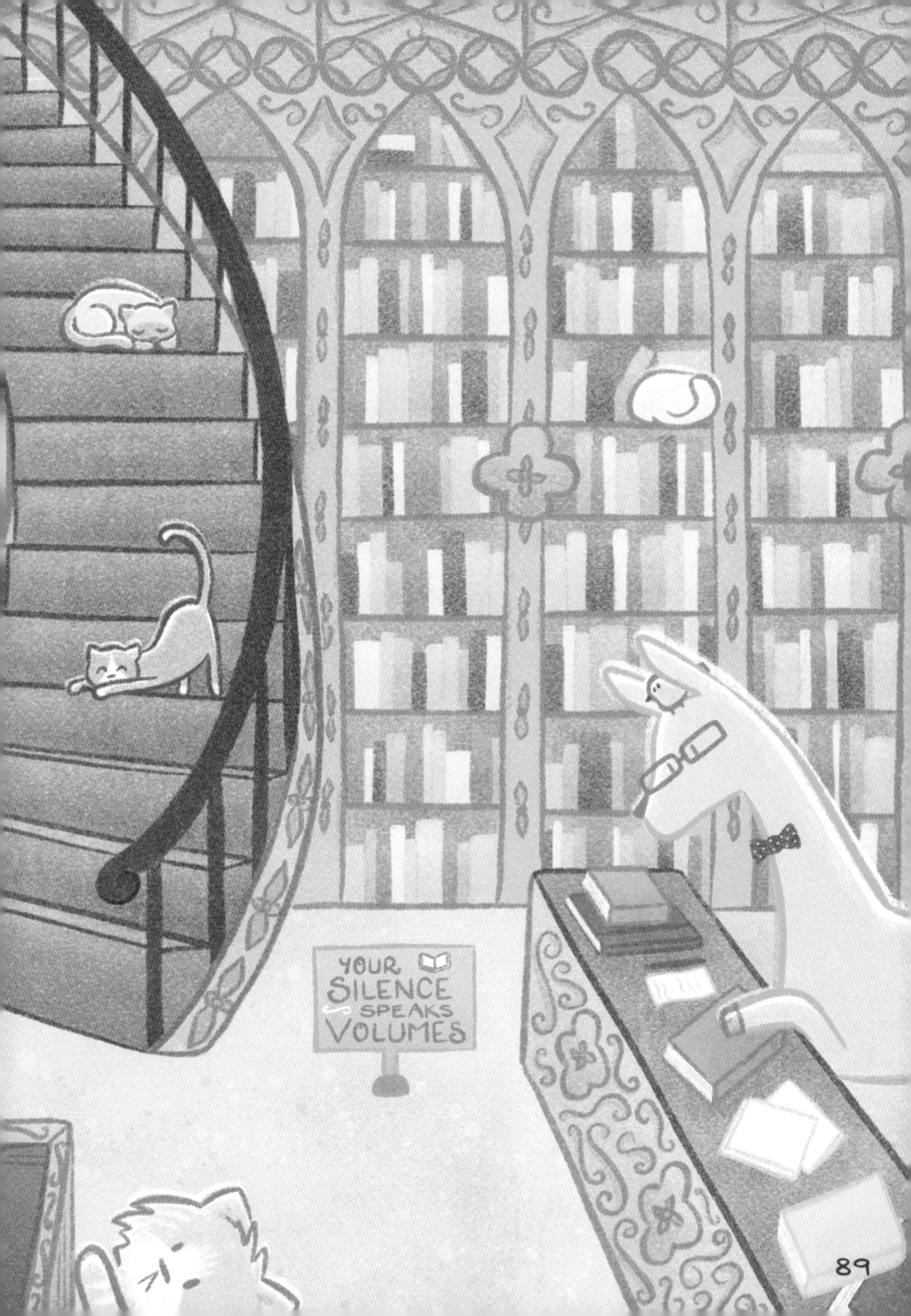
YOUR
SILENCE
SPEAKS
VOLUMES

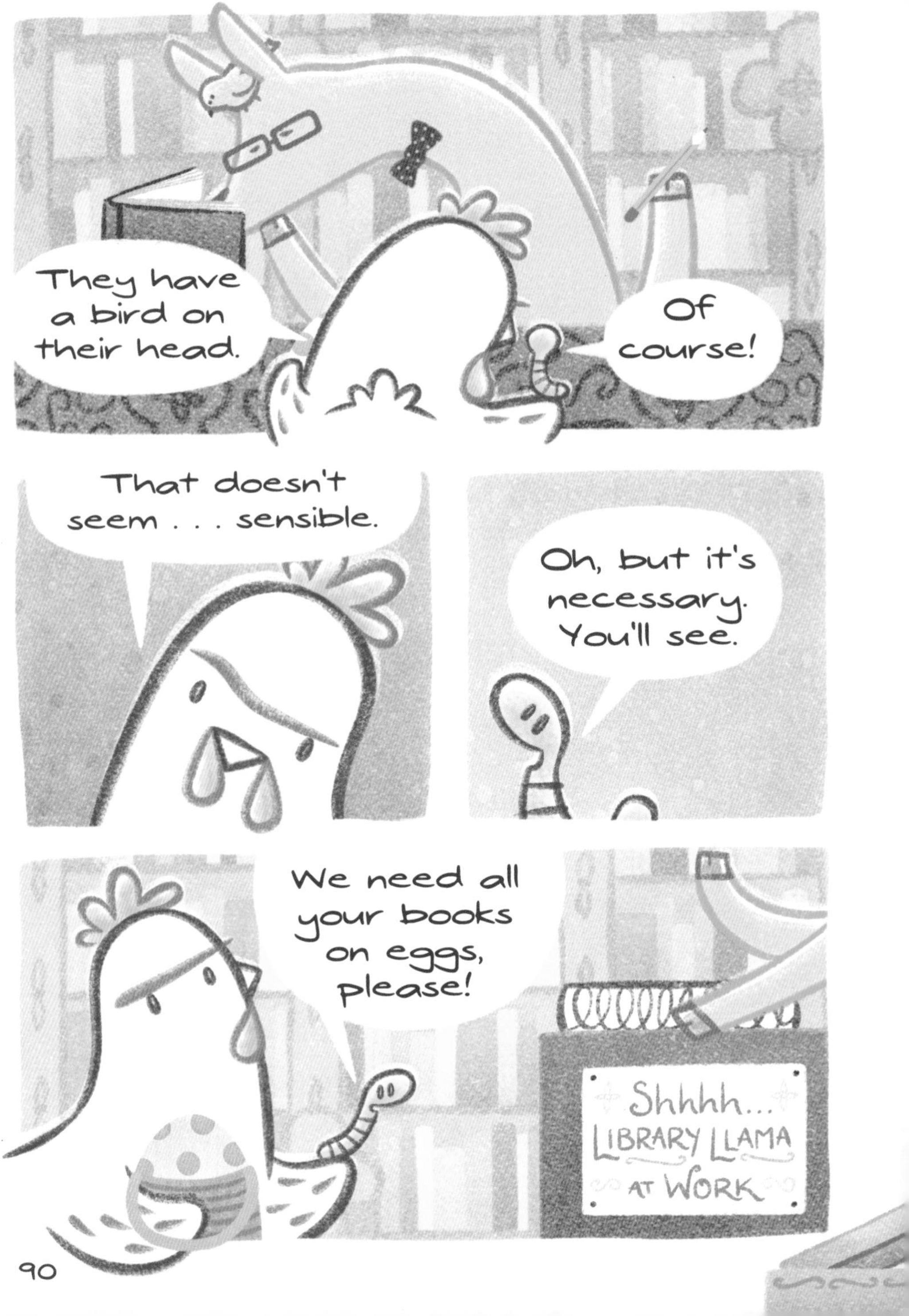
They have a bird on their head.
Of course!
That doesn't seem . . . sensible.
Oh, but it's necessary. You'll see.
We need all your books on eggs, please!
Shhhh... LIBRARY LLAMA AT WORK

SHELF 42
44
43
42
Thank you!

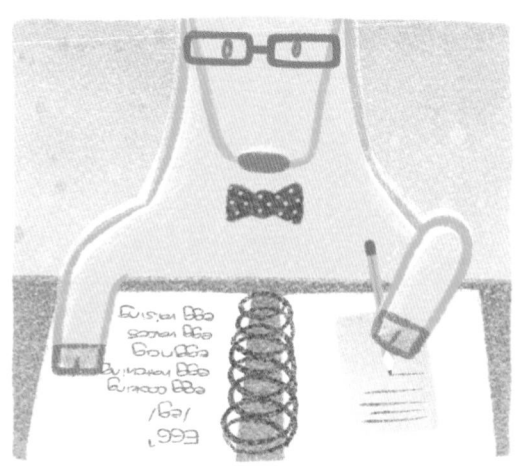

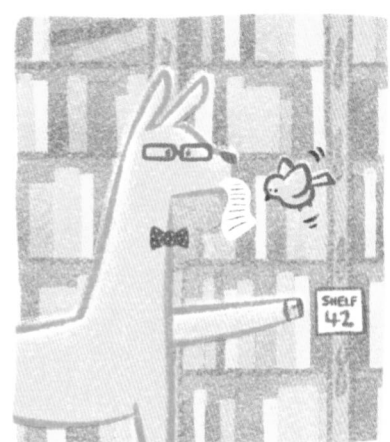

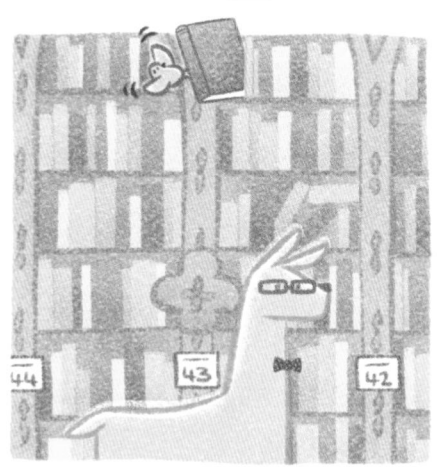

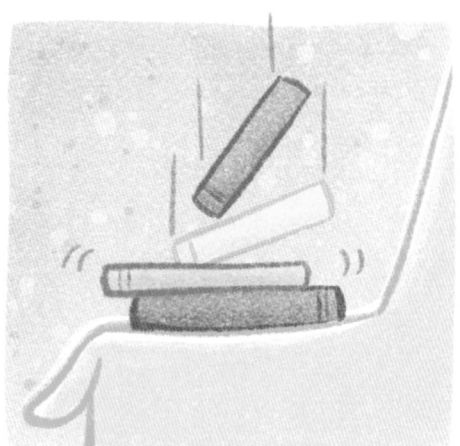

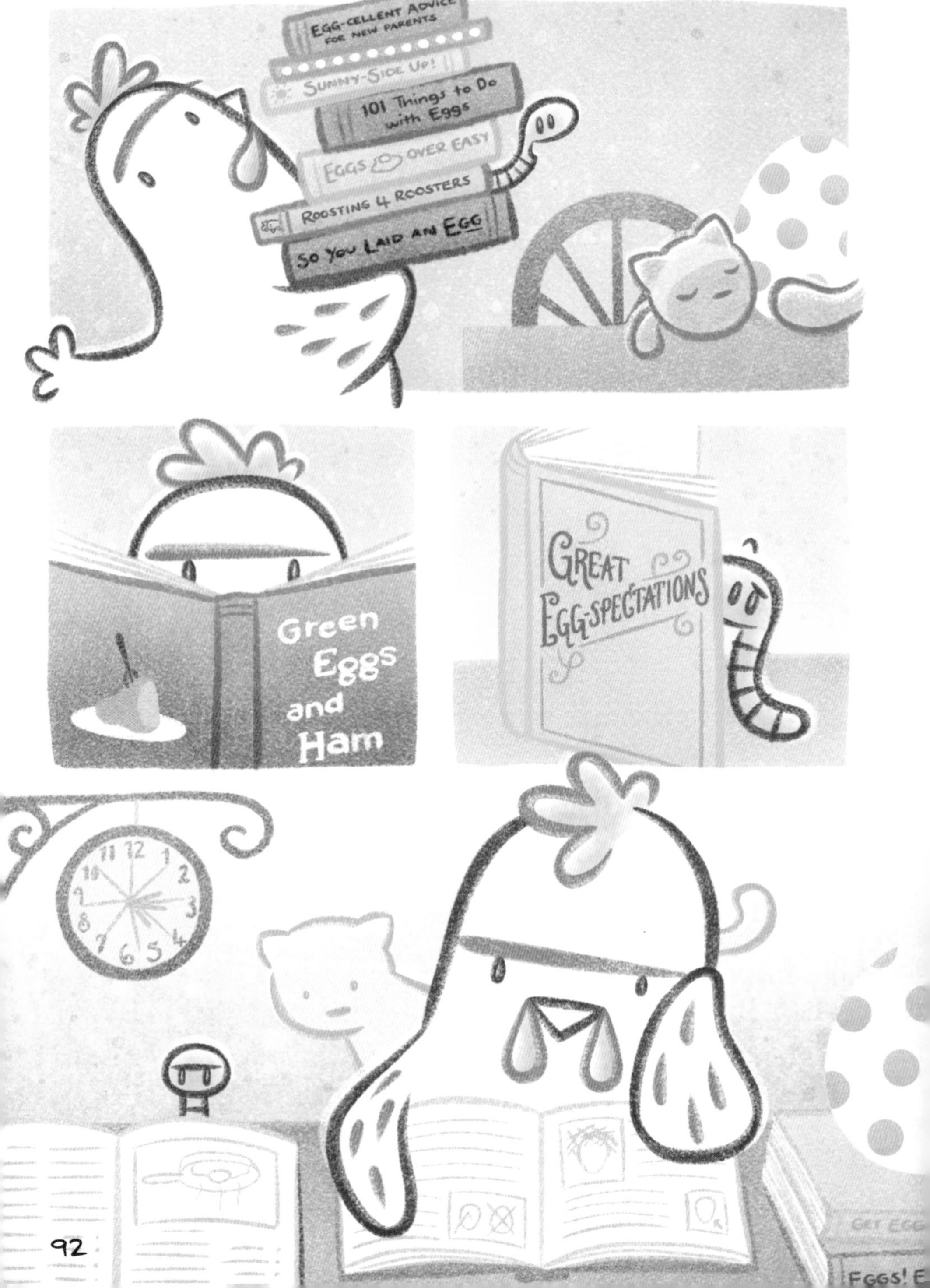
EGG-CELLENT ADVICE FOR NEW PARENTS
SUNNY-SIDE UP!
101 Things to Do with Eggs
EGGS OVER EASY
ROOSTING 4 ROOSTERS
SO YOU LAID AN EGG
Green Eggs and Ham
GREAT EGG-SPECTATIONS

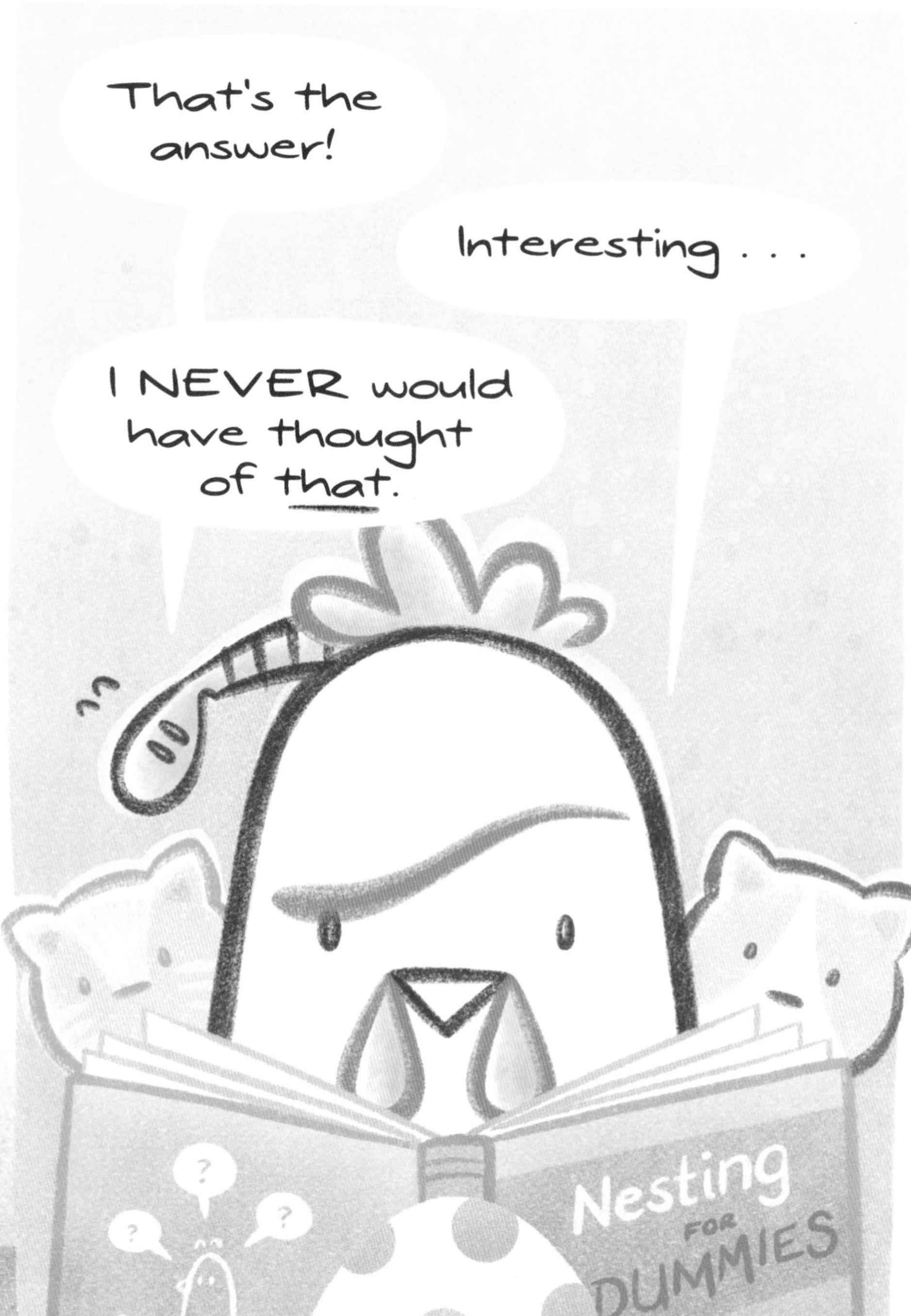
That's the answer!
Interesting . . .
I NEVER would have thought of that.
Nesting FOR DUMMIES

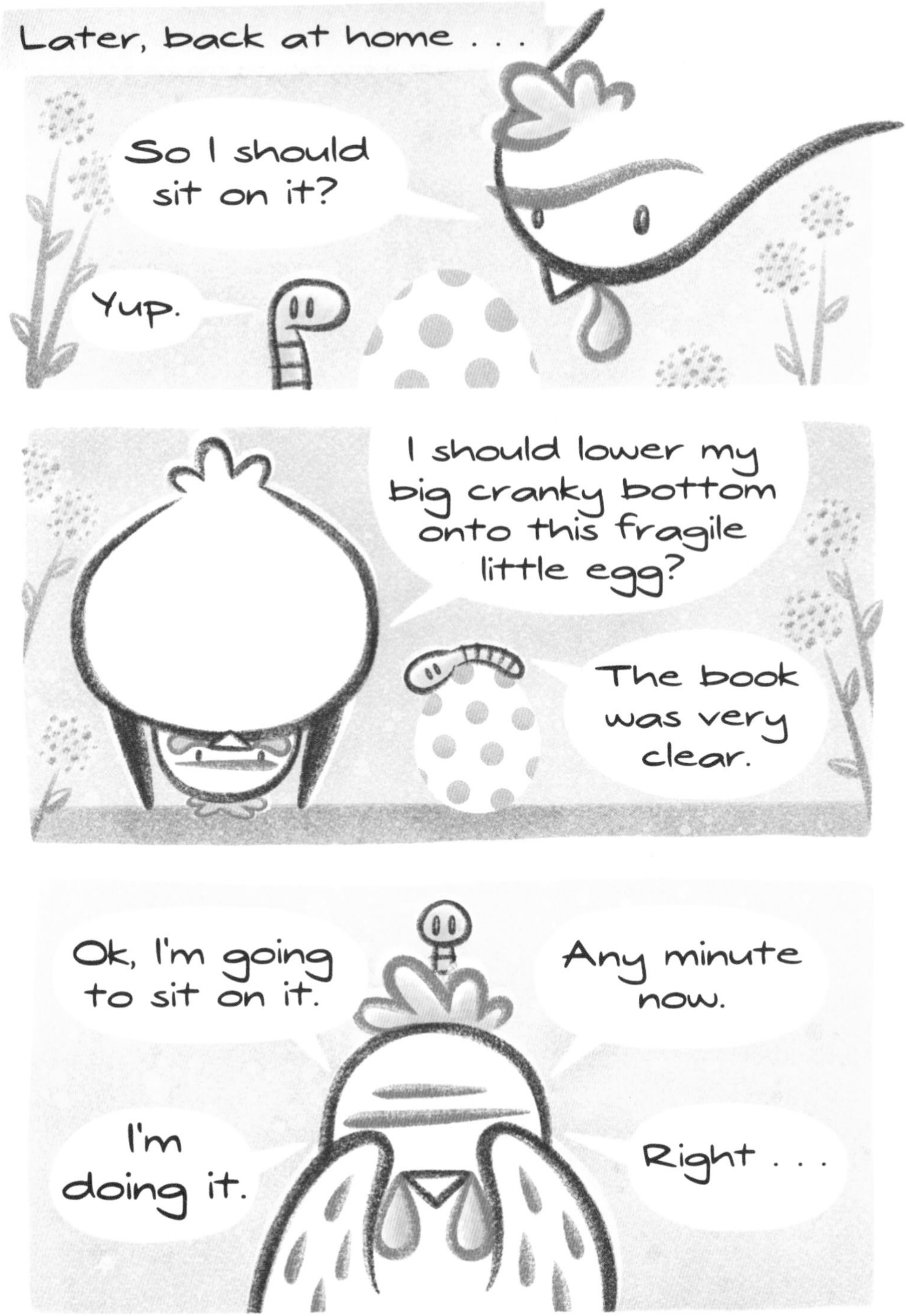
Later, back at home . . .
So I should sit on it?
Yup.
I should lower my big cranky bottom onto this fragile little egg?
The book was very clear.
Ok, I'm going to sit on it.
Any minute now.
I'm doing it.
Right . . .

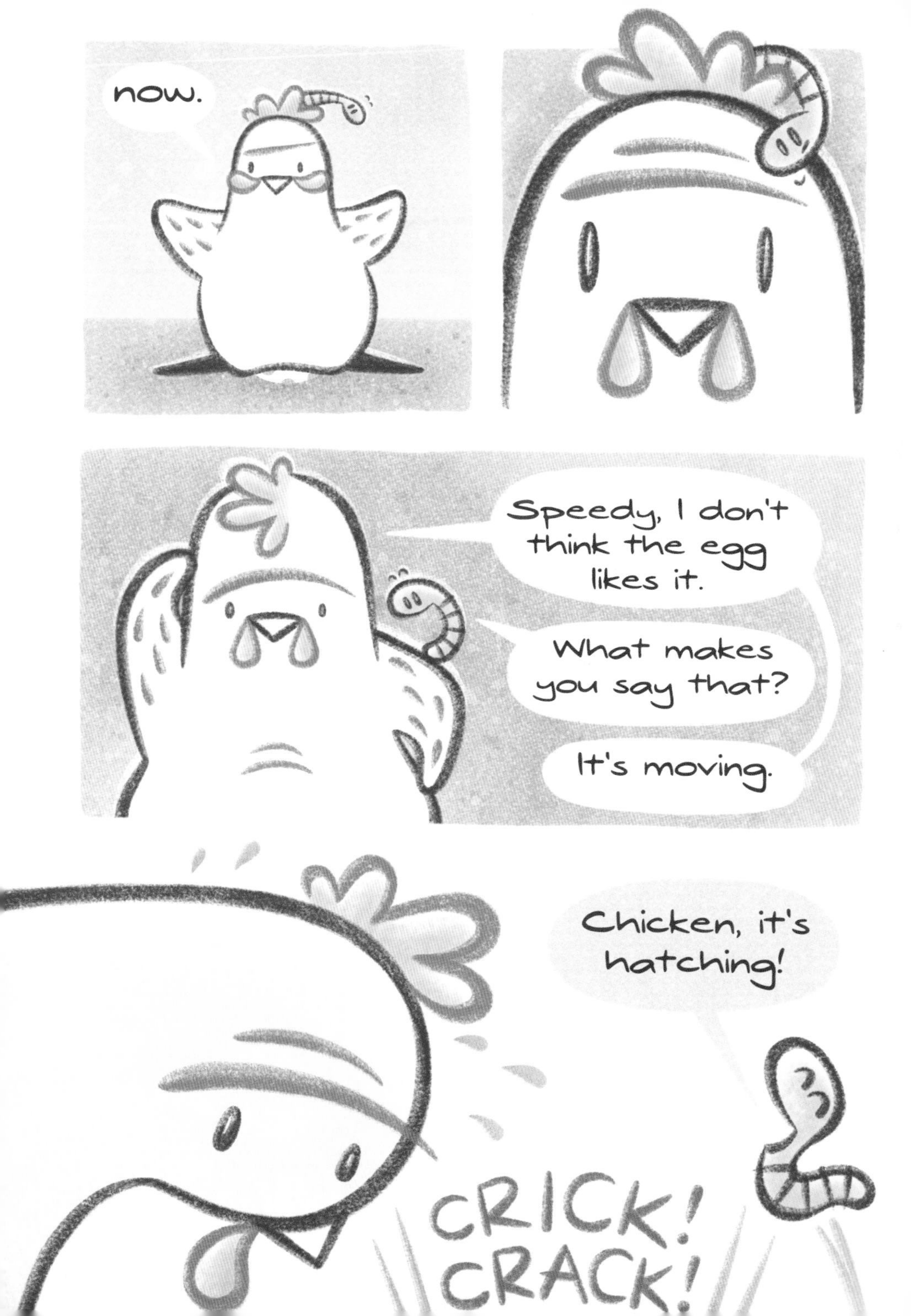
now.
Speedy, I don't think the egg likes it.
What makes you say that?
It's moving.
Chicken, it's hatching!
CRICK!
CRACK!

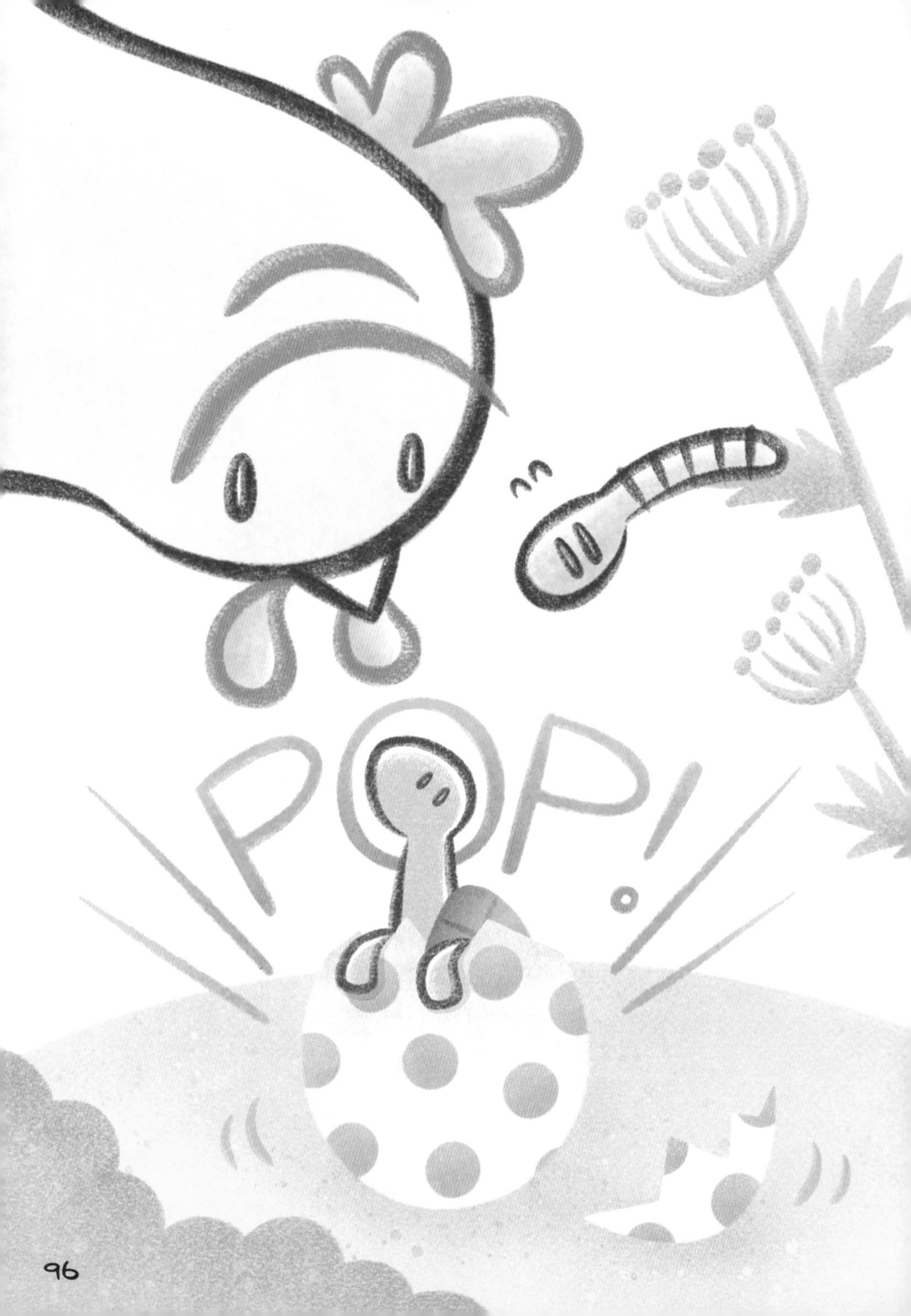
POP!

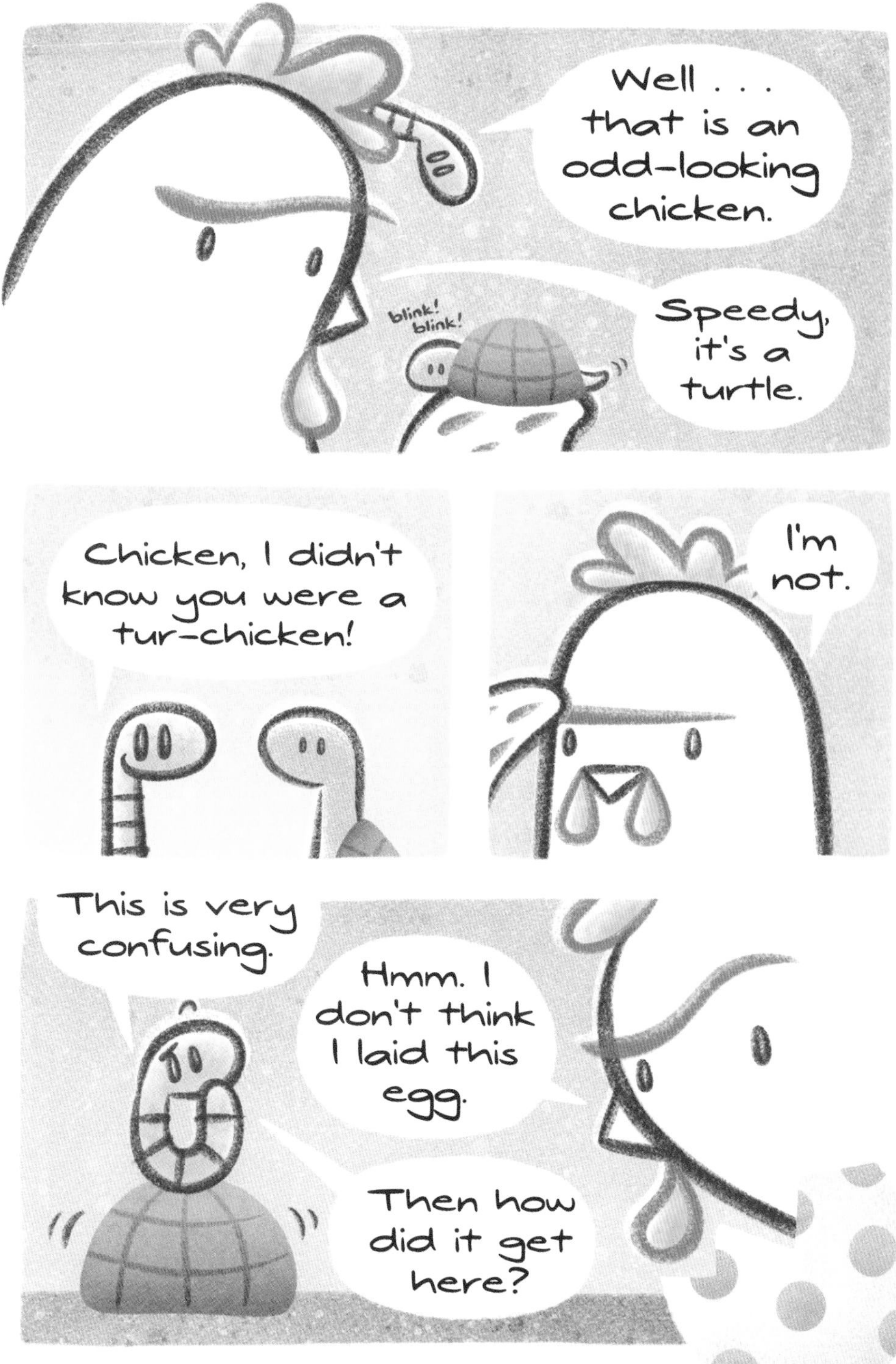
Well . . . that is an odd-looking chicken.
blink! blink!
Speedy, it's a turtle.
Chicken, I didn't know you were a tur-chicken!
I'm not.
This is very confusing.
Hmm. I don't think I laid this egg.
Then how did it get here?

What REALLY Happened . . .

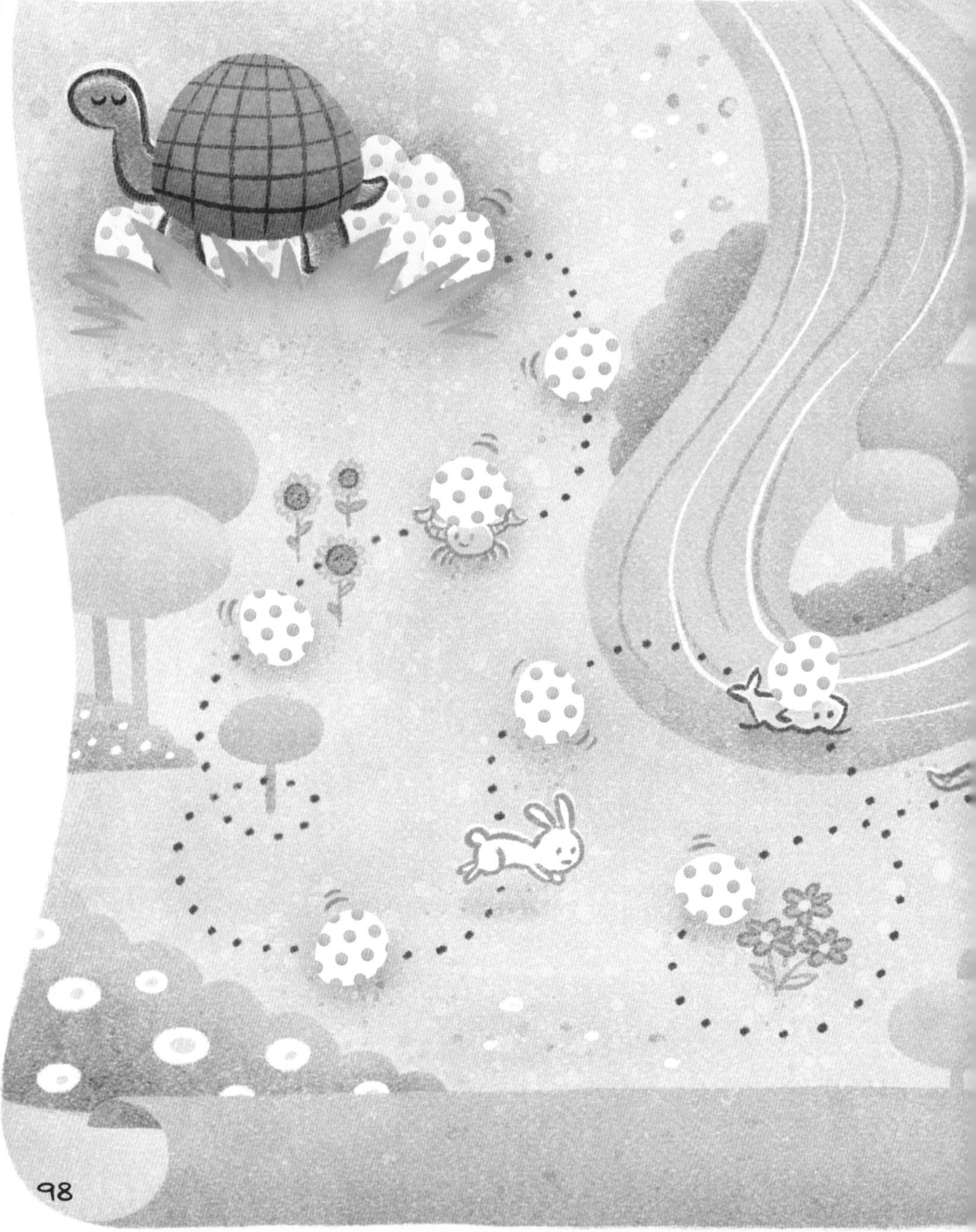

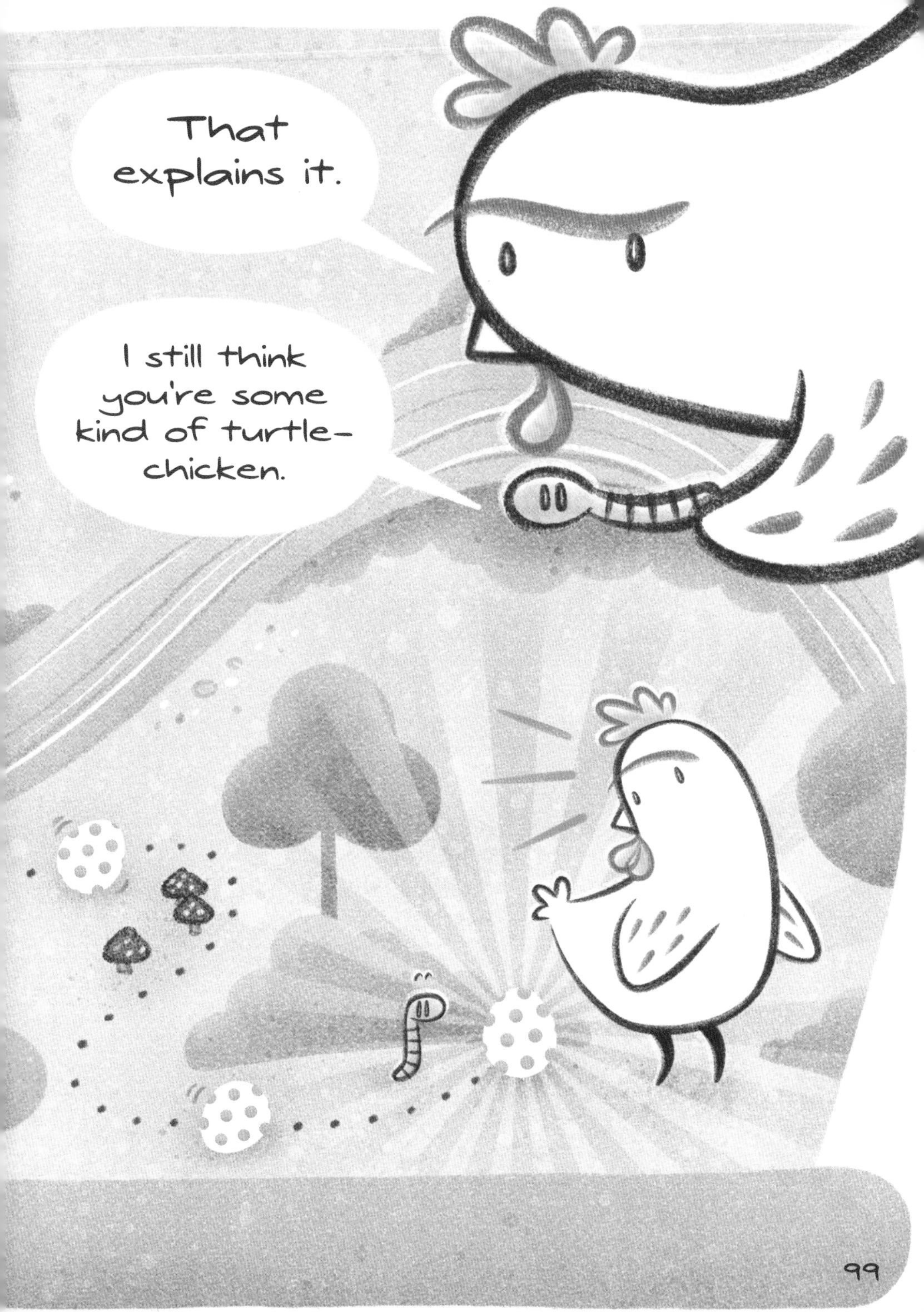
That explains it.
I still think you're some kind of turtle-chicken.

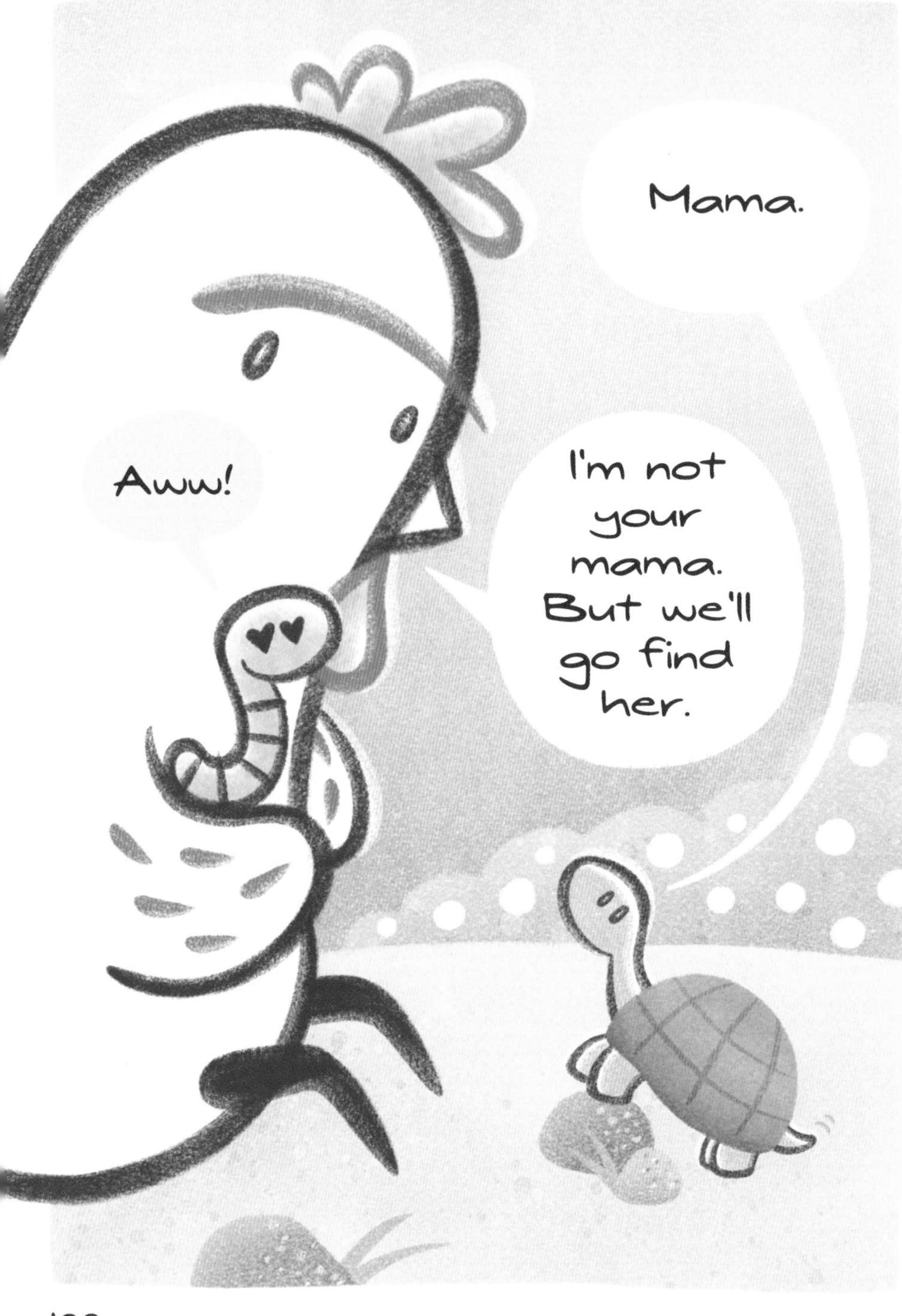
Mama.
Aww!
I'm not your mama. But we'll go find her.

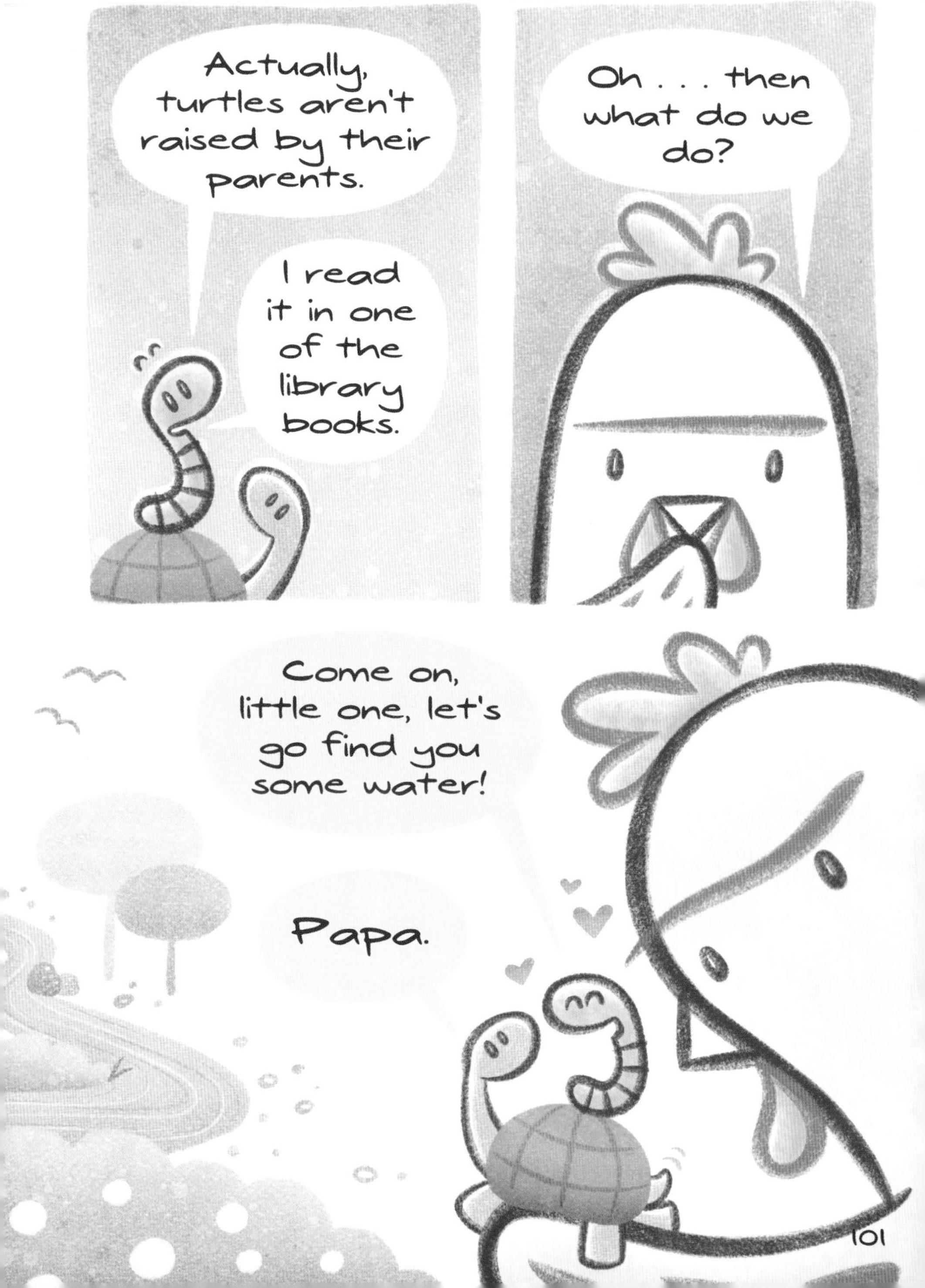
Actually, turtles aren't raised by their parents.
I read it in one of the library books.
Oh . . . then what do we do?
Come on, little one, let's go find you some water!
Papa.

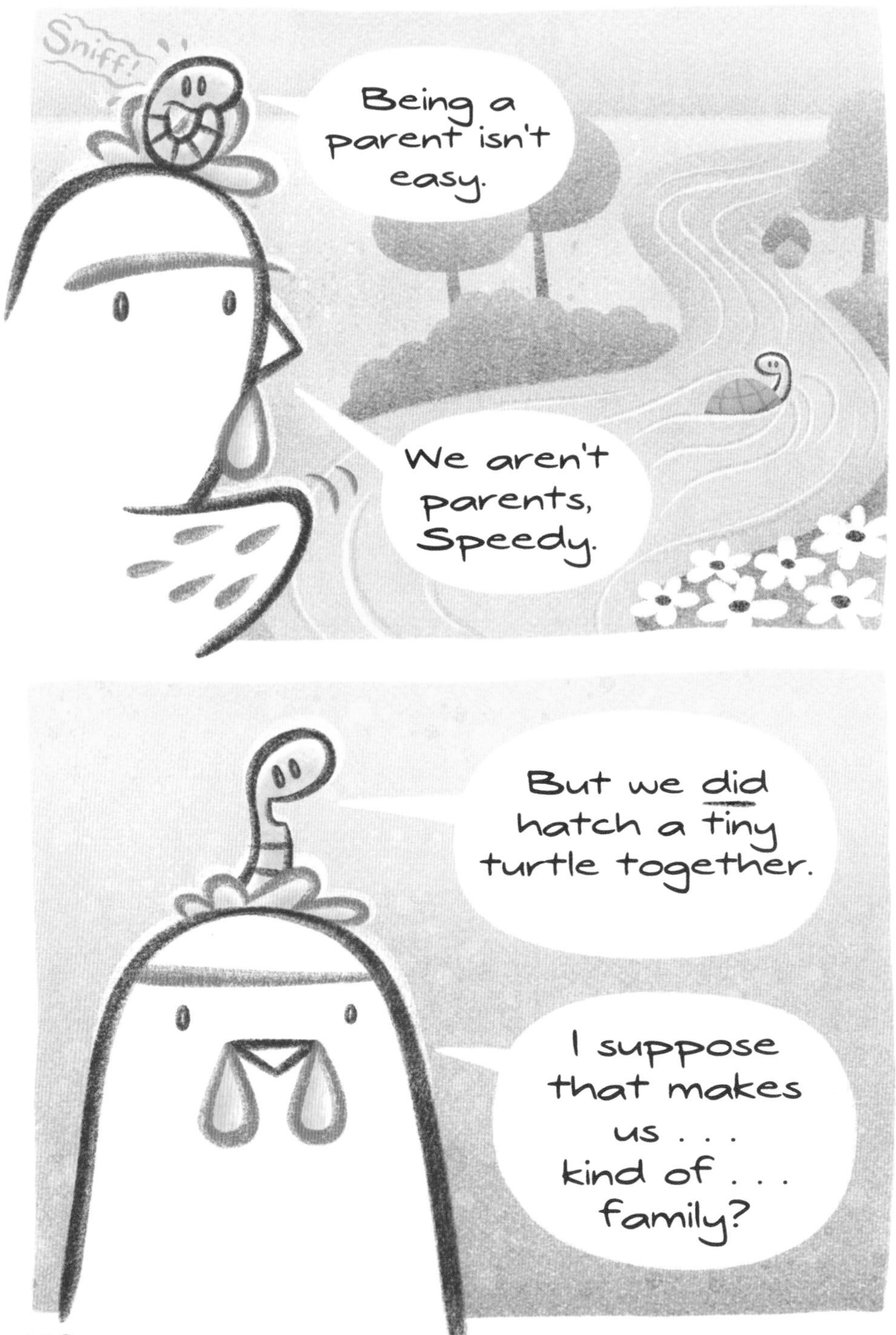

Sniff!
Being a parent isn't easy.
We aren't parents, Speedy.
But we did hatch a tiny turtle together.
I suppose that makes us . . . kind of . . . family?

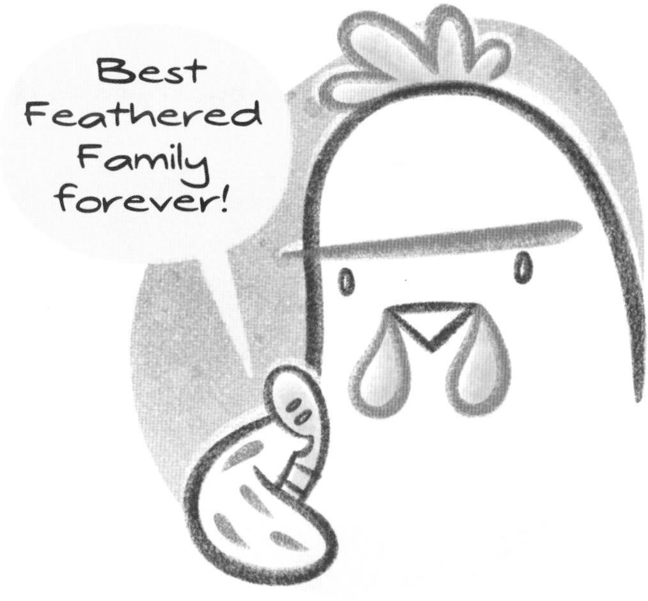
Best Feathered Family forever!

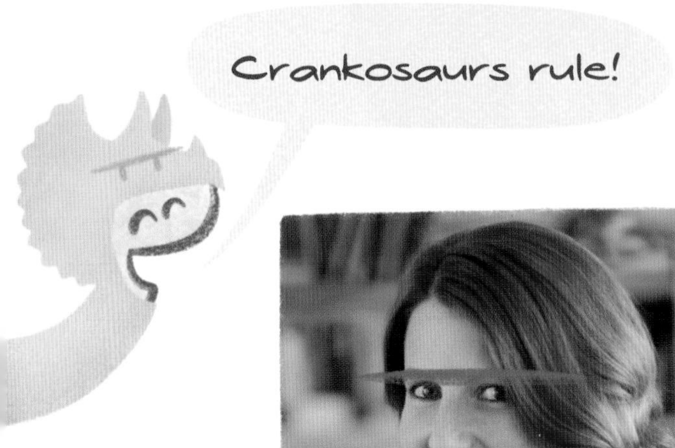
Crankosaurs rule!

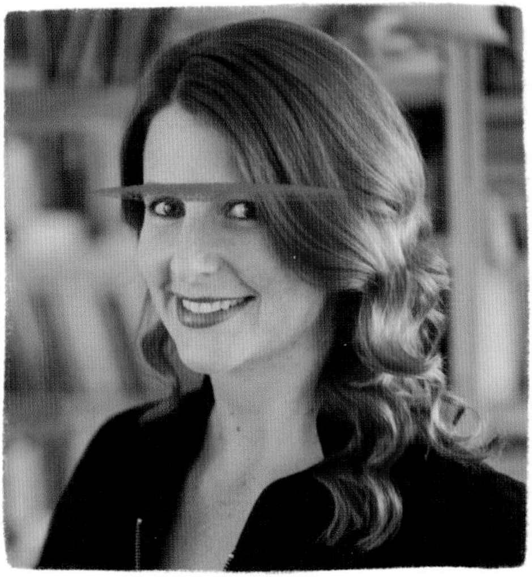

Katherine Battersby

is the critically acclaimed author and illustrator of a number of books, including *Cranky Chicken, Cranky Chicken: Party Animals, Perfect Pigeons,* and *Squish Rabbit,* a CBC Children's Choice Book. Her books have received glowing reviews in the *New York Times* and starred reviews from *Kirkus* and have been shortlisted for numerous Australian awards. Katherine is Queen of the Crankosaurs and can be found grumbling about interrupted naps, exclamation marks, and windy days. She lives in Ottawa, Canada. Visit her at KatherineBattersby.com.

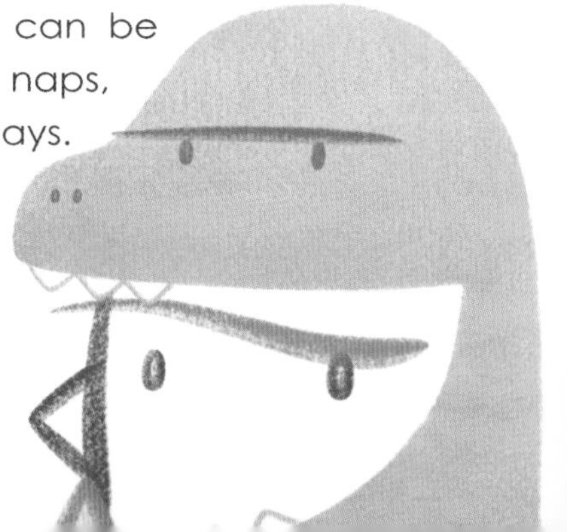

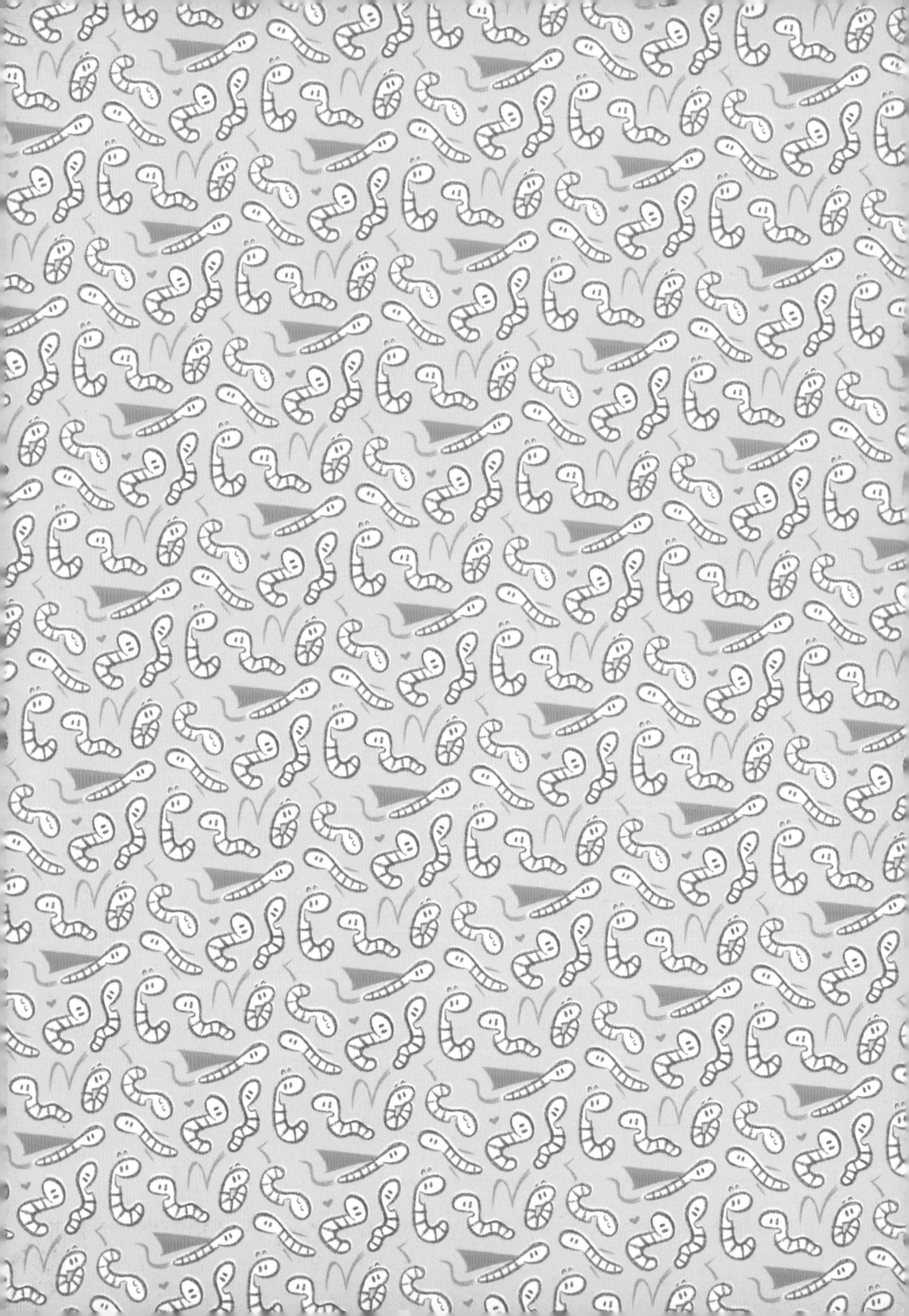